The Lap of Luxury

The Lap
of Luxury

A NOVEL

William

Hamilton

THE ATLANTIC MONTHLY PRESS
NEW YORK

For Sandy Walker

Published simultaneously in Canada
Printed in the United States of America
FIRST PAPERBACK EDITION

Library of Congress Cataloging-in-Publication Data

Hamilton, William, 1939–
    The lap of luxury : a novel / William Hamilton.
PS3558.A4444L37   1988   813'.54—dc19   88-22617

ISBN 0-87113-342-3

Design by Julie Duquet

The Atlantic Monthly Press
19 Union Square West
New York, NY 10003

FIRST PRINTING

Part 1

Chapter 1

Quite soon after he began what was at the time just a drawing of an American eating in a restaurant in France, Vincent Booth realized he would make a painting of it. He'd been sketching a lot, hoping to come across a subject to enlarge upon, and at last he found something important and fascinating enough to raise up in size and color into a painting.

From first lines this drawing was full of pleasant surprises. A hand gesture he'd never drawn before, nor ever recognized as telling, suddenly appeared with great effect. It beckoned him toward further subtleties. It waved him into a better drawing. Everything came easily—even solutions to perspective, which usually only annoyed him. But what convinced Vincent he had the makings for a painting was the main subject. The young woman was so clearly and confidently American that her presence galvanized her surroundings in a way no less pointed than the effect the Madonna and Child had on the barn, hay, and kings in a Renaissance *Adoration of the Magi*. There was something out of context about her, and not only out of the French context. She seemed out of time as well as out of place, like the subjects in masterpieces.

Vincent wasn't good enough to paint a masterpiece, but he was aesthetically acute enough to feel their secrets, and this woman, popped out of time and circumstance for some transitory reason, whispered in his ear: This is what it is like. He was doing so much better than usual that he tried not to notice so he wouldn't get distracted and lose it. But it did not seem to be a fragile drawing. It didn't matter what he thought about. His sketch just kept on working along beautifully, promising everything.

Mary Brigham wondered whether the attractive person in the beret staring at her in the bistro was really drawing her picture or just trying to get her attention so he could go after her money. "He couldn't possibly know about it," she reasoned one minute; and "This is a new approach" the next. That beret was so stagy.

She was self-conscious to begin with about eating alone in this restaurant. The waiter had been awful to her since she walked in alone, and this staring person only made matters worse.

She was here to lunch because she hadn't felt like getting up at dawn with her companions to bicycle to the prehistoric site. Instead, Mary allowed herself the luxury of sleeping until after ten and dawdling around what she considered just another bony, stony old French town. It had its big rock carcass of a cathedral, its pots of geraniums, outdoor cafés, and slimy-looking river, just like so many others.

By one she was hungry enough to decide on a real indoor luncheon instead of the lighter fare of the outdoor cafés. On a narrow street she'd spotted a restaurant with lace half-curtains, old enamel paint, and crumbling gold letters on the black glass of its sign. Mary found these attributes propitious enough to brave a solo entrance. She was hungry.

The instantly annoying waiter looked at her pointedly before disdainfully palming her to a table. French nannies notwithstanding, Mary's French was defiantly reluctant. He made her negotiate every point of the meal in her lockjaw accent. Despite his animosity (she began to realize he hated only women more than he hated Americans), she found the food richly delicious.

During the *gigot d'agneau* she noticed the artist glaring at her with the intensity of an exhibitionist. In Palm Beach, Mary had recently aborted the fruit planted in her by what had tragically revealed itself to be a gigolo, Count Cleomenes "Cleo" Hunvalfy. The horror and heartbreak of all that was in fact the cause of this European jaunt. The last thing she needed was a man directing the distinctive sniper's stare of the fortune hunter at her. And that's just exactly what she saw coming from under that obvious beret.

Hunvalfy had first advertised himself as an escaped Hungarian boy freedom fighter, then as a disenfranchised aristocrat. He had manners as ritualistically acrobatic as a fencing match. Mary never completely decoded his bowing and kissing programs—

who got a bow and an air kiss versus a two-handed wrist kiss, or a one-cheeker, or the full two, or just a bow or no notice at all or a kiss on the lips.

Everyone warned her he was after a rich wife, but she was twenty-nine, and his kissing was not restricted to the upper body. Mary was experiencing a strong biological urge to have a baby, and Hunvalfy came on like a bee in a bed of roses.

"Just don't marry him," was her mother's final dictum.

"That one's a European carpet crawler," advised her father.

"He *is* handsome," said her friend Alison.

He had a luxurious wardrobe, a very expensive car, and he'd taken Bobo Legree's house for the winter. He was the only man describing himself as an investment banker who in Mary's experience was always in a good mood.

The first time she found herself in his bedroom, Mary had asked who the man in the old snapshot on his dresser was.

"My father," he had said. Then, as an afterthought, he picked up the photograph and added, "Count Pav" in a voice filled with the modulation of great respect. At a dinner he gave for Mary's parents, this photograph had been replaced by a completely different, but equally European-looking man in uniform. This new photograph was mounted in a silver frame with armorial bearings. She heard her fiancé's "my father" as he drew her mother's attention to it. Then Mary saw him pick up his new progenitor and add "Prince Kiril" with the same modulation of respect that "Count Pav" had called up in him on that earlier occasion.

Mary rationalized her beau's ancestral switch by telling herself one picture was probably Cleo's grandfather and the other his father. Who doesn't mix things up in foreign languages? He was fabulous in the sack, and Mary wanted a baby night and day. But other photographs, and then miniatures and paintings, began to arrive at an embarrassing rate, as Cleo's family expanded and elevated its noble position with each arrival.

The telltale "Oh, my God, I forgot my wallet" had already occurred three or four times before he asked for a loan to pay his rent. Mary kept all these giveaway shortcomings of her betrothed a secret until she found her friend Alison's bathing suit under some shoes in Cleo's well-stocked closet of entirely new clothes.

The abortion had caused Mary such depression that she fled to a psychiatrist for relief. When that hadn't exorcised her guilt, she'd gone to Europe with her twenty-year-old cousin, Margaret, and Margaret's equally disgustingly young friend, Missy Ferguson. The damn bicycling was meant to firm both her resolve and her thighs.

The handsome young man's stare in the restaurant reminded Mary too vividly of the no-count count who had so horribly fulfilled her parents' dire predictions. Damn old Europe and its creepy counting counts and starving artists. They're bred and born to go after your money. But she felt weak and attracted at once. That staring and sketching under that beret looked as phony to her as retrospect had illuminated Count Cleomenes Hunvalfy's hand kissing and antique-store ancestors to be, and yet, in a completely annoying way she found him interesting.

It was Margaret and Missy Ferguson who got Vincent over to the table. Mary had told them about the restaurant she'd discovered when they returned ravenous from bicycling. Margaret and Missy nudged each other and then whispered about him when Vincent entered the restaurant at suppertime. He was so good-looking, and apparently alone.

He went to the bar, from which he looked around the dining room. His gaze stopped when he saw Mary. He smiled and raised his glass. Though he was young and handsome and happy, like the people in advertisements, Mary wasn't about to be swindled again.

"Do you know him?" inquired Margaret with girlish glee.

"He was drawing me at lunch," replied Mary evenly.

"Let's invite him over," suggested Missy.

Mary found it all ridiculous and ludicrous. Her cousin and her friend were young and cute. Mary would just as soon the sketch artist kept to his side of the room, especially considering that dangerous twinge she felt returning.

It was plenty disturbing. Despite the unhappy, hospital light of her last experience of manhood, she knew she would not enjoy watching the attractions of her youthful companions turn his head. Hadn't she found him?

"What is he? He doesn't look French."

"Probably another fucking Hungarian," Mary growled.

Margaret, who knew of her cousin's recent misadventure, gave her a piteous look. But already Missy had brazenly gone to the bar and invited him over.

"He's American." Missy grinned, presenting Vincent Booth to the subject of his triumphant drawing.

Chapter 2

*A*fter his artistically momentous lunch Vincent took his picture to the room he'd rented for the summer—a room in which he'd arranged his few effects much the way Van Gogh had decorated his quarters. He propped it on his bed and grinned. It was a real picture. He closed and swung his fist, making a clashing noise in his throat as the orchestra in his mind struck a congratulatory chord.

After a while Vincent decided he couldn't see his picture anymore for having looked at it too much, so he decided to take a walk. In his present state of mind everything outside looked like great pictorial raw material. Up until this breakthrough, Vincent, who was officially in France as an art historian, not as an artist, had been intimidated by subject matter he kept recognizing from master-pieces. How dare he paint what geniuses had already revealed? What did Vincent Booth have to add to the revelations of Cézanne, Corot, Van Gogh, Poussin, Chardin? But today, after his success, he wanted to try showing that row of poplars his way. They didn't look like the Impressionists' exclusive property anymore. He could feel the mechanics of those trees, and sense the colors to use. He felt like an artist instead of an art historian.

Now he wished he'd used his grant to study eighteenth-century French painting to paint instead of study pictures. In fact, he'd finished his scholarly work and found time left over for this vacation, but his newly aroused artistic sensibility allowed him to feel like a rebel and a rogue—a real artist, helpless to be anything else. He decided that when he returned to New York, he'd paint a series of women at the hairdressers' that would be funny and mysterious at the same time. The old—or should she be young?—yes, a young woman, and the man beautifying her hair—he'd paint them in coincidental antipathetic selves with signals from the cultural aftermath of modern America all around; Roman columns meant to simultaneously suggest classical beauty and Hollywood costume epics, the tubes of ooze emblazoned with scientific graphics to give the consumer confidence . . . no, not that, Vincent decided. That's getting academic again. To think like a critic offended the artist. Vincent picked up a real rock to throw it at his beauty parlor idea. How could he go back to being so shallow, so cute, now that he'd been given a true artistic inkling?

He skipped the stone across a pond. Now that was what he decided to paint—nothing sophisticated about that: the stone skipping with three splashes in physically fated graduations from the oldest to the most recent, bottom to top respectively, the succeeding generations of rings spreading farthest in the oldest splash, widest and weakest like aging . . . no, not that, either! Just paint! Don't think. He had, after all, begun a real picture today. The pictures would paint themselves unencumbered by a lot of bright-young-man style consideration and scholarship.

Vincent skipped another stone and fell to brooding about whether his picture was really any good. Maybe the truth was that he was only a hobbyist painter who should stick to his acclaimed beginnings as an art historian. He'd won two prizes. How could he work as a painter with his scholarly self looking over his shoulder as he tried? Vincent sighed and clasped his knees under his chin. Odd how excited you can get over something coming up out of you, through your hand onto paper.

In kindergarten Vincent had drawn a horse with a soft-leaded, thick brown pencil on a piece of newsprint. The teacher took it in one hand, and him in the other, when his mother arrived to pick him up after school. He remembered their praiseful conversation as he mouthed the chrome sill of the car door.

The horse in this kindergarten drawing was trotting. It was Princess, whom he mainly hated. His mother always wanted him to ride her whereas Princess always wanted to throw him, and Vincent always had to climb back on to show he wasn't afraid, which he was. Princess may have tormented him as a horse, but as a drawing she signaled his gift. Like a singer's voice, an athlete's coordination, or a mathematician's tenacious endurance of logic, his drawing of Princess became from that day on Vincent Booth's edge. Drawing gave him the attraction necessary to advance in popular esteem, romance, and education.

* * *

At Yale, in the dramatic Mr. McLaughlin's History of European Art, Vincent fell in love with the subject. The professor singled him out from the big crowd at this popular undergraduate course because of an exceptional paper Vincent wrote on Dutch painting. McLaughlin liked his student at once, and he furthermore liked Vincent's paintings. He doted on him, thinking Vincent every bit as brilliant as Vincent thought the professor was.

"If you were a Dutchman in the seventeenth century, you probably would have been one of the masters," McLaughlin told him as they drank endless cups of tea at the Elizabethan Club. Vincent wished his professor wouldn't say this where others could hear it.

"Now art is celebrated as a sore," McLaughlin continued. Vincent was relieved to hear the professor shift his focus to the general subject of art. The modulation of McLaughlin's voice was closer to what it was in his public lectures. A classmate of Vincent's carried in his teacup, paused, ladled back a visor of hair that had fallen over his eyes, and joined them, correctly perceiving the public lecture note McLaughlin had fallen into.

"Art has become the burning sore we deserve for our foul living," McLaughlin now roared, and two more undergraduates alighted to listen to the celebrated professor.

"The sore gets poked like a pimple, and it gets wildly, medically expensive as it spreads, and all sorts of low-grade sons of bitches who couldn't make it in the philosophy department of Oral Roberts University start explaining it to us. The art dealers get rich. The so-called artists get rich and the critics keep explaining why—and art, the sore, gets worse and worse, and everybody hates it more and more. Then they get to hate themselves for having that for their art. Art is all hatred and disease now."

Two other professors, sipping tea at an octagonal table in another room, stopped their own modulated conversation as McLaughlin's speech rebounded off the walls. These two raised their eyebrows and tipped cups over their sarcastic smiles. The undergraduate at their table excused himself and went to join the charismatic art historian's growing audience.

"Irish," said one professor to the other, nodding toward the other room.

"I've been thinking how illiterate societies vivify images of speech in a way that dies out when the inevitable verification caused by the printed word calls its bluff," said the other.

McLaughlin made a personal cause of Vincent. He got him the grant for graduate school and, afterward, the prize to France. He couldn't get over how Vincent could both think and draw. In predicting fame and fortune for this young man he was right, of course. But McLaughlin never would have guessed what fame and what fortune lay in store for Vincent Booth.

Chapter 3

*A*fter his contemplative walk Vincent was famished. He debated whether or not to return to the restaurant where he'd drawn the girl at lunch, reluctant to spoil imagination's pleasures with the disappointment of actuality. Maybe the restaurant wouldn't look as he'd seen and painted it, and this would no doubt end his lovely fancies. He looked again at the picture on his bed and felt pleased. Clearly there was nowhere else he could possibly dine than where he had fed so well at lunch.

As the artist arrived at her table, Mary Brigham found herself remembering how her own cousin, Marcy Phillips, had been ruined by a so-called artist—a womanizing, coke-driven painter who had the effrontery to actually charge Marcy a million dollars for divorcing her.

"I drew your picture at lunch," said the artistic, attractive stranger.

"Yes," Mary said, "I noticed." She didn't ask to see the results. This actually increased Vincent's admiration for what he regarded as her powerful independence—the very quality on which his picture had turned.

"You never get to come over and introduce yourself to a still life or a landscape afterward. I mean, you can, but the response is kind of depressing," he joked as Margaret gestured him down into a seat at their table. Margaret and Missy bit their lips so as not to giggle.

Smart, thought Mary to herself. Very attractive and obviously smart. She decided her best course was silence.

Her bubbling companions on either side did most of the talking. Everybody's interests and itineraries were revealed. Mary wondered which of them he would select. She was sure Margaret would be only too pleased, and Missy Ferguson, after all, was the one who had walked over to the bar and picked him up. This was an extremely attractive young man.

"Une bouteille de Chiroubles," he told the waiter with an impressive-sounding accent.

"Hungarians can speak any language," spoke up Mary. She watched for a sign of Hungarian recognition but found only a slight confusion in the face before her.

"Excuse me?"

"Are you by any chance Hungarian?"

"God, no," he said. "I'm from West Virginia."

"I thought you looked Hungarian," she explained.

The wine was good, the food even better. Everyone was talking away except Mary. More and more pointedly Vincent felt her silence was attractive. Especially when everyone else is nattering, silence has authority. He also liked her plain, decent looks. Excessively good looks caused problematic personality distortions, he reasoned, knowing he had them. He liked to think he had never allowed himself to be drawn into the silly shallow advantages offered by mirrors.

As he contemplated his model, Vincent decided that he had enough looks for two. The generosity of pairing up with a homely girl pleased him. There was something chivalrous about it. Anyway, she wasn't that plain—and she was his inspiration.

"Would you let me draw you again?" Vincent asked after generously paying for all four meals. Mary agreed before she even thought about what she was getting into. Mostly she was pleased he hadn't gone after Missy or Margaret. This, she decided, was a situation she could handle. After all, hadn't she learned her lesson in the very hardest of all possible ways with Cleo?

As for Vincent, he thought about painting the whole scene of himself and the three girls as a judgment of Paris.

Mary recognized the inspiration of the decor in Vincent's rented room. "Van Gogh slept here," she said.

The picture was propped on his bed, and she did a real double take when she saw it, which complimented Vincent more thoroughly than anything she could have said. She glanced, then looked, then looked away, and then looked back at the picture very closely, even squinting. Then she looked up, apparently astonished.

"That is really good," she said.

She must have thought he was just a jerk in a beret, mused Vincent, drawing junk in restaurants in France.

Unlike her fellow cyclists, Margaret and Missy, Mary was wearing slacks instead of shorts, because she didn't feel her legs were equal to such competition. She wore a gold Georgian signet ring, no makeup, and a scarf to keep dust out of her hair. That hair was her one really beautiful attribute. It was rich, heavy, and plastic, a dark brown that in dim light could look black.

She had it tied up in a bun under the yellow pennon of her scarf. As instinctively as he'd know how to draw Mary, Vincent pulled out the pins holding her hair in its bundle. She immediately blushed and breathed fast, scared and enchanted. At first she froze like an animal suffering some human indignity beyond its understanding. Then she began to relent. She felt her hair fall like a trap door beneath her in a dream as she turned into Vincent Booth's enclosing arms.

Since it was foreign France, they could both translate themselves into anyone they wanted. Their actual identities were of little consequence, and the world was a lark. Neither of them could get enough of the other.

"Why don't we travel a little?" Mary suggested one afternoon. Vincent wasn't doing much besides being with her. His grant was soon to end. He had a new idea about how to finish his year abroad. "Would you like to go all around Europe and look at art?" Vincent asked Mary. His hands were moving and his eyeballs darting, as if he actually saw it all before him. "Sure," she replied.

Margaret and Missy thought it was great that Vincent was carrying Mary off. Margaret said her farewell like a mother sending her daughter to school—some school—and bit her lip so as not to giggle when Mary and Vincent finally left.

"I wonder if he knows?" she said to Missy.

"What?" her friend asked.

"That Cousin Mary is absolutely loaded," Margaret explained.

France seemed to find the couple attractive: the stolid Mary like a cigar-store Indian, and the Byronic Vincent with his ludicrous but somehow winning beret. He was much taller than she, and looked a little younger. How she had enchanted him interested the women, and how carnal his devotion seemed won men's approval. *"Je crois qu'il a un professeuse,"* opined Vincent's landlord to his wife.

"I'm really having a good time," Mary admitted to Vincent against her better judgment.

"When I drew you, I felt like I was drawing for the first time in a hell of a long time," he answered.

This alleviating romance seemed spectacular good luck to both of them. Mary was showing Vincent much he didn't know, and he was teaching her all about European art. The only word in the proximity of their mutual enthusiasm seemed to be love. In Nice, Mary said "I love you" in a matter-of-fact way that immediately seemed too naked to her, so she threw "very much" over the private parts of her declaration. Vincent beamed and held her close.

"Let's stay at the Negresco," she suggested, pointing to a block-long pile of turrets and balconies overlooking the harbor.

"Forget it," replied Vincent, who was running out of money much too fast already.

"It's free."

"I don't understand."

"My father's company has a suite, and there's nobody in it," Mary lied. She wanted him to have a treat. She thought it was adorable how he kept trying to pay for everything, how they'd been living like a pair of little mice on little crumbs in little rooms.

She'd just told him that she loved him, reason enough to back a little celebration. Besides, she wanted to relax in a way only very thick walls, big bathtubs, and a lot of staff could provide.

"What does he do?" Vincent asked at dinner. They were dressed up, looking out at boats jostling at their moorings, drinking an old bottle of Haut Brion that tasted like the history of night. Mary had explained that the wine also belonged to her father's company.

"Mohican Trust," she muttered.

"Is that a bank?" Vincent asked. He saw she didn't want to talk about it and wondered whether he should just let it go. But it was quite a suite they had; the great four-poster bed was caparisoned in heavy, new yellow silk, the same as the tree-tall draperies on windows overlooking the harbor.

"It's this thing he's in," said Mary, referring to a family trust that administered a sum financial magazines often speculated in billions of dollars.

Mary didn't want to spoil things and immediately regretted arousing his suspicion. She didn't want to bring the damn money into it. Why had she put them in the Negresco? Because she had wanted that good long bath. Couldn't he just enjoy it and stop sniffing for clues? Anyway, it was all borrowed time and holiday, so the menu was disguise, costume, and fancy dress.

"Actually there's this rich family, and Daddy's a friend of this man and it's his, but he just wants us to enjoy it anytime we're in France."

"Are you kidding?"

Mary smiled, shaking her head and placing her hand on Vincent's. "Daddy saved his life at a shooting accident," she uncharacteristically embroidered. This was the right answer, and it put them back on holiday.

In Avignon they stayed in a much cheaper old hotel whose water closet was in the hall. Vincent had been continuing lunch's wine all afternoon. He disappeared into the hallway from their room looking for the facilities, and Mary soon began to feel he'd been gone too long.

She opened the door, sensing a commotion a few ribs down in the skeletal structure of the old hotel. She heard French shouts and rapid-fire bursts of pursuit on stairs, then Vincent suddenly rushed up with a wild, hilarious, winded grin. When he saw Mary, his face bloomed with joy, filling her with love. She could see at a glance he knew she was his salvation.

"Thank God you opened the door," he whispered breathlessly. "I was lost." He held her face and kissed her lips as he panted. Mary felt like the embodiment of nursing, succoring, womanhood.

He had locked their door, turned out the lights, and buried both of them under blankets before they heard footsteps pause at their door.

No doubt the French couple outside had seen the light go out in the transom over the Booths' door and were debating mightily whether or not to disturb the guests within. The

French whispering was sibilant from the high pressure of exasperation and indecision. Deciding against an inquiry, they ran on and ascended the next flight of stairs. Then, grumbling, the pursuit unsuccessful, they passed Vincent and Mary's door once more and continued downstairs, whispering angrily and scuffling into silence.

Vincent laughed until tears came to his eyes and explained that the hall toilet was occupied, that he'd gone down a flight to find the same problem, then up two flights for another lockout, then down three or four, looking for a vacancy until all he knew for sure was that he was drunk and lost somewhere in France.

"Just when I was completely desperate, I saw it—a real beauty, and the right size for me."

Apparently Vincent was in the basement, enthroned on a top-loading washing machine, and the hotel manager, hearing noises, had come down to investigate, initiating the now concluded chase.

"They never saw my face." He laughed helplessly. "Just my ass."

It was that look of rapture on his face when he saw Mary as his safe haven that convinced her to marry him.

The next day, he held her hand as they toured the Palace of the Popes. When they stepped into the Chapel of the Inquisition, where he wanted to see the murals of Simon Martini, Mary felt like a bride.

Vincent talked about perspective and the Sienese School. Mary found the people in the murals all looked alike, as if the artist could do only one basic face, but she loved the way pictures excited him. He would probably, she projected in the chapel, make a great dad.

Chapter 4

*V*incent's romance with Mary in France was soon directed toward Italy, because he wanted to show her the great wonders of painting that he hadn't seen himself.

Because she had no confidence in her intellect, Mary didn't say much. She was thoroughly intimidated by his conversational facility and intensity. Her own education had been desultory; they'd handed her through boarding school hoping for a dormitory (she gave them a theater), and she left college after two years, much to the dismay of the development office.

But Vincent's sexual naïveté delighted her, especially after the Hungarian's theatrics. She enjoyed surprising and even amazing him. When they weren't in museums and restaurants and churches, they were in bed. Mary began to wonder if she could get back out of love with him once the trip was over.

"Can you imagine how technological a thing like that was in the quattrocento, the power it gave?" Vincent said as they left another church in which tourists milled obliviously past old ladies praying. "The church could show holy pictures in 3-D to peasants, just wow them and cow them because artists could paint perspective." Mary was relieved to get back out into sunlight.

She found the Picasso Museum in Antibes a break from the dour, damp, and cold church murals. Following Vincent through the gloomy shafts where he looked for art, she had begun to feel like a coal miner. The Picasso Museum was bright and decorative, capturing the fish, melon, mythological lechery, and *les fruits des mer* that seemed to make up life on the Riviera. Compared to the religious agonies depicted in the sewerlike churches and boring, scruffy museums, it was so refreshing, clean, and uncomplicated that Mary privately decided to look into buying a Picasso when she returned to New York.

In Monaco, something in a shop window brought an enormous smile to Mary's face, and Vincent tracked her gaze to a bride's gown. On a piazza in Florence she drank a cappuccino, which made a mustache when she pulled her cup quickly down to peer at the diverting, merry appearance of a wedding party spilling out of a church, down stone steps, to cross right in front of them. Vincent was struck by her reverent intensity. And when he parked the car in Siena, she didn't get out right away because she was staring at the wedding cake alongside them in the bakery.

The idea of marriage, Vincent noticed, now seemed to be

following them like a clumsy detective. He was disconcerted, barely out of the educational institutions to which he'd been indentured at the age of five. Couldn't they just live together? Did they have to put on uniforms and swear oaths? Couldn't they remain civilians? Then they would both hear cars honking, and Mary would look at him and smile, and sure enough, a bride and groom would drive by with a string of well-wishers' cars braying behind.

Eventually Mary got Vincent to inspect his beloved art without her. To relieve herself of the dank mysteries he was after felt luxuriously truant, like an excuse from school. She also liked having him disappear for an afternoon and then come home like a working husband. With Vincent off looking at art, Mary could walk around the pleasantly safe little European cities, especially keen on observing mothers and children.

Vincent was skipping lunches. When he left to travel with Mary, the French landlord had refused to return his month's advance. Even with her paying everything involving the car and splitting food and lodging whenever she remembered, his money was coming to an end. He had to get all the way back to Paris for his return ticket to be valid.

Obviously Mary felt no similar pressures. In fact, it was becoming apparent to him that she must be rich. Vincent considered all this as he looked at a rich young man in a fresco painted by Pinturicchio. With a rich wife a man could paint all day. The fellow in the painting wore crimson tipped with furs. He was as beautiful as an object. With a rich wife, Vincent considered how he wouldn't have to work as a scholar for wages. He could find out if he really was a painter. Mary was the model, and maybe also the means, for him to begin to paint.

When Mary said "That looks divine" about a restaurant in Genoa, Vincent suffered a serious financial qualm. She was already marching in before he could look around for a cheaper alternative.

"Don't you really want anything?" asked Mary when Vincent scowled at the menu and shook his head, handing it back to the waiter. "Vino Rosso," he replied.

Mary realized he'd probably run out of money, which she found endearing. That the guy was probably starving himself just to keep up with her seemed really sweet.

Excusing herself from the table, Mary found the owner in the kitchen opening clams and berating a waiter. She pointed out their table and said she wanted the best.

"Best?" asked the harried owner, considering what an ugly, barking, spitting language English was. They negotiated a meal by pointing and gestures. Mary signaled top quality successfully by employing thumbs-up.

Vincent looked sweet and stoical as she approached him from behind. He was eating gouges of bread and drinking wine slowly to make things last.

The feast arrived like a conflagration. Vincent thought there had been a mistake.

"No, no, no," he objected. But a drool broke over his chin, making Mary laugh. The waiter expressively indicated Mary's patronage by gesture and wink.

"Thank you," Vincent said meekly.

Mary patted his hand. "How much have you got left?" she asked.

Vincent shook his head.

The fine food made him sleepy, complacent, and unargumentative. After lunch Mary pushed two varicose travelers checks at him. Each was for five hundred.

"Let me have a turn," she said. With this kind of money they could see everything and eat and sleep where they wanted. They could go to Rome.

"I have to get rid of some money before I go home," she said. "Otherwise it just sits around with American Express getting rich off the float."

"Jesus, the Pantheon," said Vincent, surprised as they turned a Roman corner. They entered the ancient domed space and looked up at the oculus and around at the niches in which saints had replaced Roman gods. Mary stood stone-still in the monochromatic light shafting down from above. She could be a statue herself, thought Vincent, a goddess. She was so still and grave. She seemed suddenly quite nobly handsome to him. Should he propose right now? An entire life of making love and painting opened before him, making an avenue straight through the Pantheon into a wide, bright haze of infinite possibility. He looked deeply at her, trying to say the first word of a marriage proposal, "Please . . . umh, uh, Mary? Will . . ." She looked up at his inquiring face.

"I'm starving," she said.

They now made it a point to find really exceptional restaurants. A few turns from the Pantheon they came to a piazza in which a long restaurant with a lobster on its sign made them nod simultaneously at each other.

A lobster dish was the specialty, and the place was crowded

with devotees—with good reason, discovered Vincent and Mary. A pair of newlyweds entered and caused everyone to look up; the bride blushed and the groom tried to look maturely stern. Everyone could tell they had just changed out of their wedding clothes. The customers all smiled and winked at one another. Mary beamed at the bride, who smiled back, blushing again. Vincent grinned and shook his head at Mary. Marriage was everywhere outside, and now inside him too.

People looked away, resuming their late-afternoon luncheons, to give the newlyweds some privacy. Suddenly the chef rushed into the dining room, red, perspiring, carrying an empty bowl and, Mary noticed, dressed all in white like a bride himself. He went right to the couple, and, astonishing Vincent and Mary, he burst into tears.

He expostulated to the young couple and held the bowl beneath their noses. Whatever he said caused the nearby diners to laugh and applaud as the chef returned to the kitchen.

Vincent discovered from their waiter that the chef had run out of his specialty just as those who deserved it most, the new husband and wife, entered his restaurant. He was heartbroken. He wanted to apologize personally and wish them a long life and many babies.

"There is no more, and he bring out the bowl for them to smell how good it was," explained the sympathetic waiter, shaking his head and issuing the inevitable, significant, but indecipherable Italian gestures describing the limitations of fate and vagaries of the human condition.

Unlike his inconclusive deliberations in the Pantheon, Vincent's proposal to Mary in the maze of a garden below a villa was offered automatically, on one knee, before he even knew what he was saying. His sense of preordination had become overwhelming. His knee knew more of his fate than his mind. Mary accepted simply, with "Sure."

"Maybe we could get a loft or something," Vincent said as they backtracked, hand in hand, the garden maze toward the villa. "I've got a lot of painting to do."

"As long as there's not a lot of naked models," answered Mary. She laughed and put her head on his chest. It landed on him like an orphan in a basket.

Mary had a vague idea about lofts. The elevators were dreadful, and people built artful homes in the great, dreary spaces where workers in rows had once sewed pants. Well, if it made him happy, why not? It would drive her parents crazy and astonish her friends and be fun, like this surprising bicycle trip to Europe where, thank God, she didn't have to bicycle anymore. Lofts probably got grease on you and snagged runs in your hose, but they wouldn't have to live in one forever.

Mrs. Vincent Booth sounded like a fine name. He'd been to good schools. He could draw very well, although Mary would rather he did something a little less leechy than be an artist.

She was unexpectedly happy. She couldn't pull back her smile. So she was going to marry the sketch artist in the beret. How do you like that?

"Great garden," she said to the Countess (who was also a princess) at the villa.

"We're getting married," said Vincent. The generous host and hostess were overjoyed that their house had sponsored such a wonderful, significant event. The Count shot in Scotland with Mary's father, and he and the Countess-Princess had both stayed with the Brighams in Palm Beach. This was the first Vincent knew of the Brighams having a house in Palm Beach.

The Count found something old and rare to drink, and everyone grinned for hours. The toasts, the beautiful villa, the wonderful trip, and the unthinking matrimonial determinism of the whole romance made Vincent sure he had stumbled upon his destiny. Mary telephoned her parents in two calls to different houses. She was pleased by their worries and confusion.

In West Virginia, Vincent's mother reacted loyally by saying she was "tickled pink," though privately wondering whether her son was about to ruin his life with an early marriage the way she had.

"I've got to get back to Paris to fly home," Vincent told Mary that night in bed. "That's where my ticket's from."

"No, you don't, darling," said Mary with a kind of authority Vincent hadn't noticed before.

"What do you mean?"

"Well, let's just go from Rome."

"That's what I'm telling you—I can't. I have this ticket from Paris."

"It's all taken care of," Mary insisted with her new, rather bland tone.

"You mean, you're going to pay?"

"Remember what I told you about that Mohican Trust?"

"You mean, back in Nice?" asked Vincent.

Mary nodded. "That's actually Daddy," she said. Vincent did not sleep that night. He paced about and drank the bottle of wine the Count gave them as a wedding present. Mary was glad it troubled Vincent, that he didn't light up the way Count Cleo Hunvalfy had on walking into the oversize Brigham place in Palm Beach.

"Well?" she asked him the next day. It had been a long, restless night.

"Do you want to go through with it?"

"Sure." Vincent grinned.

"Good," said Mary, "because I'm pregnant."

"Are you kidding?" asked the astonished father-to-be.

"Come here," she replied.

Chapter 5

*M*ary's father, Alfred Bent Brigham IV, regarded his family as a grand and deserving, but
importuned and envied, enterprise vulnerable to
tabloid exploitation, fortune hunters, and crackpots.
People were always trying to break off bits of the
Brigham splendor to stuff into their own nasty little
pockets.

Alfred had become a fine wing shooter, at least
partly because he suspected people might someday
come at him, trying to get at his wealth. Another
reason for his enthusiasm for the gun was the
schedule it offered for his life. He shot in a pro-
grammed round from Scotland, South Carolina,
Canada, California, and Wyoming, then back to
Scotland. Often he would improvise shoots in more
exotic places, such as Costa Rica, Iceland, and, until

it became unhealthy, Africa. But his basic round gave Alfred's year its structure.

He might have shot Count Hunvalfy if Mary hadn't been otherwise persuaded that the man was a fortune-hunting *poseur.* His first impression of Vincent Booth was less murderously enraging, but not entirely happy, either. If he didn't feel the same instantaneous compulsion to collapse the young man with a shot that Hunvalfy caused him, he was still very sorry and annoyed that Vincent was five years younger than Mary, had no money, and wanted to be an artist. Furthermore he distrusted the fellow's brainy talk and good looks, realizing his daughter couldn't match them.

Alfred had been taught that the leverage of wealth raises its possessors much higher than ordinary people, but that such a height makes for ludicrous, hilariously received falls if one were to lose his balance up there. "Everybody laughs when a rich man falls down, Alfred," his father had growled in the high, shadowy library of the old house (which Alfred sold because it was so obvious).

His wife felt differently. Delila cared mostly for good looks with which the young man, unlike her own husband, was abundantly blessed.

"He is seriously poor," said Alfred.

"Oh, who cares? He's so attractive," his wife retorted. "Besides, I didn't have any money, and you married me."

"You, Lolly, are a woman."

"There is such a thing as women's liberation."

"But it doesn't include men," persisted the displeased wing shooter.

Although, counting infants, the Mohican Trust had a hundred and five heirs, it wasn't equally divided or distributed among them, and most had no conception of its dimensions. All they knew of its existence was the dew of checks regularly condensing in their mailboxes.

It was a fortune so big and abstract that instead of belonging to anyone, people belonged to it. Alfred was the main beneficiary, and he'd devoted his entire life to being the very rich man it made him. All he'd added to this fated identity was marksmanship.

"Pull," he called, and a disk was thrown from the tower. Alfred powdered the blip so close to its source that fragments ricocheted against the machine that had flung it.

"Pull," called Vincent, and for the tenth time the spinning round of low-fire clay completed its trajectory unscathed, each miss like a blow hammering his prospective father-in-law's opinion of him lower.

Afterward lackeys gave the shooting gentlemen report cards. Both were perfect in opposite ways: Alfred hadn't missed a shot and Vincent hadn't made one. And in the station wagon returning from the shooting club for lunch, Alfred hadn't much to say.

"How'd it go?" Mary asked in the mudroom of the Brigham's country house in Connecticut. She didn't actually have to ask; her father's face was florid and jowls down, and Vincent's rather foolish-looking.

When Vincent stepped farther into the house, he heard Alfred Brigham muttering. Turning around, he saw that Mary's father was cleaning Vincent's gun in an angry, disapproving manner that clearly implied any real sportsman would attend to his piece upon retiring from a shoot.

Happily a butler with a tray of Sunday Mornings appeared, to chemically reduce the tension. Vincent followed Mary into the library, where most of the books didn't look as if they'd been opened since the bookbinders finished their work and shut them centuries ago. Vincent spilled a bit of his drink when he suddenly noticed on the wall an inestimably great and important Gauguin picture of a Tahitian girl in a pink shift. She squatted on a shore of orange lapped with blue. He immediately loved the picture with the helplessness and sincerity a beautiful thing can cause a mortal.

"Gauguin," said Mary.

"Geez," said Vincent, squinting at it and breathing through the open mouth his gasp of surprise had left him.

"Left his wife to be an artist," Mary elaborated, "then died of syphilis." It was a story she hadn't forgotten. Vincent just kept staring at the picture, astonished.

"It's up to you, but broke people don't often work out very well," Alfred said to his daughter outside the library. Mary knew her father was thinking about her sister Sarah's marriage to Holly Boatwright, who soon thereafter had spread out his own name with two new middle ones and then furthermore added on a Roman numeral at the end. His girth began to expand just as grandly, with his wife eating herself into parallel corpulence. There were no children.

Holly had insisted on living in one of the family's more ostentatious nineteenth-century houses and had ordered a Mercedes delivered the day they moved in. It was a roadster, which, standing at the foot of steps leading to columns, completed the advertising world's image of unattainable elegance.

Holly, by now a fat man, had descended the marble stairs to his prize. He wedged in behind the wheel and couldn't get out. Alfred wished his daughter had left him that way, a monument to the wrong man.

Now here came his other daughter, tracking in another example from the moneyless majority. Alfred knew his daughters were not beauties, but they were extremely well fixed. Why did they have to go outside wealth to marry? Broke people, in Alfred's estimation, were alien. They were vulgar, envious, greedy, and unpredictable. They always wanted your money, and there were so many more of them that it was plenty dangerous enough already without allowing any of them any closer.

"At least he's not queer," said Mary, defensively referring to another of the marital defects of her sister's fattening husband. Her father scowled and shut the fine shotgun Vincent had misused and then abandoned.

At the Brighams' luncheon, Jonathan and Natalie Bushwick, "Maine friends out from Cincinnati," were in tennis clothes. Like Pepe Deschamps, "the interior decorator," "Lolly" Brigham was in riding clothes. The butler wore a piped mess jacket. Only Mary wore clothes bespeaking no particular morning activity.

"How was the shooting?" asked Lolly in a low, drink- and tobacco-cured voice. Her once envied and sought-after body had not been entirely submerged by the avalanche of aging.

"I was terrible," Vincent confessed.

"There are more important things to be good at," replied Mary's mother in an even deeper voice, causing the attentive Pepe to cackle admiringly.

Over the wooden Georgian fireplace was a horse picture

that had to be by Stubbs. Vincent felt as if the velvet rope guarding a restored room in a museum had been lifted and a costume party—himself miraculously included—had entered.

"Is that by Stubbs?" Vincent asked.

"Good for you," said Alfred Brigham from the other end of the table.

"No, good for *you,* Alfred," Pepe quipped.

"Delicious," Vincent said upon tasting wine. It was in a decanter, so Lolly asked the butler to bring in a bottle for Vincent's information. "If you're getting married," she advised him, to the decorator's further glee, "you have to know what to tell the liquor store." The butler brought in a bottle, lying in a napkin. Its label was a fine old engraving speckled with age spots.

The main course was a tasty ptarmigan stew made possible by Alfred Brigham's marksmanship in Iceland. Vincent had never lived as they had been living since he and Mary arrived the previous night at what daylight revealed to be a splendid Greek revival estate an hour and a half from New York City. Out the dining-room windows was a gentle hill gridded with Aberdeen Angus cattle like cloves on a ham.

Vincent watched Mary, who was silent and adept at the mechanics of luncheon service. The decorator relentlessly gibed, especially at Alfred Brigham, whom he seemed to serve as court jester under special license to tease the king about such sacred subjects as wealth and shooting skill. The people from Cincinnati seemed blandly familiar with this surrounding grandeur, which Vincent had no idea was even legal in a democracy.

"Alfred's cousin, Dickie, is chairman of this big railroad that just merged all over the place out West," Lolly was saying after Pepe asked about a trip the Brighams had just taken.

"And we all had our own private railroad cars all the way down from Seattle to Mexico City. It was really quite divine. Every couple had a cook and a maid and their own car. We'd stop and meet the most important people in every town along the way."

"Is this the trip where you had the little picnic airplanes?" asked Pepe in a high, guttural pitch of hilarity.

"That's right. At the Grand Canyon we each got our own little plane—each couple—didn't we, Alfred?"

"Cessnas," Alfred said. "They rolled out the red carpet. "Jimmy, we're running low," Alfred interrupted the anecdote. He tapped his glass with his trigger finger. The butler whirled in with more.

When Dolly finished her report of the lavish railroad odyssey, Alfred Brigham observed, "And it was all free," with the delight of a man who usually pays for everything.

"Was it very bumpy?" Pepe asked.

"No, not especially," answered Alfred.

"I should think it would get really bumpy when the stockholders started throwing themselves on the tracks to stop the train," said Pepe, producing a surprising great laugh from Jonathan Bushwick of Cincinnati.

Walking with Mary past the anthracite-black cattle on the hill after lunch, Vincent was just about to tell her he had no idea people lived this way in the twentieth century and that he'd missed every shot with her father. But instead he said, "I would really, really like to paint these cattle." His voice was high and thin, so he cleared his throat.

Vincent wondered why he'd changed what he was about to say. It seemed to have come out differently all by itself, like his unpremeditated marriage proposal. Then, before Vincent could examine his motives, Mary said, "Watch this," and turned on a fountain issuing from the center of a circle of life-size figures.

"Rodin," she said.

Chapter 6

*I*t was a sunny afternoon. Speeding along the asphalt gash running between New York and New Haven through what had once been New England towns, Vincent couldn't help but feel that everything coming his way was salubrious. He was traveling to New Haven to talk out his marriage plans with Professor McLaughlin, who he expected would have some hard questions. Vincent reviewed the best reasons for marrying money. He came up with such examples as Portia from *The Merchant of Venice*, Catherine de' Medici, Cleopatra, Martha Washington, Oriana from Amadis of Gaul, Queen Victoria and Peggy Guggenheim.

In the midst of his speculation, it occurred to Vincent that the cars around him were all transporting humbler, simpler lives than the one growing in scale and magnificence just ahead for himself. When one of them tried to cut in front of him after sneaking down the road shoulder to bypass a traffic jam, Vincent indulgently permitted it. What was a car length to someone soon to be measured in tens or hundreds of millions? In his present mood Vincent was anxious for everyone in the world to have a nice day.

Without money to worry about, the mind could occupy itself otherwise. The painter Balthus, whom Vincent admired, was said to be loaded. The life a painter could lead with magnificent means would be a joy not just for himself but also for others—for the entire world, if he were really good. Vincent was happy he'd thought of Balthus. As if to encourage him in this speculation, the traffic opened up wide.

Mary's car was a beautiful gloved-fist of German power. "I like a nice car," she said, "but I hate to drive." Vincent, however, did like to drive. He couldn't resist taking it over a hundred just for a few seconds, even though cops and radar abounded on this busy road.

Smooth-shouldered leather was molded all over the interior, which smelled like an expensive handbag. Pieces of wood trim were polished up like gemstones. The engine was a fiend buried in distant steel, and the ornament at the end of the hood reminded Vincent of a cross-hair sight.

When slowed by tolls and traffic, Vincent was acutely conscious of how people looked at the driver of such a car. Who got one of those, anyway, and how? Is he a prince, a financial genius, a star, or a gangster? Vincent shook off the pleasant feeling of being an object of curiosity and directed his thoughts back to the wealthy, aristocratic Balthus.

However morally debatable his repetitious, erotic little girls were as subjects, Balthus was a consummate painter and a literary, intellectual sort of artist—just the sort Vincent imagined he might himself be if he utterly pursued painting. Imagine having an intellect like Balthus's without being hung up on little girls! Married to wealth like Mary's, Vincent would have the opportunity to paint his complete potential. Enjoying these conjectures, Vincent was pleasantly startled at the tollbooth he'd revved down to enter. "Nice car," said the man. "Thank you," Vincent answered.

Balthus lived in a palace—Vincent had recently admired pictures of it in a magazine—and not everyone could comfortably occupy a palace. It takes a certain grandeur, a seigneurial confidence, considered Vincent, rising up to improve his posture at the wheel of the expensive car.

Did he love her? More than anyone he ever met. Mary was like a dark little key pressed into his hand. He'd instinctively turned it correctly and watched the world light up from the radiance coming through the door he'd swung open—the door to Ali Baba's cave.

"Asshole!" yelled Vincent at a blockhead who cut him off by changing lanes without checking the rearview mirror. Some people, Vincent decided, were simply unaware of life outside themselves.

Chapter 7

Much to Vincent's surprise, Professor McLaughlin greeted him with "Well done, Vincent!" a conspiratorial wink, and a light, congratulatory punch on the shoulder. Clearly, Professor McLaughlin already knew all about the Brighams. Just as clearly, he was not going to debate Vincent about this forthcoming marriage. He seemed to view it as an intrinsic success.

"How about a drink?" McLaughlin offered. His voice retained its lecture-resonance even offstage, but he looked somewhat different to Vincent, a little tattered and distraught.

"Some Scotch would be great. Little soda."

"Ice?" queried McLaughlin, turning again and smiling at Vincent.

"Please."

Driving up, Vincent had been rehearsing his

dialogue with his old mentor and champion. He wanted to talk in the starkest way about the implications of marrying Mary Brigham. Was he marrying for money? Were men with rich wives ever taken seriously? Might her fortune emasculate him? What were the pitfalls, and how should he prepare himself for this luxurious test of character? But McLaughlin apparently had no doubts. Vincent was disappointed, having planned the evening to test his resolve.

"I disapprove of marrying for money," said McLaughlin over their drinks, "but a fortune is another matter." He laughed in such a way that Vincent felt he must accompany him.

A pregnant woman entered the room, bringing two young boys with her. Vincent had forgotten that the old Mrs. McLaughlin had been replaced with a new one, and now he recognized her as another professor's wife. The charismatic Mr. McLaughlin had wooed her away from an assistant professor of European painting, a young German with a large forehead and a finely pointed nose. When Vincent first heard of it, the scandal had seemed glamorous, rascally, and romantic, but here in the flesh, the situation appeared extensively domestic and nearly prosaic.

"Franziska, this is Vincent Booth."

"Herbert has said so much about you," said Franziska. She had a firm grip and a humorless resignation about her, and her dark green tunic was fastened with a streamlined silver gob. Her hair was pulled back so tight that it looked like it might hurt.

Her sons were clearly no kin to McLaughlin. They were as German as bullets, and in the same room with them, the professor seemed more Irish than usual. Vincent wasn't finding out about marriage, and in fact had begun to feel as if he were at a great archaeological excavation of the institution itself—

marriage spread all about him in shards, fresh from the earth as yet to be reassembled, restored, or fully comprehended. All he could glean from the spectacle of McLaughlin's new marriage was a sense of considerable expenditure, agony, and undiscovered shape and purpose.

Out by the barbecue, Professor McLaughlin demanded that Vincent start calling him Herb.

"Odd, isn't it, how men want to burn meat on fires clear to the end of the twentieth century?" said Professor Herb, staring at the glistening meat and the hissing screws of smoke it sent up.

"I've been thinking whether or not to paint or go to a museum or something," Vincent said as they stood musing over the fire.

"Just stay away from universities," advised McLaughlin. "They're too damn in-time. Here, let's get some more whiskey. The thing is, Vincent, you're a free man with a hell of a talent. You could do damn near anything now. It's a wonderful thing. I was ecstatic when I heard the news. It was all over the campus as soon as somebody in the endowment office read about it in the *Times.* You know, most big money goes to the damnedest things. It grows its own parasites and they run it straight down the old drains, but Christ, with you—"

"Herbert," called Mrs. McLaughlin from within. The professor sighed, handed Vincent the fork he'd been brandishing, and went inside. Vincent waited in the backyard listening to the meat spit.

Vincent hadn't seen Professor McLaughlin in a year, and he was taken aback. In his newly married incarnation the professor looked like a harried husband, a mere dreamer, and a noticeably vain and theatrical personality. Where was that intellect Vincent had journeyed to New Haven to see illuminate his doubts and questions?

Instead of that passionate lecturer contrasting the domes and hollows of a maternal Mediterranean with the spears and towers of the cold northern plains on a lecture stage backed by gorgeous slides, Vincent found a man in his fifties barbecuing in his backyard, complete with a pregnant young wife.

"You'll soon be at it, too, my boy," said Vincent's returning host, bringing fresh drinks. "All the puking and pissing and crying of married life—all yours, when is it, next week?"

Vincent nodded, smiling appropriately.

"The pecker's the main thing," McLaughlin explained. "You get to understand why they can't keep the poachers from killing those rhinos in Africa so old Chinamen can buy some horn and hope for a hard-on. What's more important to an old man—the survival of rhinoceroses or one last fuck? Fucking is your last righteous scream with the black velvet curtain coming down upon you." The professor stared again at his fire. He flipped the steak and patted it affectionately, seemingly pleased by the handsome shell cauterized by the coals.

Vincent had the feeling his host had been drinking before he'd arrived. And as his own drinks reached his brain the harshness of McLaughlin's remarks and the uncomfortable undertone of this unsettled home seemed to diminish. "I get along fine that way," he offered.

"Then you haven't got a problem in the world." McLaughlin fixed him with a broad smile. "Follow your pecker as long as it still points."

"I've got this offer at the Met," said Vincent, anxious to

change the subject. He did get along with Mary the way his professor was talking—not the way they had in Europe, but still, as recently as two weeks ago, there was sex.

Vincent didn't really mind not making love as much as they had. After all, he reasoned, Mary was pregnant. Even so, she still seemed to expect him to make love, creating a command-performance aspect to sex that he found almost distasteful.

"What offer is that?"

"Assistant to William Willoughby."

"He's a growing force down there. What do you want to be, a curator?"

"I like scholarship and I like to paint." Then Vincent told his professor about the drawing of Mary he'd made before he knew anything about her. "It was like fate," he concluded.

"Fate's a tricky bastard," said McLaughlin. "It has a way of getting you to feel welcome, and then, once it lures you inside, it turns out you're still outside.

"The boys want it rare," called Mrs. McLaughlin from the kitchen door.

"Take this in, will you Vincent?" said the professor, laying the California-shaped piece of steak on one platter and then forking a larger, African continent of London broil onto the grill.

At the adult dinner Professor McLaughlin opened two bottles of wine. Franziska placed her hand over her glass, signaling that she wasn't joining the drinkers. She was months farther along than Mary, and her pregnancy looked trying. Vincent wondered whether McLaughlin, with all his talk of sex, was still sleeping with her. He doubted it. He then wondered how avidly Mary would continue to expect him to make love to her.

McLaughlin refilled both their glasses again. Maybe

McLaughlin drank and talked about sex because he didn't like it with her now. At least Vincent hadn't broken up a home on Mary's account.

"There are three areas triangulating love," observed the professor. "The head, the heart, and the hard-on—excuse me, dear—the loins." Vincent noticed some sarcasm in the correction McLaughlin directed toward his wife.

"In common forms of love—infatuation, for instance—any combination of two of these elements comes into play. The loins and the heart may agree about somebody and then the head refuses to go along, or the head and the loins agree and the heart refuses, or the head and the heart agree and the loins won't play. Two thirds of love is as common as water. But three thirds, ah —that's love, Vincent. That's when you have to have her." McLaughlin was roaring as he reached across the table for his wife's hand. She blushed and smiled when he kissed it.

In the kitchen Vincent heard one boy say something in German that made the other one laugh, and he had the feeling it was a disparaging remark about the man who had taken their father's place.

"You mustn't, you must not drive," Franziska said as Vincent thanked her for dinner. "Herbert, do not let him drive."

"Mary's expecting me," Vincent answered, wanting to get away as soon as possible. The professor had disappointed him; Franziska depressed him. He'd hoped to sort out his marital motives with the help of that keen mind he remembered, and all McLaughlin could manage was to drink and spout off.

"Stay here. Lie down a while. Rest, O warrior," said McLaughlin, pushing Vincent into a guest room and shutting the door like a warden.

Vincent wasn't really tired and wanted only to drive alone

through the black night to New York. But he did lie down for a while, until the apartment was quiet. The urge to drink a beer with the great black cape of night flying about him was overwhelming—he'd seen beer in the McLaughlin icebox, German beer for the German wife. *Ja, das liebe bier.*

Vincent tried to remember to drive unobtrusively. He glanced obsessively at the speedometer and looked around before knocking back a swig of beer. It proved to be an excellent, Wagnerian idea, driving back down the big thruway in the late night alone—very Wagnerian, especially considering the German car and the German beer.

McLaughlin's new marriage was obviously strained. Those boys didn't like him, and poor Franziska seemed a little martyred. Evidently, from what McLaughlin said, sex had been a strong factor in his decision to marry this assistant professor's wife. She was a lot younger than McLaughlin.

Vincent reconsidered his own motivation. The sex had been excellent and wasn't it bound to return to top form after Mary delivered the baby? Having a baby would probably be easier for him and Mary than it seemed to be for McLaughlin because money brought more domestic help. That was the kind of advantage Mary's wealth provided—those helping hands to keep your own from tearing your hair out. Vincent's circumstances with Mary obviously could be spectacularly luxurious. And didn't he and Mary get along fine? But should he paint, or should he be a scholar? And what was this red suddenly flashing over the car's glass-and-metal surfaces, even making the creamy leather upholstery blush? The light source would seem to be behind him. Vincent looked in his mirror: nemesis, the police.

"Give us the alphabet backward," one of them said. The

other was clearly delighted when he found the two bottles of beer Vincent had tried to bury under the seat.

"This is very embarrassing," Vincent said, adopting an attitude of indignant composure.

"Can't do the alphabet?"

"Well, *Z*, of course, X . . ."

"Let's see you walk down that line," requested the same cop, and Vincent took a few halting steps, feeling that was quite undignified.

"Get in the car."

Apparently they meant their police car. "We just leave this?" said Vincent, gesturing to Mary's now vulnerably expensive-looking car.

"Give me your hands," answered one officer as his partner talked into the spitting radio.

Good Lord, these were handcuffs. Vincent was a prisoner.

After a sleepless night in a cell with three fellow imbibers, one of whom suffered diarrhea, Vincent was charged with drunk driving and informed that he was free to go. Incidentally, his car had been stolen. Vincent's fatigue, shot through with a hangover, made each minute unrelentingly sore. He signed things about the stolen car. They gave him back his wallet after he signed something else. A policeman who couldn't have been much more than Vincent's age dropped him off at a car-rental agency due to open in two hours.

Chapter 8

*T*he world looked plain and ruthless to Vincent Booth this morning. The streets of the hamlet where his arrest had taken him were scruffy and vapid. The evidence suggested it had once been a village, but economic forces beyond its powers had distended, violated, and littered the original entity into an urban vagary hanging off the thruway like a wart. It was presently composed of unrestored, hideously augmented Colonial crates, battered Victorian brick pretensions, failure, and franchises.

Torpid as flies coming out of hibernation, the unemployed emerged to populate the stoops and sidewalks. Insectile salsa music jittered in a car at the light. Vincent's own recently projected new world of wealth seemed like a hallucination in this setting.

The car-rental franchise opened slowly, with sullenness. The clerk arrived but kept Vincent

locked out while she set about arrangements inside, which included a leisurely breakfast of coffee and what looked through
the window like a baked wound. Finally she let him in and,
without looking at him even once, took up her position. They
dealt with each other through the glass partition by means of
a tray and microphone, the way it's done in prisons. This
protection was arranged for the reasons that soon became obvious.

"Yes?" she finally said, making it sound like no.

"Have you got something cheap?" Vincent asked.

"Wizard number?"

"What?" asked the baffled supplicant.

"Reservation?" she continued, alluding no further to wiz-
ardry.

"Well, no."

"Compact?"

"Yes, please. The cheapest."

She tapped her keyboard. "No compacts."

"Whatever you have."

"Nothing unless you got a reservation."

"How do I get a reservation?"

"Phone."

Someone had urinated in the phone booth—perhaps generations of people. The 800 number cheerfully accepted Vincent's
request for a reservation. Perhaps the 800 operators worked far
away in a pleasant village in the Midwest. They didn't actually
have to see their customers, which must improve their disposi-
tions. The 800 operator assigned Vincent a car in the very office
that had just refused and rejected him. Now the glass between
him and the clerk was justified. Had it not been there, he might
have been returned to jail on an assault charge.

The complimentary map from the car-rental office revealed to Vincent that he had departed New Haven in the wrong direction. If he hadn't been arrested, he would soon have arrived in Boston, wondering why there was no longer anything familiar about Manhattan. On his exhausted journey back toward New York, Vincent wondered whether this misadventure was a sign to him not to be so sure of himself, his marriage, and his luxurious future.

Chapter 9

*D*espite the lesser figures originally discussed when Vincent signed the rental agreement, the total calculated by the clerk in New York was well over two hundred dollars. The large, glowering grouper in the agency's New York glass tank blandly recapitulated a multitude of reasons for the price rise, most of them revealed in fine gray print on the contract Vincent had signed. He was exhausted and furious after a long trip in a hot, tinny little car blistered onto a sleepless night in the drunk tank. Vincent felt like a baited animal. He even considered shoving his face against the pane protecting the clerk, twisting it into some loathsome distortion, or possibly weeping.

The local lawyer Vincent called from the room he'd taken at the Yale Club for the sake of matrimonial appearances advised him it would cost at least a thousand to defend the drunk-driving case, and that at worst he would have to spend a week in jail. Vincent looked around the little room he was expected to keep, even though he stayed with Mary at her parents' apartment. The bill for this ornamental room was growing every day. He'd only taken Mary's car to save himself train fare, in the end saving twenty dollars to owe well over a thousand. There was a week to go before the wedding, and Vincent was grossly overextended.

His mother had exorbitantly overextended herself to give him a thousand dollars and her own mother's engagement ring. But this windfall was gone, and financial panic bit him inside his stomach. Vincent paced the Spartan bedroom, raking his head with both hands formed into claws.

Her car was stolen. His money was gone. All the wafting ease of his cartographically longitudinal ascent toward New Haven from New York—he'd gone to "New Haven" to discuss his "new home," an irony that set him to chuckling a day earlier —now recurred to Vincent as a chimera, the delusion of a fantasist.

One day earlier there were no problems, even when he tried to stir some up. Hadn't he been disappointed not to get raked over coals of suspicion by McLaughlin? He was looking for something rough against which to rub his smooth plans so he could get a feel for his fate. The very next day, so blandly similar to its predecessor in terms of weather and world news, all that lovely puff was deflated. Vincent was broke, Mary's car was stolen, and a drunk-driving rap was reaching at his perspiring skull from the gavel of an angry judge in a village that could only imagine it was fellows like Vincent in big cars from New York who had ruined it.

Chapter 10

*U*nlike the recent police, drunks, and rent-a-car clerks, the uniformed functionaries at the River House (where Mary's parents' apartment lay in a tower so formidable-looking that it made the East River look like its moat) seemed loving and hopeful and specifically concerned with Vincent's wishes. They all acted like happy supernumeraries —spear carriers in the opera of wealth.

"Oh, Mr. Booth!" exclaimed the gracious, elderly Swedish housekeeper who opened the door to the Brigham apartment. Vincent had to ring the doorbell because he'd lost his key, as well as Mary's car and all his money. And he hadn't even married her yet. Vincent felt vulnerable and out of place.

"We were so worried," she confided with a warm grin before disappearing into the starker, staff quarters of the extensive apartment.

"Darling, is everything all right?" asked Mary, thumping down the seashell spiral of stairs.

Vincent looked terrible to Mary—exhausted, bedraggled, and haunted, or maybe hunted. He was pale and greasy. His eyes were red flowers floating on gray lily pads. What the hell was wrong? she wondered. Was this the famous "cold-feet" syndrome that imminent weddings can sometimes cause in grooms-to-be?

"The car was stolen."

"Are you all right?" she answered at once. How sweet, he thought, and how misapplied in his case. He imagined she guessed there had been violence—that the car had been wrestled from him on the threat of death. He realized the first thing he would have thought in her place would have concerned the car. How superior she suddenly seemed to him. She didn't worry about her expensive car. She worried only about him.

He'd ravaged her possessions. He'd failed the alphabet and white-line tests. He wasn't just in over his head. He was way out over it, out where you order bad dogs and Adam and Eve to go, and where he should be sent instead of being welcomed in this way.

"Mary, I got into trouble," he began.

As he talked, he reminded Mary of how he seemed when she'd rescued him in France.

"Take a bath," she said with simple authority when he finished.

Mary adored Vincent this way. He reminded her of the wounded bird, the wet kitten, and the stray. Small creatures with dangerous problems had won her heart since childhood, because they alone reflected her dilemma of pain in a material paradise. Poor things. It was so hard to be a poor thing if you were, in fact, a rich one.

Vincent lay in scented water, with hours and walls of tile between him and the drunk tank where his cell mate had diarrhea. "Whatter yinfor?" the diarrhetic had asked. To Vincent this man was astonishingly unembarrassed, talking away as he sat on the open toilet in their cell.

"Drunk driving," Vincent answered.

The human body, no matter which human is its landlord, conducts an inevitable industry with no apparent affection or interest in its patron. The enthroned drunk began to seem a mere accessory to his body's crime. His big, inexorable body—the very thing that had gotten him drunk—was clearly having nothing to do with him. That body cared no more about him than a carriage horse must have considered its driver in the old days.

"I'm in for drunk walking," he said without laughing.

"Excuse me?" said Vincent.

"I was so drunk, I got arrested for drunk walking." This remark apparently caused fuses to burn and switches to be thrown in the incarcerated pedestrian's body, which quickly rose up with its own noises and effects. Vincent said nothing, feeling not so far removed from the mind-body dichotomy displayed before him.

The body exploded and stank, and wasn't pretty and never would be. Out of it came the voice of its prisoner, deluded into believing he was master, landlord, and driver of the disappointing flesh. Vincent considered his own insubordinate and inevitable flesh and how it had brought him there and laid him low.

In the drunk tank he'd thought extensively about the restless, uncontrollable, unpredictable mass extending under his high-riding head. It seemed as dangerous as Princess, his mean, precarious childhood mare.

In the luxurious bath at Mary's this recent traitor was happy and loyal. Warm water reduced its specific gravity and comforted it. Mary sponged him, reaching into the safe pocket of enamel in which she'd placed him.

How nice. Vincent was rosy and smiling. His body, he now reckoned, was his own adornment, once again the mount of a reckless, dashing cavalier. Rising from the tub, he pressed it wet into willing Mary.

"Hi, Dick," Mary said somewhat later to her lawyer in the bedroom. Vincent, the accessory and subject of this call, stared at her. Mary explained everything. Then she handed the phone to Vincent. He recapitulated his experiences of returning in the wrong direction from New Haven.

It was all fixed. Mary didn't even want to discuss it further. The lawyer—whose voice seemed to Vincent to sound of suits, paneling, and rows of identically bound law books—had received Vincent's problems, placed them before himself and smashed them away with a gavel more powerful than any judge's.

There was no more drunk-driving charge. A new car was on the way. The unpleasantry was removed like a stain by this splendid domestic. Vincent was both relieved and indebted.

Chapter 11

*V*incent was privately glad he couldn't paint as much as he wanted because of his job at the museum. This gave him something to complain about, a flaw in the smooth gold walls of Mary's wealth, and also offered him some excuse for his persistent frustration in the studio Mary had given him for Christmas.

His painting just wasn't coming, no matter how he tried. The fine, flax-smelling Belgian canvas was as willing as a whore to do anything he desired, but only because he'd paid her, not because she loved him. When the painting of Mary at the café—which he expected to look at least as grand as Manet's Girl Bartender at the Follies Bergère—retreated from his every touch, he figured he must have overthought it and decided to put it aside until his facility was back in order.

He began to experiment with his other idea, a picture of a woman having her hair done. Mary's hairdresser, a delicate Filipino with an astonishingly deep, volcanic voice, was only too delighted to give Vincent the run of his salon. "You can sit under the dryer with your sketch pad and no one will notice," he boomed. And the effect of such a voice from such a tiny creature was like a diesel engine running full-throttle inside a Chinese figurine.

Vincent decided such a disguise would be too distracting for him to perform. Instead of the dryer offered by Mr. Rico, Vincent took a chair in a corner and was amused to find that the customers assumed him to be Mr. Rico's boyfriend.

Women acted differently here, Vincent discovered. The sexual neutrality, and the effeminacy and make-believe quality of the hairdressers encouraged the customers to act up to it. The women were prancing and camping contrapuntally to the stylists.

"I don't b*elieve* it!" crooned a man whose weak baby face belied the bodybuilding torso he presented in a black T-shirt.

"Isn't it *unbelievable*?" responded his customer, a hogan of a woman in her fifties. Her voice was deeper than his. Heard on a radio, Vincent would have pictured the client as a wise and mission-weary bomber pilot in a World War II movie, and the hairdresser as the girl with whom he was flirting in a pub.

Vincent's studio was in a part of Little Italy getting more little still as the neighboring Chinese population grew larger. Except for a weekly mah-jongg game after midnight a floor below, it was quiet and big enough for a tapestry-size Rubens. There was a skylight, a sink, and a toilet. Vincent had enjoyed selecting an iron bed and a couple of chairs from a used-furniture place nearby. It was a Spartan space. There was no phone. Only art would happen here.

Vincent wanted to find the timeless essence of identity which glanced out of hundreds of great pictures at his new workplace, the Metropolitan Museum of Art. His mind was full of awareness of such artistic accomplishment. He laid out his sketches of Mr. Rico's clients, and drew the first line, the one he quickly felt his subject's forehead resting against, on the fragrant gessoed linen.

Her eyes required him to move that foundation forehead line several times. Her nose called everything further to order. Perhaps he had it—the eyes were great, that nose was right. Of course he had it, just as he had Mary's face a year ago in France! No—over a year ago. Time was galloping . . . and then the mouth. It's hard to paint an eternal mouth, a Mona Lisa mouth that jacks a picture up out of time. Mouths are so relentlessly expressive, so transitory and definitive. Vincent wanted the simplest of mouths, the most bare and anatomical of mouths—and he could not get one to appear.

He decided to move quickly to his subjects' surroundings, to come back to the mouth after the picture was extensive enough to overpower and control such a small part. He told himself that the wonderful idea of a woman having her hair done, not to mention the witty surroundings, would eventually hound that mouth out there where it belonged.

Seven hours later, everything looked overworked. Although the leopard spots on a chair were great, the central figure, the point of it all, had been lost as the infection of doubt had spread from the virulent failure of the mouth. Vincent rubbed out the whole overworked face.

Maybe that was a picture: a hairdressing salon with a customer whose face was rubbed out. Very funny, but not a picture. Not Vincent's picture. How had the picture come out so badly again? His intention was powerful enough for him to have spent two weeks sketching at Mr. Rico's. His inspiration was focused on a woman's face, a face he saw inside himself but couldn't seem to deliver.

Vincent threw his brush at the picture, hoping it all would shatter and fall, the picture, the whole studio, and the mahjongg game now shouting and slapping a floor below—all of it into rubble from which he could forever walk away.

At home all the lights were on, as they should not be at three in the morning. The bedroom was empty. Vincent found himself apprehensive, then scared. The door to the nursery was open, and the crib was empty.

"Crib death" they called it. Europa, their four-week-old daughter, had expired like a raindrop on sand. She was dead and gone. She was barely there before she was no more.

There were doctors and nurses and sedatives over the ensuing weeks. Mary cried all the time. When he closed his eyes to sleep, Vincent kept seeing that pitifully small box marched into Christianity's ceremony of finality. Mary began to seem and feel alien.

Vincent gave up trying to paint in the studio. To be alone there was simply unbearable. The place seemed to Vincent like his daughter's coffin from her dead point of view—a cubic, eternal emptiness surrounding him.

That emptiness made him glad he had his job at the Met. He was grateful for the interruption and human intercourse it required. All day long there were people to ask him questions, matters to be settled, and the very great pictures to look at.

Part 2

Chapter 1

*F*lorida, Laura Montgomery's cat, was black with three white boots. She'd found him beside a road in Key West, an abandoned kitten staggering nowhere in a box step, meowing interrogatively to her empty car.

Now the kitten was a cat pinned down under a sofa in the combat conditions of a cocktail party in Laura's New York apartment. Big male gunboat shoes cruised past Florida's hiding place. Bright, impaling high-heeled shoes fell about like bayonets. Florida studied the low martial horizon from his sofa bunker, praying for some break in the deadly, thundering formations of feet through which he could scat for Laura's bedroom, the safest place in the apartment.

Laughter boomed and rattled from unseen emplacements hidden in the smoke and roar. Florida crouched like a loaf of bread, tail tip twitching and eyes half shut. He was purring, not because he was relaxed but because cats bluff calm as a last resort. Cornered by puppies, their last move is often to blink lazily, trying to seem irrelevant, knowing that a show of fright can cue the kill.

Laura Montgomery's old schoolmate, Missy Ferguson, was in one pair of the high heels Florida feared. They were new and more than Missy could afford, but they were perfect with the dress she couldn't afford, either. Missy had decided that an invitation from Laura required such extravagance. Laura Montgomery was the most fabulous girl Missy had ever known. Even at school, Laura's beauty and connections implied a much grander world than the campus, or books, or even movies could offer. Who wouldn't buy an expensive outfit to go to a party thrown by the beautiful daughter of the famous movie director James Montgomery?

When Missy spotted Laura outside Saks Fifth Avenue, she regrettably had jerked into a very exaggerated pose of greeting with one hand on her hip, the other in a frozen wave, and a chortling grin on her face—all of which would have been funny if her old schoolmate had recognized her, but Laura had just kept walking, looking away from Missy as she would have from an unwelcome beggar.

"Laura? It's Missy Ferguson," Missy had to insist, catching Laura's arm. Laura was nice after that, and even invited Missy to this party; but it had been an awkward moment.

Laura had quit college, something Missy could no more imagine herself doing than not brushing her teeth before bed. Even at college Laura had led a postgraduate sort of life. Rather famous men telephoned, wrote, and came to see her—men from the real world of tested success and celebrity, instead of the clawing, panting boys trailing beer bottles who were Missy's lot.

The first names mentioned in Laura's conversation didn't require last names in order to be recognized. Laura actually knew these people, who were named over and over again in newspapers and magazines. She went to parties and nightclubs with them. It put considerable distance between her and her schoolmates. Leaving college early seemed natural for someone like Laura, who had never entirely arrived there to begin with.

Laura wasn't only the daughter of the famous movie director. She was also the daughter of a bishop's daughter, and through her mother related to a well-known family of Easterners who had not only made money but had also been distinguished academics and clergymen. Socially, you just couldn't ask for more family advantages in America. All that and her absolutely staggering beauty made Missy once say, "Maybe all *men* are created equal, but . . ." and jerk her head toward a dormitory window, beneath which Laura was passing with a French film star, kicking fall leaves and laughing. The remark was quoted by Missy's schoolmates for a year.

Missy had an extraordinary reason for her determined recapture of an old acquaintance outside Saks. Because of her work at an admired and popular literary magazine, she knew one of the writers was at work on a profile of Laura's father. She felt Laura would be interested, and that the author of the profile would be too. Both these possibilities couldn't help but raise Missy's lot at the magazine, where she currently served in the typing pool—a scullery where filthy, change-encrusted manuscripts were washed clean—dreaming of eventually writing and editing instead.

Laura's invitation led Missy to grateful extravagance in the store outside which the scene of their reacquaintance had taken place. She wondered if the dress she were buying would bring romance. Missy figured that the men at a party given by Laura Montgomery must be much more interesting than those she had met so far in New York.

So, for both professional and personal reasons, Missy was thrilled to enter Laura's party. Her first sight of the place and people was anything but disappointing.

Missy's studio apartment would probably fit in one of Laura's fireplaces, which were so big and grand that they made Missy think of Bach organ fugues. Absolutely incredible. It was an apartment of African wildlife proportions. Those fireplaces were as big as rhinos. Square feet of space stretched out to the horizons like grazing herds.

Laura sat on a great leather pouf in the middle of it all, princess of the evening. Instantly Missy wished she'd worn something less stodgy and conventional than her brand-new bank-straining dress and suddenly suburban-seeming shoes. Laura was in a silk blouse and pants. She was so outrageously beautiful, her boy-angel face with no makeup, her short, fashionable hairdo, her great big breasts and slim, leggy body— Laura Montgomery made Missy feel like a member of a subspecies.

Loathing every square inch of black taffeta hissing about her as she made her way toward her hostess, Missy still felt elated to be there, even in what she now thought of as a prom-queen outfit. But what the hell, she reasoned, even in slacks and a silk blouse she wouldn't look like Laura Montgomery.

"Do you know Vincent Booth?" Laura asked when Missy arrived and greeted her. Laura rhymed Booth with smooth.

"Missy Ferguson and . . ." Laura gestured at the other member of their group, a young woman who looked artsy to Missy. She wore layers of organically dyed hand weaves. Her extended hand was ornamented with jewelry undoubtedly pounded out by squatting brown men a world away from here.

Missy sensed Laura's hostility even before the woman's next remark explained why.

"Apartment cats eventually jump out the window. They can't take the confinement. There's an extraordinary amount of unreported cat suicide," said the artistic woman with accusatory solemnity.

Missy knew about Florida, Laura's beloved cat, because during their fateful encounter outside Saks, Laura had explained how an operation on the cat had cost $212. How could Missy forget that when it was the exact sum she had paid for the very shoes she now regretted standing in? The woman in the hand-loomed layers seemed to be lecturing Laura on the inadvisability of maintaining a cat in the city. How impertinent, thought Missy. What a stupid bitch.

"They can't stand it anymore, and they just, like, go for it."

"Meoww . . ." said the man, Vincent Booth, who seemed tight and humorous. He made his meow trail off, as if a cat were plunging into the Grand Canyon.

"Oh, don't," said Missy. "I have a cat I love, and so does Laura."

The tall, facetious man turned back to the woven woman. "I'll bet yours jumped out the window because you were boring him to death," he said sweetly. Laura laughed magnificently as the woman sailed off.

"I never heard of cats jumping out windows," said Missy.

"Sure, it happens all the time!" Vincent grinned. "They just turn into doormats when they hit. Lots of taxi drivers carry spatulas in their glove compartments."

Laura laughed and laughed. It was clear to Missy that this man had enchanted her, and he was especially enjoying himself. He was handsome and he was tight—all the makings for a romantic disaster. He began to look familiar to Missy, who wondered whether this was because she'd met him before or because he was a celebrity.

Don't I know you?" she finally asked, cocking a robin's eye at Vincent Booth.

"I hope so," he said, but only out of cocktail gallantry.

Out of the corner of her eye Laura saw Florida dash from under the sofa for her bedroom. He carried his tail like a brandished saber through the battlefield of guests.

"Kitty," she burbled in the high, baby-talk voice in which she addressed birds and animals. Her drinking had been goaded along by Vincent Booth's.

"What do you do?" Missy asked Vincent, quickly regretting the banality of her question. "It's such an American question," a world-weary Italian had groaned when Missy asked it of him at a party given two weeks earlier by Alitalia, the Italian airline, to sponsor Italian cheese—an event Missy had attended in hopes of writing it up as an anecdote for her magazine.

"I work at a museum," he said, sounding surprisingly grim.

"The Met," said Laura. "He's very brilliant or something." Vincent laughed.

Missy felt way behind them, both socially and chemically.

Would her gaffes never end? Overdressed, asking people what they did—maybe she just wasn't sophisticated enough for Laura's parties. Maybe Missy shouldn't venture beyond beginner-level parties where bottles as varied as a sidewalk crowd stood among cracked plastic glasses in which cigarettes swam next to ruptured ice and pretzel bags.

The last party Missy had gone to was given by six men who pooled address books, rented and cleaned a loft, and provided the party staples. The guests all brought something. Men brought bottles and women brought food—some of it personally prepared and symmetrically arranged. Such parties were crude, atavistic premarital rituals; the men thumping down their phallic bottles, the women spreading out nurturing bowls of potato salad and symmetries of raw vegetables and dip.

Laura's party had no such youthful, simple themes. Here, there was a variety of age and sexuality. On a refectory table draped in gorgeous weavings, food was dramatically displayed in beaten copper basins and terra-cotta vessels. Drinks were served in dark, unusually heavy glasses. The objects at Laura's came mostly from firelight civilizations. Looking it over, Missy made a mental note to use much less light next time she had people over. Everything was rich, romantic, and remote, as if they were celebrants in the tent of a Bedouin who collected modern art. How could someone walk into such a party wearing black taffeta and ask people what they did?

"Aren't you doing something in television?" Vincent suddenly asked Laura, ameliorating Missy's regretful reflections.

"Yeah. In fact, it sort of looks like I may do *It's Morning*. Do you know what time you have to get up?" Laura said. "Like three-thirty or four," she answered herself.

"What kind of love life can you have on that schedule?" Vincent asked, smiling broadly. "Night watchmen and vampires?"

"Married men," suggested Missy, causing a surprising silence, and then simultaneous guffaws from Laura and Vincent. Missy guessed right then that Vincent was married, and that Laura and Vincent either were having, or were just about to have, an affair.

Perhaps there were some advantages to love affairs with married men, considered Missy. Married men would give you plenty of time to yourself and wouldn't leave you for somebody else, since that's what they had already done. Still, Missy wouldn't do it. But it was typical Montgomery.

A familiar face was looking their way, a face Missy recognized—that heiress, the cousin of Margaret's. They'd all been bicycling together in France five years ago. Seeing someone at the party she'd at least met made Missy feel more ratified as a guest. Laura's party was now part of Missy's world too. She excused herself from Vincent and Laura and crossed the room with more authority to find out what had happened to Mary Brigham in the five years since she'd taken off with that guy in the south of France. Wait a minute—she looked back at Vincent Booth. Yes, he was that very guy, wasn't he! Missy was pleased to realize how well connected she was—even at parties thrown by the beautiful daughters of famous movie directors.

Florida awoke with a start. Suddenly his final bunker was lurching. Was nowhere safe tonight? Laura's shoes fell into view, then a man's. The bed began to stir, squeak, and jerk. The lights went out. Florida jumped up but knew of no better place to hide than this very one now threatening to come down about his ears. With no hope of refuge Florida crouched down again, still except for the disapproving tail tip. On his face was the fatalistic dignity of lower intelligence.

"Vincent, I want to go home," commanded a woman's voice at the bedroom door. The bed stopped rocking. "Vincent?" asked the voice, then it shouted, "Vincent!"

"Just a minute," he shouted back. Four feet found the floor, and a light came on.

"Leave it off," whispered Laura violently. The light went back off. Florida's pupils dilated instantly. In near panic, Laura and the man began to fight with their clothes, forcing them back on. Then the man disappeared into a slap of light from the door. The door closed and it was dark again. Laura sat down on the bed as Florida emerged from underneath.

"Kitty?" Laura said in a tiny voice. She made the trilling noise she seemed to believe bridged their species. Florida, pointed at the incised rectangle of light around the bedroom door, jerked his tail in a couple of ferocious but graceful spasms, showing Laura what he would do to anyone who dared to make her unhappy. She gathered the cat to her breast. He shook his head when a teardrop pelted his ear. He could smell perfume and desire.

Laura washed her face and looked at herself in the mirror. Short hair was a durable style for lovemaking. She was red-eyed and snotty, like a person with hay fever. People always wanted her, and sometimes she wanted them, too, only it always turned into a mess, like the sight in her mirror.

With passion's ravages repaired, Laura returned to her

party, glad it was there to distract her from the surprising sadness kissing Vincent had caused. In no time another man was before her, assaying her like a trophy. This one had a beard. He was an archaeologist headed for Mexico to a dig.

"You have to be very neat on those digs, don't you?" Laura asked him. "Don't all the little pieces have to be numbered and put in rows and everything?" She was so incredibly good-looking, the archaeologist grew instantaneously passionate. He nodded but kept his eyes staring directly into hers. "Itz-papalotl," the archaeologist murmured to her.

"What did you say?"

"Itzpapalotl. Obsidian Knife Butterfly, Star Goddess of Agriculture." He found he had to clear his throat, which desire had clogged. He taught her to say the word, nodding slowly to encourage her efforts. It was getting late. Guests were receding.

"Once we went to this dig in Anatolia," mused Laura, who seemed to have an anecdote for every subject. Whenever she used the pronoun *we,* she assumed people understood she was speaking of herself and her father. She further assumed this man knew perfectly well that her father was James Montgomery. "They had a temporary museum on the site of the dig—this sort of Quonset hut with all the best things from the dig in it."

The archaeologist stared intensely and impassively, his nostrils flaring a little, like a predator waiting for a calf to straggle off from the protective herd.

Laura was smiling broadly, knowing already how her story was going to come out. "And there were these guards all around, you know, intensely Turkish-looking, and the little man who showed us through the museum had a pistol. They all had these pistols and mustaches," she said, touching her upper lip with two of her long fingers.

Jewish men were particularly vulnerable to Laura because she looked so magnificently and unassailably Anglo-Saxon. She inevitably caused Jewish men to regress historically into the Old Testament, thinking of war chariots and conquest. She was fully aware that this archaeologist was hearing the tribal ram's horn calling him to arms.

"And when we came to the end, he asked us if we wanted anything," she continued.

The archaeologist kept nodding until he realized she was waiting for him to say something. The clangor of the Bronze Age army rising within him had deafened him to her actual words.

"I'm sorry," he croaked. "I wasn't listening. I mean, I was listening, but I was listening so hard, I couldn't hear anything."

This made them laugh together, as she had earlier with Vincent Booth.

After she'd found out from Mary Brigham what had happened five years ago in France, Missy wanted to tell Laura everything about Vincent Booth—to warn her and inform her of the surprising amount Missy now knew about him. Missy had been right there when he met Mary Brigham, and in fact she had introduced them! Now Missy was even more integrally a part of this glamorous world of Laura's party. If she hadn't run into Laura at Saks the day before, all of the events she now realized were contingent on her own personal existence would have fallen like that philosophical tree in the forest, making no noise unless somebody was there to hear it.

Missy was sure Laura would love to hear her fabulous information, but now Laura was talking to yet another guy who was obviously completely crazy about her. Laura was unbelievable. Mary Brigham, now Mrs. Vincent Booth, had angrily left the party with her husband, who Missy could tell had really been getting it on with Laura. To think this party could have happened without Missy even being there! It was frustrating not to be able to tell Laura everything right then and there, but there was always tomorrow and the phone and a renewed friendship that looked like it might keep opening up more and more splendid doors.

"Good-bye, Laura. I had the best time. I'll call you tomorrow," Missy said urgently.

Laura could feel heat on the side of her profile nearest the archaeologist as she bade Missy farewell. Oddly, the laugh she had just shared with him created an obstacle for seduction. It reminded her of what had transpired earlier that same evening with Vincent Booth, and it made the thought of sleeping with the archaeologist seem a little sordid. Yet she had set out to sleep with a man tonight, if only because she felt the situation demanded it. "If someone turns up and I feel like it, I'm going to bed with him," she had actually told Florida the night before. "Because I'm so sick of that little bastard Toby Hyman, I can't see straight."

Laura now turned back to the archaeologist, who was staring at her like a child at a magic show.

When Missy left, Laura finished her anecdote of the dig in Anatolia. "He was offering us the stuff in the museum, you know, to buy . . . anything we wanted from the dig."

This time the archaeologist laughed uproariously and nodded with vigor. The first laugh had opened one gate, and now they were laughing down the next.

"My father told the Turkish people who were showing us

the dig about the guard offering us the contents of the museum. And the next morning, when we walked out of our tent, we found the guard had been hung by his thumbs. It wasn't very pleasant."

Now they were alone. The archaeologist's name had come out, but Laura, buzzing with wine, had forgotten it. He was making scrambled eggs and coffee. Laura admired his excavation-learned patience.

"Didn't you ever want to be in the movies?" he asked.

They all asked that sooner or later, and Laura just shook her head.

Laura's facial expression made the archaeologist regret having asked it. It took her out of his company into what appeared to be a painful, private world. He was scared he might have lost her interest.

Once, diving at the Well of the Maidens, a pool into which sacrificed virgins were dropped, along with other presents for the complex and horrific gods of the Aztecs, he had gently fingered up from the silt a figure of Chalchiuhtlicue—she of the Jeweled Robes, a magnificent find—only to drop it, flailing at it in underwater slow motion as it receded into an opaque grotto, never to be found again.

"Good eggs," Laura said in a languid voice, restoring the archaeologist's hopes.

Florida was running around with nocturnal energy, relieved the party was over. He entwined himself around Laura's legs, purring like a generator.

Laura and the archaeologist ate standing up in the kitchen while she told him about her job at the network. "I think I could really contribute," Laura said, talking about being anchor-woman of the network morning show.

Anchorwoman of the network morning show? National stardom? A face in the supermarket magazines? He disbelieved her only a moment. A look at her changed his disbelief. This woman was incredible—she could have anything she wanted in the world.

She was intensely, ridiculously beautiful, with her long legs flashing like scissors, her big, high-set breasts, her cameo of a face. He rose, reached out for her arms, and tasted the eggs in her mouth. Hell, maybe she'd quit her job and come with him.

The archaeologist, giggled into his fist. It seemed so impossibly wonderful. Now they were naked. She had jumped off the bed and closed herself in the bathroom to arrange birth control. The luck of it all staggered him. Invited to a party the night before he must leave for a dig in Mexico, he winds up making love with the most beautiful woman in the world. Who had asked him? Somebody he knew from Colombia. It was something he'd only done because there was nothing better to do. And now this!

Women in bathrooms always seemed to take longer than expected. The memory of her naked form blazed in the dark all around him, like the perfectly preserved Mayan murals in his boyhood fantasies of archaeological discovery. She was the most beautiful woman Bernie had ever seen in his life, aloof as a tower, fine as a gem, magnificent as Montezuma's headdress, and only moments away from conjoining him to earthly paradise.

When she opened the door, she turned on the bedroom light and marched to her closet. She pulled on a robe and sat in a chair, closing off her sex with a defensive leg-crossing.

"Look, I'm sorry," she said.

"What's the matter?" Astonished, he rushed to crouch beside her and stroke her arm.

"It isn't you, it's me, but you'll have to get dressed and go."

"What?" he said, shooting to his feet like an exclamation point. He was enraged.

"I'm very sorry, but I'm not doing this, and I hope you will just please go."

"What the hell is this?" He snarled, fisting up. She rose, strode past him, and locked herself in the bathroom.

On his way out, a cat started bowing up around his legs as if to trip him. He kicked out. The cat twitched in a midair spasm that enabled him to land on all fours, off which he shot at once in a vector aimed under the couch.

Chapter 2

*A*fter the party Mary Brigham Booth did not wait for her wayward husband to pay for the cab. Neither did she wait for him at the elevator. Vincent was left alone in the lobby. The night doorman discreetly stared out the door until the elevator that had borne Mrs. Booth aloft returned. When the elevator doors closed over Vincent, the doorman laughed out loud. Serves the son of a bitch right, he thought to himself. Domestic trouble is a great democratizer, and a great relief to someone standing up for the rich all day.

Sensitive to anyone's opinion of him, Vincent considered other possible explanations of his wife's desertion of him in the lobby; diarrhea and an emergency phone call occurred to him as plausible examples. The elevator man nodded at each airy concussion from a passing floor, as if in obedient agreement with Vincent's unspoken defense. The elevator man, too, was steeped in discretion.

When the doors opened at his apartment, Vincent and the elevator man grunted "Good night" simultaneously, though the latter added "sir."

United in the lobby, the elevator- and doormen shared a hearty laugh.

"He better watch out, 'cause she's got the money," the doorman noted. The elevator man nodded solemnly, because the subject of money can sober any conversation.

What had Mary actually seen or imagined when she came to the bedroom at Laura's party? In retrospect, Vincent realized there was no actual confrontation; it wasn't as though they'd all been looking at one another. He was anxious to discover what Mary thought had happened, but the taxi ride home had been silent. They'd sat as dynamically separate as the North and South Poles, and now they'd sleep in the same configuration in the big linen cloud of the marriage bed—unless she kicked him out, of course. He listened to the hydraulics of her preparations for slumber.

When she emerged, he stood up.

"Mary, I—"

"Good night," was her total, uninviting reply.

Vincent exited the bedroom. In the hallway he stopped to stare at the doorway behind which lay their new baby, Wallace, and his nanny, Mrs. Keswick. Tears came to Vincent's eyes but didn't run. He shook his head and set off to make himself another drink.

That goddamn terminal, unedifying "good night" of Mary's was a perfect example of what Vincent felt he was up against in the ever solidifying imprisonment of marriage. Perhaps the drink was too strong. He added more soda water in a gesture he considered virtuous. Her "good night" did not condemn Vincent or open an argument or question or even particularly include him. It was polite, and polite was her method for doing anything she wanted. Vincent marched into the great sitting room of their apartment, turning on the lights. He held his highball chest-high, scowling intensely like a naval officer coming on the bridge in enemy waters. Mary had an oceanic fortune and good manners, a combination against which there was no argument. Vincent sighed, turned off the illuminated grandeur, and walked back through the entrance hall.

In the guest room, where he'd considered sleeping, he thought out the effects of such a retreat. This was just where she was putting him, exiling him, until time covered his breach of behavior at Laura's party. Deciding he must not relent, he drank down the rest of his highball and returned to the master bedroom, flinging on a light with confrontational abandon.

But Mary wore a sleep mask and did not flinch.

"What the fuck am I sleeping with—the Lone Ranger or a fucking raccoon?" he snarled, not unpleased by his sarcastic wit. She rolled away and pulled a pillow over her head. Vincent undressed noisily and climbed into his side of the bed.

In the dark, withdrawn to the very edge of the marital bed, Vincent alternately chastised himself and justified his actions at Laura Montgomery's party while he listened to Mary's repetitious breathing. No longer did anything seem capable of interrupting the inexorable patterns that grew up around Mary and him, stronger every year. The thought of her husband with another woman was apparently not enough of a shock even to make Mary lose sleep.

If only they hadn't lost the first baby, or if only he hadn't stayed on and had a second, or if only he'd kept painting instead of going to the Met, or if only he'd gone out with Laura back when they'd met in undergraduate days, or . . . Vincent expelled a steamy sigh into his pillow. He'd quit painting because no paintings would come in that perfect studio she'd given him. He loved baby Wally and was happier that Wally had come into this world than he was about anything else in his life, and the museum wasn't so bad, and he couldn't have had a romance with Laura Montgomery back at college because at that time she had the irrelevance of pure unattainability.

Since nothing was said by Mary, nothing had happened. This was Mary's way. She had not actually entered Laura's bedroom and caught them. In fact, she had only knocked on the door and said she wanted to go home. Perhaps she didn't know how he and Laura had so sweetly yet roughly gone at stripping and peeling each other, how smooth and tender parts were exposed and . . . Vincent felt a buzz of desire. But maybe Mary really didn't have any idea of what he'd fallen into with Laura in her bedroom. Maybe she thought they were just talking about old times, or that others were in there with them. Of course not. Of course she knew. She had to know.

He clenched his teeth, bunched his pillow, and butted his forehead against this linen protagonist. Mary was now perfectly the creature of the established social programs she once implied she couldn't stand. As it turned out, she couldn't change. The great oxen of her fortune dragged her inevitably into the ancient family rut.

Her family had become his fate. Its expectations and migrations patterned his life. His wife's majestic trust funds patronized and codified their behavior. Like a group of grazing nomads, they moved on rounds from the city to the country, then to the coast of Maine, then to that of Florida, with periodic diversions to Europe. At every destination there were examples of enviable real estate, happy friends, relatives, and employees to receive them.

Why couldn't Vincent just go along with such luxurious good fortune? Why must he strain against the pull of oxen, a hopeless contest?

Laura sprang up again in his thoughts. Her apartment had appealed to him enormously. It was plainly her own and not, like his, the formula of an interior decorator applied to the inventory of estate executors. Laura's was at once funky and extravagant. There were pieces of bright cloth, modern art, Victorian extravaganzas, and Bauhaus novelties. It did not immediately suggest expense and possession the way Vincent had come to feel his homes with Mary did. It was inspiring and creative instead of relentlessly magnificent. Now Vincent considered how even Laura's decor measured out his mistake for him.

Unwittingly Vincent had too quickly clasped Mary's fine old furnishings to his bosom. He had been thrilled by the glamour of these grand old trophies—booty beyond the reach of all but the richest collectors. It derived from the sea captains, slave brokers, mining engineers, financial speculators, and marriers of wealth who had been gathered up into the Mohican Trust by a great turn-of-the-century manufacturing fortune. The things were beautiful. The accumulation was stupendous. Wally would be a rich man. It was wrong to kiss Laura. It was wonderful to kiss her.

Judging from his own grunts and sighs, the kisses of Laura Montgomery had loosened an enormity of conjecture Vincent had only guessed existed within himself. People had acted as if

Vincent's life ended the day he married Mary Brigham. Her wealth represented conclusion to everyone. Appropriately, marble at once began to spring up everywhere around him. From the very aisle of the church where they were wed to building lobbies, apartment bathrooms, mantels, clubs, and hotels, Vincent found himself more and more frequently among marble, the stuff of cemeteries.

Of course, Mary thought it was fine for Vincent to work at the museum. It was, after all, marble. Here Vincent muffled a bitter snort with his pillow. Working at the museum gave him something to do in well-cut suits. It didn't matter how little they paid him. She had, after all, plenty for both of them.

All the men at the museum were rich, with the exception of certain impoverished scholars whose penury seemed as appropriate as their arcane university degrees and concentration wrinkles, and of course the guards and janitors. The lawyers and curators, and of course the director and the president, were all wealthy men for whom the museum served as a pleasing metaphor of moneyed civilization.

Cajoling funds from the rich was best done by the rich. For the poor to seek funds for the trophies of wealth would be unseemly and out of place. The egocentric old oil gnome; homely, thin-lipped heirs of a spectacularly greedy Civil War draft dodger; the former whore who probably killed the old auto manufacturer; the cretinous woman from Texas . . . All of them required wealthy beseechers. They had welcomed Vincent as an appropriate addition to the museum, that is, to the fundraising festivities and congratulatory convocations for which the museum provided a theme.

Another abrupt twist of his body bounced the bed and seized at the covers but did not interrupt Mary's steady and relentless breathing. His life with Mary, Vincent reflected, was only a coincidence of two separate enterprises: her fulfillment of a richly funded, tested, and proven way of life; and his own halted, impoverished experiments.

Since childhood Vincent had figured a recurrent pattern behind closed eyes in the dark. A tiny constellation of violet specks framed in a filigree of light passed by. He could jerk it by squinting, but in no other way could he interrupt it, move it from its trajectory, retain it as it disappeared, or summon it back to his perception. He had tried without success to make sense of it both as a common experience of mankind and as a personal omen.

This tiny, private spectacle arrested Vincent's insomniacal writhings. He'd contemplated it as a small boy. He'd marked it ever after, in school, college, and on his travels. Although it had never boded anything he could make out, it reminded him how his identity continued. To find himself perceiving it tonight led him to consider the minute spectacle a form of punctuation for in life. It must mean the story was to continue despite an abrupt change.

The change would, of course, be Laura. Thinking of her as Salome in her barbaric tent, of her face, her breasts, and her ankles, of the touch of her, Vincent was overwhelmed by desire. Now three of them shared the Vincent Booth marriage bed: wife, husband, and, like a mole popping up to wreck an orderly lawn, the husband's desire.

Reason would have these three become one. A blessed trinity. He should turn over again, cross over, sweeten, soften, and enter his sleeping wife with the strong, sudden presence joined to his loins. This, after all, was exactly the celebration of family communion. But his member did not point to his wife, his family, their security and future. This dowsing rod strained at another spring. Oh, Laura!

Vincent squeezed the thing and it jumped. He pleased it further. In a sock gathered up from the floor next to the bed, he released his seed and was quickly ashamed. Empty and ashamed. His wife impassively slumbered on. His shortcut through emotional complexities into a sock was appalling and humiliating. He dropped the assaulted stocking near its cuckolded mate.

Chapter 3

*L*aura shut off her alarm and awarded herself a few minutes more in bed before either entering the problematical day before her or reviewing the problematical evening just finished. She was exhausted. Unpleasant heats and pains and memories, the burned villages left by the previous night's passing army of wine and hectic entertainment depressed her. She fell back asleep and dreamed Vincent Booth was with her, declaring his love. The dream became erotic, poked her eye, and she awoke with a jump that sent Florida flying.

"Kitty?" she called out apologetically. "Florida?"

Florida had saved her life. She was going to be late, anyway, but had Florida not stepped across her face, Laura undoubtedly would have slept until afternoon. Laura put water on to boil and showered. Out the corner of her eye she had seen the archaeological remains of her midnight supper. She didn't even want to think about that one. The maid better show up and clear it all away, Laura warned the mirror.

This was a day to clear many things away—Toby Hyman, for instance. Today was Toby Hyman Day. She should have finished the affair even before he'd offered her the opportunity to host *It's Morning*. Anyway, now it was impossible. For the host of *It's Morning* to be involved with its producer would be extremely unprofessional.

Pouring tea into a cup that other women might save for display, Laura watched a few minutes of what she had begun to think of as only the present version of the morning show, which she was going to drastically improve. It seemed customary for people in television to have state-of-the-art receivers in every room, Toby Hyman had television receivers all over his apartment, but one was Laura's stylistic limit.

That morning the present anchorwoman, Sally Anne Coombs, whom Laura now regarded almost like a romantic rival, was interviewing an English actress/authoress who was plugging her book, *Return to Romance*.

"You point out that romance doesn't have to be expensive," said Sally Anne, leading her guest to expand on her product.

"It's really just as simple as candles at dinner," enthused the authoress in an English accent. Lace, centered with a cameo, bandaged her throat all the way to her chin. Her hair was a stack of ringlets tied with a velvet ribbon.

Sally Anne was a blonde of Laura's age who was threatened with a weight problem. She dressed plainly, in neutral clothes chosen by the image architects of the show to set off guests.

Laura couldn't help but consider the revolutionary difference she would soon make on this stupid, stupid show. Instead of an obvious, self-promoting pinhead like this lacy piece of artifice, Laura could get people like the Dalai Lama or the Lesbian superstar athlete who had made a pass at her at a party to which Toby Hyman had taken her.

"I confess that after reading your book I put candles on the table last night, and when my husband got home, he was afraid he'd forgotten our anniversary or something," Sally Anne admitted jocularly, as if she were gossiping over the phone. Laura smiled sarcastically. Sally Anne Coombs always dragged reminders of her marriage and motherhood into her interviews, no doubt to ingratiate herself with an audience who had probably just gotten rid of their working husbands for the day. Laura gave the morning-show audience more credit. She was sure they would enjoy fare more interesting than Sally Anne's coffee and doughnuts.

Sally Anne Coombs's impending weight, her reference to her husband and baby, her plain good looks and Heartland blonde hair all looked to Laura like a gathering of attributes suggested by polls and market samplings rather than the effusions of a specific personality. Wouldn't viewers prefer character and intelligence to such a bland creation of consensus?

Sally Anne didn't listen to the people she interviewed. She cattle-prodded them along, just as she was doing this morning with the professional romantic swathed in Victoriana. The show was so wooden, predictable, forced, and banal that Laura kept sighing and shaking her head.

Laura had discussed the shortcomings of *It's Morning* avidly with Toby ever since he had groaned at a bad patch of Sally Anne Coombs one morning and said, "You know, I bet you could do a hell of a lot better than that."

"Seriously?" Laura had replied. She felt as if a switch had been thrown, changing her life in an instant. Hosting a television program made perfect sense to her and for her. It would make professional use of her looks, her background, her acquaintances, and her mind. And it would make her famous, like her father.

It's Morning had declined in audience ratings from a solid first to barely second among the three network eye-openers. Sally Anne Coombs had been thrown in six months ago to bring the show back. She had failed, and Laura frequently and enthusiastically explained why to Toby, who would set his jaw and glower whenever she did so.

"She's just so obviously targeted," Laura said, "as if the marketing department had put her together like Frankenstein." Toby clenched his jaws and ground his capped teeth. "She doesn't listen, and she gets asshole people on as guests. The audience can tell. It's a drag."

Toby soon regretted his provocative suggestion that Laura might replace Sally Anne. Now Laura wanted to know exactly when she would begin. To put her off, Toby had recommended she take voice lessons. He felt his passionate romance was running down the drain of her ambition. Moreover, she showed much less respect for him. If she ever did get such a job, she would probably consider herself his superior. Toby stalled for time, trying to get as much of her wonderful body as he could before she would have to be dismissed.

Toby Hyman wasn't merely the producer of the show. He was also the executive vice president of the corporation, and he sat on the board of the foundation. He was a broadcast pioneer. How such a dull, greedy man had risen so high was astonishing to Laura. How could this twerp boast such grand credentials?

The successful people she had known all her life were much more civilized and graceful. Toby Hyman talked about money. He ate too quickly. His clothes were too natty and he was a quick and selfish lover. "Mistake, mistake," Laura said to Florida as she left her apartment on the morning she decided to officially end the relationship.

How had it ever begun? You simply do not accept men who wear crocodile shoes and cry to get in bed with you. She never should have let him. She never would again. In the taxi Laura reviewed the history she had decided would be concluded today.

When she accepted Toby's first dinner invitation, at his apartment in town, she expected a party, or at least certainly the presence of his wife. Instead Toby alone was present. Laura had correctly identified the picture over the fireplace as a Jawlensky. Nodding furious congratulations—"Right, right, good for you, that's right"—Toby was clenching the lever of an ice tray with the clumsy passion of a murderer breaking his first neck.

"Fucking ice machine is broken," he exclaimed, giving another jerk. The lever sprang and ice bounced all over, leading her to notice his reptile shoes. After this ice breaking, he was quickly at her. She resisted in proportion to his assault.

He pushed; he wheedled and begged. He promised and swore, and ultimately he cried.

"I love you, goddammit. I love you, what can I do?" He meant it. He was crazy about her. But his eyes were not softened by tears; they sparkled like jacks.

Loving Laura drove Toby Hyman to extravagance. This beautiful, well-born, intellectual, and sophisticated creature, a head taller than he—yet, in practical matters, a head less—brought forth all his bounty. But he soon realized he should've kept his largess flowing from sources outside the network. Suggesting she would make a great anchor for *It's Morning* was a hideous mistake.

He had intended it merely as a compliment, but she had taken it as an offer. Her acceptance was so instant and definite, her gratitude so charged with emotion—more than any he'd ever seen her display—that he foolishly fed her hopes. He joined her in enumerating her advantages over the incumbent personality: how well read and acquainted she was, how intelligent and beautiful, how superior—all the attributes, in fact, that made her completely unsuitable. Even though he ran her down all the time, Toby Hyman still wasn't ready to get rid of Sally Anne Coombs. She was homey, and who wants Laura Montgomery-style snotty superiority at seven in the morning?

The inevitable, encroaching finish of their romance added to the intensity of what he felt for her. He couldn't resist brightening her glow, turning up the current of her expectations. He was lamenting this very thing when she walked directly into his office with neither appointment nor announcement, as she infuriatingly had been doing ever since he started seeing her. He loathed that easy license she took for herself. It demeaned his office. It advertised their romance. What did she know of struggle and merit? All she knew was privilege. He loved and hated her for walking in on him the way she did, like a queen.

"Toby, I'm sorry to tell you this," she said, looking at him frankly, "but I've fallen in love with someone, and I'll have to stop seeing you. And, anyway, it isn't right with me doing *It's Morning.*"

Though aghast and outraged, Toby coolly looked away from her and pursed his lips, a business tic he used for stalling.

He said nothing. Finally he looked back at her with a wintry smile. "I'm so happy for you," he said softly, his eyes filling with tears.

"I'm really sorry, Toby." Laura started toward him like someone who's just dropped a vase.

Rueful but pragmatic—given the constant supply of long-legged, good-looking, and ambitious featherbrains at the network—Toby stopped her with a hand signal and revolved the leather chair away from her until she could see only the back of his head, which unfortunately brought to her attention the way he combed his hair up from its retreating sources.

"You're dead," he said so softly, she didn't understand. Afraid he was going to start sobbing, Laura withdrew from his office.

There was a message Missy Ferguson had called, inviting Laura to lunch. Laura accepted. Missy, and of course Vincent, were refreshing reminders of the good old days, an antidote to her present society. Toby had provided a flashy acquaintance of television and financial celebrities, which Laura had now decided she didn't like. They acted like a street gang, these small, coldhearted men who swore and strutted around in big apartments, limousines, and expensive restaurants. To them, everything was a deal, and women were no better than personal ornaments.

Old college friends seemed like balm. Hadn't she even dreamed of Vincent? It isn't often a person enters your subconscious so quickly. In fact, it was Vincent she was thinking of when she told Toby she'd fallen in love—not because she had but because it was the fastest and most final way she could think of to cut off Toby's attentions. Saying she'd fallen in love and thinking of Vincent Booth to authenticate her performance came very easily. Vincent did seem more attractive than ever. Age was an ally in his case, and he was bound to grow more and more attractive. God, had he fallen for her! On her bed he'd been like a man scrambling in over the side of a lifeboat from a fatal sea.

By the time Laura noticed her, a plain young office woman had evidently been looming at Laura's desk for some time. She smiled with some strange sort of affection, like that of mothers seeing their sons off to war.

"They want . . ." said this homely little woman, gesturing behind and above her at *they.* She couldn't seem to convey what exactly it was *they* wanted.

"You should . . ." The woman gestured some more, as if she were sculpting her message out of air.

"What?" asked Laura impatiently.

Although Laura recognized this person, she didn't know her name and had no idea what she did in the office.

"Mrs. Kupa . . ." said the flustered messenger.

"What is it?" Laura demanded, noticing an older woman had stepped out of her glazed work pen to observe the scene. "Cooper," Laura said to herself. This new observer was Mrs. Cooper, who had something to do with running the office. Mrs. Kupa must be Mrs. Cooper. Laura could not imagine what people like this girl and Mrs. Cooper could possibly have to do with herself.

Laura hadn't paid much attention to the engine of office management at the network, having devoted herself to contemplating the possibilities of the medium itself. Originally she'd wanted to be a producer, a behind-the-scenes shaper of programming, but then Toby's suggestion that she anchor *It's Morning* came along.

"It's like I'm supposed to help if you want me to clear out your desk," blurted the young woman.

"Why?" asked Laura, excited. Her first thought was that they were moving her to Sally Anne Coombs's office. The woman shrugged, and her palms slapped her thighs. She looked piteous. Now her gestures and expression came clear to Laura. They meant, ". . . because you are fired." Fired? When it occurred to Laura that Toby Hyman was firing her because she'd broken off their affair, she felt a rush of fury that brought her to tiptoes before she made for his office.

"He's not in there. He's in a meeting, Miss Montgomery," said Toby's secretary. Laura slammed his empty office door. When she turned back, she saw that the woman at her desk was loading everything there into boxes. Other employees made assiduous shows of office work, between stolen peeks at Laura.

"And the moral is, 'Don't boff the boss,' " opined the young woman assigned to empty Laura's desk to three riveted girlfriends in the booth of a bar that evening. This young woman had often told them about Laura Montgomery, implying a close personal friendship. Laura Montgomery, she needlessly reminded them, was the daughter of the famous movie director.

Chapter 4

*V*incent's immediate superior at the Metropolitan Museum of Art, William Willoughby, caught up with him on the steps. Vincent was amazed by Willoughby's overcoat. It was leather and an acrid shade of beige familiar to Vincent from the time he'd spent around his son's diaper changes. The sight of it gave Vincent's flying hangover a dizzying swoop.

Willoughby never would have sported such a garment if he hadn't been passed over. At a recent dinner Vincent and Mary gave, Willoughby had brought a young man who sold women's clothing in a department store. Like this startling coat, the young man was a display of Willoughby's new attitude. Slighted in his bid for the museum's presidency, he felt less compunction to be circumspect.

"Good morning, Vincent," Willoughby said. "Did you go out last night?"

This was Willoughby's regular query. He asked it of anyone he thought might have important or interesting evenings. William Willoughby was a scientist studying New York society, and people's evenings were his lab samples. His practical application of this science enabled him to raise more money for the museum than any other individual in its history, which is why he thought he deserved its presidency.

Even though now he never would be more than second in command, he continued to soldier. He was still always gathering intelligence. Who was entertaining last night and who was entertained?

Willoughby wanted names and news. Who was new on the social scene? What couples had formed; which couples had endured and which had not? Who was attractive and who wasn't? He followed the ebb and flow of affection and decor and loyalties and health and restaurants in New York City with clergical dedication. This rewarded him with a constantly updated overview, an archive of information he drew on to raise money for the museum. Only magnetic tape could rival his storage capacity.

"Laura Montgomery," Vincent informed him. He enjoyed saying her name. To think he'd met her so long ago and not devoted his life immediately to winning her seemed tragic. But in college she was a goddess who went out with movie stars. He'd never even considered her a contemporary, and suddenly there she was, the previous night, alongside him with that beautiful body appearing up out of the husks he shucked.

"Oh, God, yes, Laura," enthused Willoughby blandly as he took off the yellow coat, revealing a suit that had been purchased earlier than the overcoat, back when he still had an eye on higher prospects. "I know her mother."

Most people, Vincent mused, would have rejoined, "James

Montgomery's daughter." Only Willoughby, the preeminent escort of wealthy dowagers in New York society, would choose to identify Laura through her maternal line. Vincent had an impulse to call Laura at once to tell her. She'd laugh, he could almost hear it—that exceptional, fine-toned laugh. Bad laughs can put you off, while good ones are affectionate and welcoming. A great laugh is a shrine. Should he call her? You should thank people who have entertained you, and circumstances being what they were, it seemed most unlikely that Mary would take care of the courtesy.

"Doesn't she have some sort of job in television?"

"She's going to host their morning show," said Vincent with unexpected pride, as if he were already connected to her.

"Really," answered Willoughby, now distinctly interested. Television meant publicity. And in fund-raising, publicity was the yin of which money was the yang; each made the other occur. Vincent all but heard the softly clacking keyboard as Willoughby entered this new information into his memory bank.

"We have the meeting about the roof today," Willoughby informed his assistant. He announced it without pleasure but with the determination common to anyone resigned to an unpleasant duty.

A roof-raising committee faces many obstacles, since a new roof costs more than most masterpieces but lacks the appeal of a masterpiece, a collection, or a new wing. Like water, a roof is a dull, prehistoric necessity, and Willoughby's omnipresent smile was somewhat bittersweet as he contemplated the glamorless task.

Willoughby had formed a different sort of committee to

raise roofing funds than he would have for a project providing a more righteous podium for a patron's name. He'd included the avid nouveau riche he wouldn't dream of inflicting on the old guard during plummier projects. To his credit, William Willoughby was no less polite and charming to these parvenues than he was to blue bloods, which was another reason for his success as a fund-raiser.

"Medici means doctors," he informed a wealthy doctor, helping that physician to see the historical connection of his profession to art patronage. "That is stunning, is it . . . don't tell me, Givenchy?" he said to the doctor's wife. She smiled like an aborigine witnessing the miracle of Polaroid photography.

The meeting took place in a private dining room at the museum. On the wall behind Willoughby was a huge Canaletto cityscape of Venice he had chosen for the occasion.

"I picked this picture because it shows so many rooftops," he began, causing an outbreak of chuckling that allowed the members of his new committee to begin to feel comfortable and civilized.

"Actually," Willoughby continued, "this picture was donated by—what would he be, Vincent, your grandfather-in-law?" Vincent's ears tingled with a blush. Once again he was being larded with old-money importance for the delectation of rich new marks—exactly what Vincent had come to hate most about working at the museum.

At each place at the mahogany banquet table (attributed to Bullock of Liverpool, ca. 1818) was a packet of information. Accompanying the constellations of digits astrologizing the estimated bill for a new roof was a five-page list of foundations and families of great means. Willoughby led the committee through the list name by name, asking those present to raise their hands if they had any acquaintance or connection with the wealthy surnames. This exercise served another purpose besides the obvious one it proposed. Intrinsically it implied that those present were on equal footing with prior philanthropists and part of a grand old context.

"The Abbots of this Abbot family are the St. Louis grocery-store Abbots," Willoughby languidly and somewhat facetiously elucidated about the first name. "Old James L. Abbot gave us some atrocious Barbizon pictures at the turn of the century, and the family has kept up a vague connection with the museum since, though not as strong a link as we would like. If anyone knows any of them, I'm sure we could revive and revitalize their dangerously neglected connection with us." Smiling, he looked up to see if anyone could get to an Abbot. The committee was smiling as brightly as a first-grade class on the first day of school. Apparently nobody knew any Abbots, but now they knew who the Abbots were, and now they had been put on a par with them by Willoughby. "Ackerman?" he continued.

"I know Hetty Ackerman," Sondra (Mrs. Sidney) Laval eagerly called. She was exactly like a schoolgirl, bright-eyed and bursting with the correct answer to the teacher's question.

"Great," said Willoughby, noting that Sondra's suit was from the most recent Paris collection.

"I mean, not real well, but I do know her. My husband knows them," she expanded, looking around enthusiastically at the other members. But she wished she'd said *very* or *really* instead of *real*.

Willoughby marched on through the list, giving Vincent a twinkling smile and significant pause when he arrived at the Brigham Foundation.

In spite of his distaste for this use of his identity, Vincent raised both his eyebrows and his smile, signaling to the rest of the committee that, yes, he was in fact connected to the great Brigham monies, and how natural and easy he was about his advantages. He disliked himself for enjoying their respect for his connection to the Brighams. Sondra Laval beamed markedly his way.

After the meeting she came straight over. "We're friends of Dick and Alice Cooley," she said.

"Oh, great," Vincent replied.

"They think you're terrific."

"They're wonderful themselves."

"We ought to all get together sometime," Sondra suggested. She was a high-strung young woman whose extra-large breasts made Vincent think of Laura again.

So you're Sidney's reward for looting all the Wall Street money, Vincent thought as he and Sondra Laval prattled on inconsequentially. He looked up and caught an approving glance from William Willoughby.

As soon as Vincent was back at his desk, Willoughby phoned him.

"You've got to have the Lavals to dinner," he said. "I think the whole roof is right there with a little more from here and there to make them feel like they're not being stuck with the check."

Hanging up, Vincent wondered why he'd agreed to have the Lavals to dinner, why he worked at the museum, and why he'd married Mary. Because of Wally, he answered himself—so the great Wallace could crawl under the tent to see the circus of life. How can you leave a woman who's lost her baby? Shouldn't you at least replace it for her before you run off? And then you love it, too, and then . . .

The silence of the thick museum walls encouraged Vincent's brooding. Why was he unhappy with all anyone could dream of having? It seemed so unforgivable and yet so equally undeniable that he was miserable in the lap of luxury. After all, he was working among pictures he loved. They were bound to make him curator of European painting once the incumbent retired.

Was he just a pathetic example of overextended adolescence? A ludicrously spoiled Byronic depressive? Today Vincent Booth's self seemed to him to be a dull, mocking burden, a huge unpaid debt. He was ashamed of himself. All his recent acts seemed so lowly. If it hadn't started to rain and he wasn't hung over and he hadn't done what he had last night, perhaps he could do justice to his great fortune instead of regretting it.

There he was, entombed in a great marble mausoleum filled with treasure, a live version of a mummy. Yes, exactly, thought Vincent, like some Pharaoh's flunky buried in treasure—in fact, some of the very treasure extracted from the Great Pyramids of Egypt themselves. Museums were merely the new pyramids— the extravagant burial mounds of present civilization. Morticians should come in and oil and bandage him, and Willoughby, too, and a thousand years should go by uninterrupted except for the periodic scratching of grave robbers every couple of hundred years or so until some overjoyed archaeologist from a new civilization dug them all up and removed them to a still newer museum, which would also eventually need a new roof and all that went with it.

"Let's go to Le Bordello," Willoughby said to Vincent when his lunch with the widow of a magnate was canceled. He was referring, facetiously, to the French restaurant where so many museum officials, collectors, art dealers, art journalists, experts, scholars, and attendant lawyers, romantic interests, accountants —and, occasionally, even artists—had lunch. The red walls and banquettes were set off with a few execrable paintings. The bad art was an undemanding, comfortable reminder to the diners of their infinitely superior taste.

"Monsieur Willoughby," greeted the patron with a cocked head and an insider's smile, "Monsieur Booth." He walked them to a banquette, which Willoughby took at once so he could feed his insatiable social curiosity on most of the room. That left Vincent to sit in the chair opposite him, with only a peripheral view of the adjacent banquettes. Behind Willoughby was a painting of a painting of a landscape. Actually it was a painting of a painting of a painting—at least three generations removed from any direct attempt by an individual to render physical reality.

Vincent's gloom and discomfort focused most of his mind on the glass of white wine he had ordered. How long could it take to come? What if it had been forgotten or misdirected? From his catbird seat, Willoughby chatted away with the bland enthusiasm that made the evenings of older women in ball gowns fly by.

To Vincent nothing else could be as important as the apparently delayed glass of wine. Vincent smiled and recrossed his legs, flexing their muscles and craning forward with an intensity Willoughby found flattering, not realizing that Vincent was only trying to materialize a glass of white wine before himself out of thin air by mental powers.

His young colleague's ardor reminded Willoughby of his own student days. He stopped instructing Vincent when and where to include Sidney and Sondra Laval in a dinner party and switched to a discussion of El Greco.

"After early adoration, I detested El Greco for years," he said. "It was like looking at Thomas Wolfe after you grow up."

Vincent was considering an unnecessary trip to the bathroom, on which he could remind the bartender of his order.

"But lately the lambency of it has been occurring to me. How flickering and flamy and firelike his colors and shapes are. Night fire—in fact, I think his father was a blacksmith. Anyway, there must have been loads of blacksmiths in Toledo making those famous swords. I watched blacksmiths in Turkey once. They work at night because it's cool . . . torsos in the firelight, etched in grime and hair and shadow. Even the blacks in El Greco look charred."

Inspired by Vincent's brooding concentration, Willoughby was voluptuously transporting himself back to his late-night discussions in the Gothic college rooms of his youth. Specifically he was remembering Julian, the Englishman, and how their collegiate arguments had surged back and forth, late into the night. Julian had despised what Willoughby had considered sacred, El Greco. "The Bernard Buffet of seventeenth-century clerical buggery," the Englishman sneered in that accent of culture and intelligence Willoughby had come to revere and even to install in his own speech.

Then, having seen how hurt and baffled he'd left young Willoughby, Julian had softly yet manfully commanded, "Come here, dear boy." It was long ago and far away, and yet Vincent Booth's present intensity and youth reminded Willoughby of it—of Julian and first love.

Vincent's wine finally arrived. Even before he raised his glass, Vincent felt released from the limbo in which he'd been floundering. He left the glass sitting before him like a trophy a moment before his first quaff. His next worry would be how long the refill would require. He had only secondarily noted how Willoughby seemed to be rehearsing a bit on El Greco, probably for a near-future performance somewhere grand, with real linen and silver. Vincent looked around the restaurant.

Just as he turned, so did Laura. Their editing brains focused only each of them for the other, all other details of the restaurant and its occupants disappearing entirely.

Willoughby's own attention had simultaneously strayed off as he wandered through reveries of El Greco, college, Turkish forge light on muscular torsos, and Julian. Breaking off his daydream, he assumed Vincent was staring away because he'd fallen silent.

"Have you tried looking at El Greco lately?" Willoughby inquired, breaking the silence and returning to the present moment from his dear memories. Vincent didn't answer. Vincent's blue eyes were large under black brows. His skin was sleek, braced over his fine bones. Willoughby was struck by Vincent's beauty. He'd noticed traces of it before, surreptitiously, but it was so apparent at this moment that Willoughby's heart fluttered.

Willoughby masked his face with his glass of wine. Memories of his college affair apparently had unhinged him, and he needed a moment to regain his composure. Vincent looked too beautiful.

Fighting infatuation, Willoughby considered the subject of his attention. Vincent was married, apparently straight—but even more to the point, the attractive young man was himself in a fixed gaze. Willoughby's chiding reasoning demanded that he stop feeling smitten and realize Vincent was in a state not unlike his own, staring with solar intensity at—Willoughby followed Vincent's stare—a beautiful young woman. An unpleasantly familiar gust of jealousy and hopelessness rushed through Willoughby's tents. His great arabesque of emotion flattened.

"Who's that?" Willoughby asked with cold poise.

"Excuse me," answered Vincent, rising and dropping his napkin.

Willoughby was incensed. In Willoughby's lifetime, this was an old wound being reopened in an old way. He watched Vincent zigzag toward her through the maze of tables. She looked familiar, a tall, full-figured brunette with a long neck, quite beautiful. She sat with a contemporary female who looked neither familiar nor distinguished to Willoughby. Did she work for somebody? Was she related to somebody? Was she married, or had she been? Related? Yes, that's it, she was related. Now he had it—she was Laura Montgomery, whose name had been mentioned that very morning.

Willoughby felt some solace for the unexpected outburst of emotion he'd just survived from the fresh proof of his encyclopedic capacity to identify. He shuddered, relieved his feelings had been so quickly scotched. It could have been embarrassing —a disaster, even. Odd how looks you've dully accepted for years can flare up into a blaze of beauty like that. Lucky girl. She was attractive. She was the cause of it. Obviously Vincent Booth was violently attracted to Laura Montgomery. Well, that could prove rather interesting, considering his marriage to the Brigham heiress.

Victor Churrasco, a dealer Willoughby normally politely despised, came by and offered a two-handed shake for Willoughby's extended hand. The courtly old crook's face was a topographical map of wrinkles. His eyes looked as artificial as glass substitutes.

"Didn't you once tell me you knew about some El Grecos

somewhere?" Willoughby smilingly asked Churrasco. The dealer's own antic smile closed as he considered the question, then his grin returned as he nodded, vigorously, and sat down.

In this peculiar, elliptical way, the museum's Craven Fund was ultimately and unexpectedly tapped for the purchase of a pair of El Greco's studies of apostles.

When she arrived to meet Laura, Missy had no idea this was the restaurant the art crowd favored for lunch. She'd suggested it to seem sophisticated. A cartoonist from her magazine had taken her there for dinner the week before. At night it was favored by wealthy old Republicans who had looked to Missy like high society. Even splitting the bill with Laura would be much too expensive, but Missy was in that extravagant mood she associated with her glamorous friend's everyday.

What she had least expected to find was a woebegone Laura Montgomery. Missy was shocked, outraged, and subtly gratified by her friend's tale of seduction and betrayal. The rest of the college class she shared with Laura was toiling at typewriters and telephones at the first fringes of careers, but Laura had begun way up there at the very top, looking down on all of them, until this very moment, when she'd been flicked off by a lecher like a speck of lint.

"You ought to give the whole story, you know?" Missy advised. "Let the bastard have it. Call a magazine."

"I know," agreed Laura.

Missy felt exalted defending an embattled friend. Laura's advantages had been lifted away, revealing a dishonored equal. Missy wanted to step in, clean house, and do battle alongside her old pal. The first step, Missy decided, would be to cheer Laura up.

"I had the best time last night," she said, looking in her memory at the glamorous faces and surroundings of Laura's party.

"I didn't really," Laura answered. "I guess I just knew this was all coming to a head today, but I just didn't know it was going to come out like this. Shit."

"Here's to better days," said Missy, raising her glass. Laura followed suit. "You'll be all right," Missy offered. Similarly struck, she would have retreated to her apartment to nurse her wounds. That Laura could walk from a personal disaster of such magnitude directly into a restaurant was just another display of her superior hauteur. Missy wondered if it would depress Laura to hear how she had introduced Vincent Booth to his wife. Perhaps it wasn't the best subject, she decided, a little rueful that her part in the drama must continue to remain anonymous. As Missy pondered this possibility she saw Laura look at something, squint a moment, and become transmogrified. Animation filled her face, her spine straightened, a grin spread. Missy, like Willoughby, looked for the cause—and suddenly Vincent Booth arrived at their table.

"You remember Missy," said Laura in a voice Missy noticed had dropped in timbre and become liquefied.

"Hi," said Vincent.

When Laura asked, "Can you sit down a moment?" Vincent turned to consider Willoughby's current status. He was delighted to find his chair had been filled by some table-hopping art dealer.

"Are you drinking white wine? Let me get us a bottle of something," he offered.

Missy's lunch with Laura, which has started so unhappily, had become a jolly party. Despite its possible effect on Laura, Missy couldn't resist reminding Vincent of how she had introduced him to his wife. Laura seemed oblivious. Vincent's smile, however, shook for a moment. He then consumed two glasses of wine and told several funny stories about himself. By the time he returned to his own table, Laura's eyes were flashing, and her grin was ineradicable.

Churrasco, the courtly basilisk who immediately wanted to secure his proffered El Grecos, got up from Vincent's chair with the elaborately apologetic but highly pleased air of a Versailles adulterer withdrawing from a fellow courtier's wife.

"Please, please," hissed the exquisitely scaled reptile, gesturing for Vincent to assume his rightful position. "So sorry, Vincent."

Churrasco slithered deftly on through the teeming art pond as Vincent, distracted but joyful, sat down.

"I ordered," Willoughby somewhat snippishly informed him.

"Oh," said Vincent, opening the menu but failing to concentrate on its contents. The maître d'hotel was immediately at hand. He hadn't missed the tableau at Missy's table. His hatchecking niece told him to *regardez l'amour* at table four. *L'amour,* like the red walls and re-rendered post-paintings decorating the restaurant, was just what the maître d' felt the place needed.

"What's good?" inquired Vincent with the voice of a customer who clearly was about to adore whatever was set before him.

The maître d' actually winked as he inquired, "May I choose?"

Vincent nodded and grinned and handed back the menu. "And may I have another bottle of that Puligny Montrachet?"

Willoughby was jealous in spite of himself. Ridiculously, he found Vincent more beautiful than ever. This gloomy, spoiled young man—a luncheon companion only because of the cancellation of a major patron—had assumed discomfortingly large proportions in Willoughby's imagination. Oblivious to all his good fortune, his looks, his position, his rich wife, and his undeniable connoisseur's aptitude, Vincent had until now seemed to Willoughby an overgrown schoolboy who might not even rise to become a curator unless he applied himself much harder than he had—or unless he broke off a really respectable chunk of Brigham Foundation money for the museum.

Who was Vincent Booth in Willoughby's social archive? He was just a luckily wed egocentric of nonentity origins, ungrateful for the bounty bestowed upon him. He drank too much. He was undeservedly unhappy. He was not completely useless nor untalented, but he was a troublesome, balky figure Willoughby had merely endured as another of wealth's many tiresome stipulations and appendages.

Until now. Willoughby hated the feeling of helplessness that came over him after his review of Vincent's shortcomings. How could he suddenly be infatuated with a creature he so thoroughly understood and vaguely despised?

Willoughby faked a smile and, tasting the wine Vincent had ordered, realized that long-legged Laura, across the restaurant, had the very same taste in her mouth.

Chapter 5

*T*he museum administration loved the crowd through which Vincent and Willoughby returned from lunch as a statistic but loathed it personally. "They might as well be at a garage sale," Willoughby said, watching grandmothers in numbered football jerseys and adolescent girls in short shorts window-shopping the galleries.

But today Vincent felt differently about them. The crowds made life feel like a holiday. He wanted to look at the curiosities with them like a rural boy at a county fair who would close his eyes back on the farm that night and see the rides, sideshows, and passing girls slide by again.

Every picture was thrilling. Saucy Judith had Holoferne's head on a plate. Aphrodite was deeply sad; Adonis was about to leave her for a hunt, and she, being a goddess, knew he would be killed on this hunt by a boar. Adam and Eve were clearly in love; she held up the forbidden apple, urging him to take a bite.

At Le Bordello, Laura's looks had actually changed before Vincent's eyes, as if her physical presence was merely the raw material of a more highly refined idea. He had recognized her, approached that table, and watched her face pass from an identity he recognized to a purpose and goal—something filling him with as much aspiration as desire. He had glanced at Missy Ferguson throughout lunch, much as a dancer in a spin avoids vertigo by fixing on a member of the audience.

"Hi," said Vincent, forgetting all he'd thought about saying to Laura in this telephone call during his enraptured tour of masterpieces after lunch. He was drawing her face as they talked. It was coming out of him as if it had been inside him all along.

"Hi," she replied, her smile opening the word like an embrace.

The atoms composing him buzzed and vibrated. "How is everything?"

"Fine."

"I mean, about the job and all that."

"Oh, hell. That's that."

"Great."

Neither Vincent nor Laura noticed the substantial pauses in their conversation.

He finished her profile and drew a full face just as easily. "You're home."

"Isn't that where you called?"

"No, but I mean for a while?"

"Yes."

"I was wondering if it would be okay to stop by for a drink or something later?"

"Tomorrow?"

"Sure."

Willoughby entered Vincent's office in his yellow leather coat and smiled sarcastically at Vincent's blush. Obviously this infatuation was going to place some kind of a witless moon-calf where Vincent once stood.

"Okay?" Vincent asked, his blood sludging through thick swamps in his skull.

"I'll see you tomorrow," said Laura.

"Okay, then, I have to go. Good-bye."

"Bye."

She said the word with a final lilt that almost sent Vincent over backward. He hung up and clumsily angled himself in what he believed was a casual pose to receive William Willoughby.

Willoughby was holding an open date book like a saint's identifying icon. "Sorry to interrupt you, Vincent, but your phone hasn't stopped, and I wanted to make a date for that dinner with you and Mary and the Lavals. I'm going over there right now to see their new Renoir. Aren't we lucky how Renoir painted enough for everybody."

Vincent studied his calendar with a scholarly grimace and a finger running along days in the weeks and months. But he could only go through the motions of participating in ordinary existence. His vision had inverted. Instead of seeing his finger on the page and replying to Willoughby's words, he was looking down inside himself into a glowing brown shaft of self with spots like the eyes of a peacock feather coming up out of it. The emotion he felt was as awesome as fear.

"Earth to Vincent," Willoughby prodded.

"April twenty-eighth," Vincent said triumphantly, feigning membership in reality.

"Right, the twenty-eighth." Willoughby was flipping the minutely annotated pages of his leather date book, which in mere February was already richly worn. "I'll see what they say. I can do Thursday, which is perfect. I'll bring Rainey Phillips. If the Lavals can't do it, just drop it. I've got opera tickets but it's *Girl of the Golden West* and I don't care either way. Rainey is the widow of Walter B. Phillips as in Phillipine Mouthwash."

Once Willoughby left, Vincent smiled, chuckled, then burst into laughter.

Chapter 6

*L*aura Montgomery stroked Florida, who was stretched out and rhythmically fisting and fanning his front paws as he purred like a plane home. Laura felt the same way. She was sure she'd fallen in love. One minute she was dragged by Toby into the depths of despair, and now she was zooming through the fluffy pink clouds of infatuation. She looked at her telephone devotionally, as if it carried a relic of Vincent's lovestruck conversation.

"The darkest hour is just before the dawn, Fla-fla," she said, cuddling her purring cat, who dutifully rubbed his head up under her chin.

Irrelevant as it now seemed, Laura had a date that night with a young man who worked at the network on the corporate side. Should she cancel it out of faith in her new love? Laura found she couldn't, even if she wanted to, because she'd not written down the young man's name, only the theater where they were to meet. She could, of course, leave him there alone, but it would be better to show up, better manners, better for him, and after all, it was something to do. This young man had applied himself to winning this date for months, despite the many refusals Laura's relationship with Toby Hyman had necessitated, and weeks had passed since Laura finally agreed. She would have forgotten about it if he hadn't just called to confirm his good luck: a play and supper afterward; would she meet him at the theater? Yes, she would, it was the perfect distraction to end this eventful day.

Tom Harrison was a pleasant, polite young man who must have known in his ardent farm boy's heart that the likes of Laura Montgomery would never love him. But he stood fast, anyway —through a dozen refusals—until she relented. He was a methodical and determined Hoosier who wore suits all week, and a sweater and cotton trousers on the weekend. He took business seriously. He'd seen at first glance that Laura was everything he wasn't: glamorous, sophisticated, unpredictable, and well connected. He had wanted a date with her more than he wanted anything else in New York City.

"A date—but I don't have dates," she'd told him the first time he asked. He never used the word again. But even with him avoiding the disapproved word, she'd refused him over and over. Wheedling tickets from a network contact for a sold-out show had emboldened his thirteenth attempt to spend an evening with the beautiful, beautiful daughter of James Montgomery, the film director.

In the inevitably frustrating order of things, Tom Harrison

had to work late the evening of his momentous date and would have to meet her at the theater in a shirt soured and deflated by the worry of a day's business. Even with no shower and no shave, he would barely make it.

He'd seen her only at the office. Striding at night through theater crowds in a coat that seemed to have its fur on the inside, she looked almost fantastically more attractive. He sighed aloud. Tom saw nearly everyone around him, men and women alike, turn to look at her.

"Did you have to wait long?" she said, smiling, coming up closer than he expected and placing the leather-gloved fingers of both hands on his arm with the grace of a pianist.

"No, just got here," Tom answered, surprised he could speak at all.

Throughout the first act Tom reacted to the play—which he thanked God was good, because he felt she would judge him by it—with Laura in mind. The shared intimacy of a mutual laugh enchanted him. When he laughed alone, he stopped quickly, not wanting to lose any slight synchronization he might have established with her.

At the intermission he gave up the intimacy he'd felt in the dark for another experience of her illuminated beauty in the theater lobby.

"Would you like a drink?" he offered, proud to be seen with her by eyes he watched rise toward them like fish to the surface of a pond where insects descend to dance at sundown.

"Vodka," she said through her smile.

Tom muscled into the shoal of men around the bar. They seemed to be getting four-fifty a drink and expecting the dollar change as a tip for two drinks. What he didn't understand was how Laura made *vodka* sound like a word he'd never heard, at least in Indiana. When Mary Ellen Cooper said *vodka,* the word was as bare as a coat hanger. Furthermore, Mary Ellen would giggle and smirk, making a drink order sound mischievous. The bartender paused significantly before cocking his head and pointing his finger at Tom.

"Vodka and, uh, bourbon and soda."

"Rocks?" the bartender asked impatiently, already throwing two bottles over two glasses.

"Um, yeah," Tom replied, hoping Laura hadn't specified a mixer because she didn't want one. Vodka on the rocks sounded like something she'd like. "Uh, wait—I'll have one, too—two vodkas on the rocks," Tom corrected. The bartender dropped his head in disgust, ostentatiously dumped the bourbon, and made a new drink with equal emphasis, so everyone in the pressing crowd could see who was causing the delay. Tom left his dollar, which the bartender skinned up and threw under the bar in the same motion that raised his finger to point at his next customer. He didn't say thanks.

In the crowded lobby, Tom rather smoothly lit Laura's cigarette, which encouraged him. Just standing there sipping drinks with her was a gorgeous triumph.

"Laura," crooned a glamorously dressed and ingeniously painted woman in her fifties. She raised her arms for a hug, throwing interrogative glances at Tom throughout her hospitable motion. A man Tom assumed was her husband also hugged Laura.

"Jocelyn and Victor Sharp . . ." Laura announced. Then she leaned forward toward Mrs. Sharp, gesturing at Tom as she presumably announced his name to both of them. The man stepped closer and asked, "I'm sorry, I didn't catch your name," in a stagy, forced way, with his hand cupped to his ear.

"Tom Harrison," Tom carefully replied. Laura, drifting aside with Mrs. Sharp, nodded at his answer in a way that made Tom suspect she'd forgotten his name.

Chapter 7

*T*he cascade of invitations, commitments, and entertainments for Vincent and Mary were never a more welcome diversion from the problems of their marriage than they were the night Vincent arrived home after lunch with Laura, desperately in love. It was an opera night. There were drinks at a nearby apartment and a supper afterward.

Clothing changes, greetings and introductions, movements through the city, the opera itself, the audience and other preoccupying exigencies of society would allow Vincent and Mary to be together without forcing any issues between them.

Mary was bathing. Wally was being fed in the kitchen. The coast was clear of the suspicion and interrogation Vincent feared he'd find mining his home harbor.

He gratefully entered the tile grotto of his

shower. All he could think of, naked in the hot, pelting pleasure, was Laura. He incrementally increased the heat and moved his body to comb his spine with the jet. He didn't want to leave this undemanding limbo of a shower for the chills, hard corners, bruising falls, decisions, and punishments of the world outside. He wanted to stand there, his eyes closed, thinking of Laura. He let it go on and on.

"Vincent, for God's sake," Mary yelled into his dressing room, slamming the door behind her.

Now Vincent rushed his dressing. His wet hair congealed, and a cold droplet of water ran down into his collar as he came down the hall to where Mary was bent over with her back to him. In her fur coat she looked like a bear. She swiveled, holding up baby Wallace's upraised arms, standing him on his legs, then let go. The baby held his hands up like a surrendering soldier. He stamped a step toward Vincent before being dumped by gravity.

He howled as Vincent picked him up, but the wetness of his father's hair diverted him. Vincent felt the warm, smooth skin of his new-smelling son against his ear. Diapers crackled within the baby's suit as he made interrogative grunts and fondled Vincent's wet curls.

"Oh, Christ, now I suppose he's going to be a hairdresser," said Mary. Vincent laughed and looked at her appreciatively. He liked the way she inevitably chose to defuse the couturier's spectacle, the family jewels, the furrier's glamorous intention, and the hairdresser's confection with her horn-rimmed glasses and her implacably unglamorous attitude.

Mary's decency and honesty surged up in Vincent's mind. How ridiculous it would be, he thought, dangling his son in this handsome vestibule, to knock down this home for the sake of infatuation. He abruptly decided never to see Laura Montgomery again. It was out of the question. His decision felt as sound as it was sudden, offering an exhilarating sense of relief. Virtue patted him on the back.

"Let's get going," he suggested with a smile that warmed Mary's heart.

"Mrs. Keswick?" called Mary, and the nanny came to fetch Wally.

Cocktails were to be consumed at the apartment of a couple similar to Vincent and Mary in age and circumstance. Their library paneling was darker, and their choice of colors brighter. The husband loved opera and his wife enjoyed everything about it except the sound. The two other couples who would later complete the population of the Brigham box were not much dissimilar. One of them had laid on a limousine to carry the party about town, and the other was hosting supper afterward in an Italian restaurant, making the whole event a model of wealthy cooperation.

Vincent greeted the company with enthusiasm. Now that he had decided never to think of Laura again, he wanted to relish his life with Mary. These fine people were old friends.

"How's the museum?" they asked him.

"How's the bank? How are the children? How was Maine?" he asked them. On neither side was there any real interest in the responses these questions elicited.

Mary loved to play the stock market and was grilling a corporate lawyer about a publishing company in which she'd bought stock. In the fireplace behind her a polite-looking little blaze nibbled through the birch logs.

"The decorator is his own wife's beard," a woman said of a love affair about which the group, including Vincent, had been gossiping. "Isn't it a riot?"

After a hundred years of patronage the Brigham box lay in the middle of the first tier of the opera house. Each box seemed to develop its own identity as people filed in and filled them. Soon the boxes were as personalized as a row of backyards in barbecue season.

The Piggots had the box next to them, but they seldom came anymore, selling off their seats at the box office. The first to enter this box tonight was a young man wearing a huge hat, several scarves, and a flowing cape. At the top of the cleft under his nose was a carefully barbered tuft of hair. He claimed a chair in front of the box by laying his program and binoculars on it. After a glance around, he retreated into the vestibule to hang his extensive and theatrical wraps. The lawyer sitting next to Vincent raised his eyebrows and rolled his eyes, and Vincent grinned in agreement.

Vincent looked down into the dressed-up, expectant crowd fleshing out the grid of seats. The young man in the next box returned minus his cape and hat but still swathed in scarves. He sat down with delicate deliberation while the lawyer suggested to Vincent that the famous diva they were about to hear was past her prime. Mary was staring at the exotic young man in the adjoining box. When he looked back at her, she smiled warmly.

In the first act of the opera the famous diva began to sing bel canto style about falling in love. She was not a moment past her prime, and her extraordinary voice made everything else simply vanish. Reality seemed like an afterthought compared to the clear, dancing sound coming up through her. All Vincent (and a great many others) could think of was love. "Oh, Laura," he silently sang along with the voice coming from the stage, "Laura, Laura, Laura, I love you."

When the diva finished, a huge ovation released the emotions her song had stirred. People rose to their feet. Carefully the man in scarves rose too. Every time he weakly clapped his hands together, the two tendons running from his skull down the nape of his neck flexed. Whenever the door to his box opened, he hunched forward as if the draft might finish him. He appeared to be very ill. Mary turned back to Vincent and silently formed the word *AIDS* behind her hand.

Vincent regretted allowing Laura back in his thoughts. The passion set off by the love song was too big and strong to put back in the dungeon where he had so recently sentenced it for the rest of his natural life. Oh, love, he thought, and, looking at the poetical, skeletal dandy in the neighboring box who was probably dying for it: Oh, death.

During the course of the opera the great singer touched her audience half a dozen times so deeply, they were pulled to their feet to applaud. In the final ovation Vincent even considered shouting "Laura" in the anonymity of the tumult.

The united passion of the audience dissipated into individual departure. Vincent and his crowd became a privileged little band seeking their limousine among crowds finding cheaper, more demanding ways home. His membership in the joking company taking places in their big black car reminded him he was not really the lone lover who had mouthed Laura's name in the dark. He was, in fact, a husband not unlike the other husbands in the car.

"Wasn't she divine?" the hostess asked in a wealthy whine.

"Big as a horse," said another.

"I like to see a grandmother play a virgin. Gives me hope," said the lawyer.

"Great fun," allowed a male voice.

In the dark, on a jump seat, Vincent secretly began to despise the old friends around him.

Why shouldn't he leave this company he'd never wanted to keep in the first place? When he married her, Mary had agreed to follow him anywhere, but in her mind anywhere had never been anywhere but New York.

The restaurant was a chic and busy place where the cooks worked in sight of the diners. The cooks were young, educated-looking people who could as easily have been doctors or lawyers. The food was tasty, pretty, and expensive.

"Did you see that man next to us?" asked Mary, and of course everyone had.

"I don't think they should just be going around everywhere like that," said the hostess.

"It's a conflict between the right of privacy and the general good," said the lawyer. "You can't have a quarantine of a minority without it looking like concentration camps."

"I was sitting in a steam bath in Chicago," said the banker, "at a public health club, and I heard this one sort of dim shape say to the other, 'How's Bruce?' and the other said, 'He's being so brave,' and then the rest of us in there hit the doors as if somebody had shouted fire." The banker had reenacted the overheard dialogue in two different effete voices. Everyone laughed and looked around guiltily to see if any restaurant patrons had been offended.

"It must have been an incredible effort for him just to get there," Mary said.

"The scarf winding must have taken hours," joked the banker.

"He's dying," Mary said softly, "and he's planning out his last days to do everything he loves."

Vincent was both warmed and chided by Mary's decency. She saw nobility in the opera lover's lonely effort where the others saw only an outcast to fear and ridicule. She was decent, and he was crazy to be goaded by his loins into cheating her. Vincent ordered another bottle of wine when he had the waiter's eye, rudely forgetting it was not his party.

At home Vincent smoked a cigar and drank a fistful of cognac alone in the library. He might have stayed up half the night, drinking and debating himself about his purpose in life, had Mary not entered.

She sat down and lowered her head onto his breast. He put his arms around her. She was determined to make love, and he was relieved to be able to comply.

Chapter 8

*U*ntil the aging process hobbled them, both Mary's parents had strayed considerably throughout their marriage. As an eleven-year-old, Mary had been kept awake by a loud, lengthy party her parents were having at a big chalet they'd taken in Switzerland one winter. She had left her snoring nanny in the bedroom and crept through the extensively carved wooden house toward the light two floors below. Then her mother, giggling and trying to contain her bare, bouncing breasts with her hands, ran down a hallway and right into her. A strange man wearing only an evening shirt with jeweled stud buttons joined the collision a moment later. His private parts looked to Mary like a nest of gerbils.

Before that, in Florida, a Miss Campbell had

breakfast with her father every morning for a week before Mary's mother came down. Miss Campbell had her breakfast in a monogrammed gown with *C* for Campbell on the breast. The gown itself, Miss Campbell had explained to her, was of the Campbell tartan. Mary thought she was some sort of a daddy's nanny, which, in a way, she was. Her father told her not to tell her mother about Miss Campbell, and she never had.

Although Mary didn't want such a marriage herself, she knew enough about their operation and maintenance to be disappointed but not defeated by Vincent's behavior at the slut's party.

Mary had tea on her tray. She was happier than she'd been in some time. They had made love the night before for the first time in ages. He had been sweet and smiling for a change. For months he'd stalked around, clenching the little muscles around his jaw—a tic Mary believed he vainly staged to activate the scenery of his undeniably handsome face—and staring artistically at shadows and textures. For months he acted interrupted every time she came near.

Just as her father did every morning, Mary checked the stock market—not because the Brigham fortune was affected by such a piffle as the market but because she bought and sold stocks for fun. Like her mother, she wore thin white cotton gloves to keep the newsprint from blackening her hands.

Goody—Conchita finally put the homemade jam on the breakfast tray. The bedclothes were frothy in the sunlight. The market was up, and Mary loved the jam made by the nice little old lady in Maine. What a superior morning this was, she thought as she bit into her muffin.

"I think you should have married Jonathan Bushwick," her father had said to her after meeting Vincent. "I think you'd have been far happier with that one." He still said so upon occasion.

Jonathan was a neighbor in Maine. Alfred Brigham was completely conservative about his daughter, despite his own Miss Campbells and the notorious affair he'd had with Mrs. Piggot (to the point where Mr. Piggot stopped going to the opera because of the way their boxes adjoined). He had wanted his daughter to marry a known quantity.

Jonathan was somebody Mary had seen grow up with the time-lapse rapidity of summer acquaintance. As a child, Jonathan had showed her his "weenie" in exchange for a look at where he told her her own must have somehow fallen out. She remembered how adolescence came over him like demonic possession. The idea that a creature as stultifyingly familiar as Jonathan was regarded by her father as being suitable for love and marriage seemed absolutely laughable. When Jonathan had actually asked her to marry him, it had seemed both silly and incestuous. In no time at all he married someone else. Mary had found his bride was almost incidental, more like a costume Jonathan had donned for a fancy dress party than a partner he'd chosen for life.

But Jonathan and Natalie seemed rather happily married. Over the years they gained weight and had children. As Mary continued to watch her old friend's life develop and accrete in the fast forward of periodic reunions, she began to wonder if her father hadn't been right, after all.

But last night made things looks much more hopeful—and her stock was up, to boot. Mary had bought ten thousand shares of Zundstrom at six on the advice of George Wilcox, a shooting friend of her father's, and today it was up to eleven. Zundstrom made Bibles or something, religious books. Mary was very pleased. Yesterday it was nine and five-eighths, which was pleasant enough, but eleven—eleven was heaps more money. She decided to sell her shares and buy something for Vincent. Maybe she could begin to train him to repeat the previous night's conjugal performance a bit more regularly.

Chapter 9

On his way to the museum the morning after the opera, Vincent felt ambitious, virtuous, and domestically happy. When Wallace had bumped his head into his father's newly shaved and cologned cheek that morning, the baby had looked amazed and then squealed with delight, kicking his legs like a runner going over hurdles.

Vincent felt unusually in place as paterfamilias. He had breakfast with the baby, joking pleasantly with Mrs. Keswick, and then walked out from his happy home into the bounteous sunlight of a new day, encouraged by his comparatively high office in this world, and cured of his morbid doubts and dissatisfactions.

"Good morning, Ritchie," he said ebulliently to the doorman.

"They patched it up," the doorman told the

elevator man a few minutes later. The elevator man had bet a hundred that the Booths would turn out to be what the building staff called a royal straight flush—their term for a progression of elevator rides that began with newlyweds, then featured domestic quarrels, then hoisted secret lovers, then transported lawyers and, finally, realtors.

"Good morning, Horace," said Vincent to the guard after a short, brisk walk to the museum. "Be very careful of those new Italian baroque pictures in the south hall," he added with facetious seriousness.

"What do you mean?" asked the guard.

"They may try a break."

"Huh?"

Vincent nodded. "It's all over the yard—some of the Italians are planning a break. We're checking for tunnels."

The guard laughed weakly, wondering what the silly bastard possibly could be talking about.

The first thing Vincent did in his office was to call home.

"Mary? Hi, darling. I forgot about this thing. Could we ask these people, the Lavals, to dinner on the twenty-eighth? And Willoughby? And he's got what's-her-name, good old Mrs. Phillips. It's for our new roof."

Vincent got more done that morning than he'd managed in a month. By three he'd scheduled a week that would barely leave time to get from one appointment to the next. He didn't stop until six. His only doubts concerned whether he should cancel his drink with Laura Montgomery by phone, or just go over there and tell her in person that it had been a mistake. He decided the latter was the decent thing to do.

Winter's early darkness gave Vincent pause. Night was such an intimate circumstance, and he hadn't considered this when making his decision. Bouncing down the museum steps, he realized he really should have phoned, anyway, because she might not be expecting him after all. The drink had been mentioned only once, casually, in yesterday's phone call, and she probably had other plans by now.

He would have called right then from the pay phone to cancel had a taxi tiara not lit up right in front of him. Taxis were too rare to pass up at six-thirty in front of the museum. Next to the grinning Haitian head shot on the taxi driver's license display on the dashboard was the name Romeo Vercingetorix.

"Romeo?"

"Whe faux at thou?" replied the driver, obviously used to jokes about his name. Vincent and the driver both laughed. It was dark and impish on this ride with Romeo.

Baby Wallace loves me, and Mary, too, Vincent said to himself like a bedeviled maiden in a horror movie holding up a cross as the doorknob in her bedroom turns. Everything Vincent would ever need was in that rich and wonderful home on the other side of the park he'd just been taken across by Romeo. Yesterday had demonstrated that Vincent could still be a good husband and father, the custodian of his vows and expectations. So much lay ahead along the route he'd almost abandoned: a curatorship, studies abroad, maybe even a sibling for Wallace. Vincent thought about buying himself a new suit. He thought the one under Willoughby's defiant layer of yellow leather was a beauty, a rich, mature weave with some unexpected red in it.

"Hi," she said. Her hair looked different. But it was short hair before and it was short hair now. How could short hair look different? It was Laura who looked different, standing here outside, real instead of remembered. A plum-colored silk blouse upholstered her big breasts and slim waist. The enviably placed garment was open to show an inch of line dividing these wondrous, creamy globes. Vincent had seen them entirely that night in her bedroom. He'd thought about them over and over, and he'd drawn them. Her face was perfect by any standards. What would it be like to accompany such beauty, he wondered, to wake up next to it?

"That fire looks great," said Vincent, taking off his overcoat. "You know, apparently what happens when you heat wood hot enough is that chemically it turns into gasoline," he babbled.

On a large, low table in front of the fireplace she'd stacked tangerines on an ancient, pale gray Chinese platter. Next to them was a small Tibetan knife, its sheath studded with chunks of turquoise and coral. The pair of high old leather Spanish chairs he remembered stood guard on one end of the table, and a huge corduroy couch bearing big fancy pillows ran alongside it. It was like the casually magnificent hunting lodge of a Spanish grandee.

"What would you like to drink, Vincent? I think there's some champagne."

"Actually, I wouldn't mind a Scotch if you have it," he replied, wanting a strong drink to lacquer his confusion. He'd better tell her pretty quickly he was never seeing her again, before he forgot.

The place was so uncluttered and stylish. The wooden floor had been enameled off-white to set off a scattering of fine old rugs. And there was a wonderful portrait of Queen Elizabeth over the fireplace. How hadn't he even noticed it at the party?

"It's a beautiful apartment."

"Thanks," said Laura. "Cin Cin." They touched glasses,

grinning curves parallel to the ones they brought to their lips.

"That's an Aztec feather robe," she explained as he toured around, wondering where to sit. Her high heels implied a certain formality of occasion. She probably did have a dinner date, he decided. Men must be stacked out there like planes over a busy airport, waiting for the chance to accompany that unbelievable beauty, that wonderful taste and . . .

"This is fantastic," said Vincent, looking up at the Virgin Queen, bedizened with iconographic jewelry and costume. The queen's red hair and scalloped collar pointed with jewels made a second fire above the one silhouetting Laura. "I was in the Elizabethan Club at Yale. I'm crazy about the Faerie Queene." He continued to speak in the tinny, distant radio voice from which he seemed a stranger.

Vincent wished Laura would sit down, since where she sat might tell him something of her expectations. If she chose one of the Spanish chairs, it would seem this was to be just the "drink" he'd been asked over for. Of course, it was just a drink —what else could it be? He should take one of those palace-guard-like chairs himself and tell her that though, as she probably knew, he had been deeply, deeply stirred by her, nothing could come of it. Hadn't he only made that dark transverse of Central Park with Romeo at the wheel in order to advise her he was sorry for so presumptuously and treacherously embracing and kissing and kissing her at her party? Hadn't it been an enormous relief for Vincent to realize his marriage was viable and saved? His business here was to tell her he had no business being here in her marvelous apartment where she smiled into her firelight. He could tell her about baby Wallace—that would hit this occasion like a bucket of water in the fireplace, whose flames seemed already to be chattering inflammatory gossip to one another.

It was just a drink—he held the drink in his hand, the drink it all just was, standing there with her in the firelight. The Scotch in his glass flashed with reflection and refraction.

"Isn't she like a frozen fire herself?" Vincent said, startled by his new cracked voice. He cleared his throat and raised his glimmering glass toward the portrait. His voice seemed to be deliberately distancing itself from him. "A picture of a stopped fire like alchemy?"

"Don't you love her?" said Laura. She kicked off her shoes and sat down just off-center on the big sofa. The sofa! Off-center! Was it an invitation?

"I think it's a nineteenth-century copy, but it's a very good one." Vincent's voice had returned to his service. In fact, it sounded smooth and hard now, his own ruthless lieutenant.

"It's not mine," said Laura. "This place is a sublet from this professor who's a friend of my mother's, and some of this stuff is his. It's a complete steal, and he may never come back from this thing he's on." There was something breezy about her manner, a spring breeze joking with a rose garden.

Vincent sat next to her, smiling as if this all were only conversation, a drink, a social moment in the briefly coinciding complexities of their historically separate lives. A space ran down between their parallel thighs. She was leaning back and he was tilted forward, placing his glass on the table—not to free up his hands for anything untoward, just to set his drink down a moment. Pitched forward like that, his crotch seemed to him like a seashore grotto taking the spectacular crash and spumes of a mighty ocean. It was, of course, desire—so much desire that he reached for her, perfectly willing to be arrested and hanged for it. One of his arms went into the gap under the small of her back, and the other went over her. He squeezed against the heavenly shape, marveling over where it was and where it wasn't. She received and held this disreputable avalanche with a titter. She patted him on the back as he kissed toward her mouth. She didn't accept him immediately.

"Hey, Mr. Married Man," she said teasingly.

Like a surprised looter, Vincent pulled all he could of himself up away from her, but he couldn't entirely let go.

"Sorry," he said huffily. Gasps of passion rocked him. Laura tittered again and, reaching up, screwed his forelock around her finger.

Vincent came back to the great embrace he'd just tried, and felt welcomed. They kissed deeper and deeper, and as they sheared together, he pulled at the tiny, knotty fastenings of her strained clothing. He wanted his interior somehow at her interior. Their bodies were climbing and clambering about the big sofa like great beetles, matching up triggers of passion and pressing together.

"Hey," Laura said. She was grinning. "Are you sure about this?"

Vincent nodded and went back at her, understanding how dandelions could push up through concrete to get their sun.

Wordlessly Laura extricated herself and stood up. She pulled him up by the hands. They crossed toward her bedroom, their walk neither innocent nor light. Masaccio's *Expulsion from the Garden of Eden* came to Vincent's mind.

He was chagrined by the suddenness of his orgasm. Laura was thrilled by its violence. She smiled at his confusions, covering her obsolete nudity.

Now it's done, he thought. Now it's over, no going back. He loved Laura. She petted him and chortled at his astonished expression. He fell asleep a moment, or perhaps he died. When he awoke, he took account of his corpse and hers. She, too, was sleeping. He found a clock beside her bed. It was, as it would be for some time to come, much too late.

Mary was glad Vincent was late, because she decided it meant he was trying harder at the museum. Men like Vincent wanted to be the chief, and it must be galling to work for Willy Willoughby. Albert Borden said there was a homosexual Mafia assisting each other in museums, leapfrogging their lovers into top spots, making advancement difficult for straight men. And Alfred was the head of another museum—a smaller one, of course, but still he was the head of it, and he was Vincent's age. Mary would so much rather Vincent had worked on Wall Street, away from such intrigues. Why had she married an artistic man? He was so vain and impractical. In Europe he'd pulled her up to those damp old sewer paintings with a kind of wondrous anger and explained and explained and explained their glories. If she didn't know him, if she'd only met him in this excited state, she might have dismissed him as a nutcase. Mary saw only ancient personalities in the pictures, but she didn't let on. She had always been told it was important for men to have enthusiasms and hobbies.

It would have been so much easier to marry a commercial man, pleased enough to calibrate life's digits, instead of this confused, romantic-visionary type who was late for dinner. Money men just measured, Mary reflected as her husband's tardiness lengthened. Mary's millions could make money men as awestruck as pictures made Vincent.

But it was really nice how he'd called that morning about giving a dinner party, his voice so refreshingly businesslike. It made them seem like a couple useful to each other again, a team.

Mary was happy just to be called by her husband from his office. At least momentarily, everything had somehow fallen back into place. She decided to get a record of that wonderful opera where the ill man had been in the next box and they'd finished the evening making love. That opera could now be their theme.

He was now quite late, but Mary decided she wouldn't telephone him at the museum. The switchboard was undoubtedly shut down, and besides, everybody she knew was always complaining about their husbands being late—especially the lawyers and bankers whose activities now pivoted on spokes from time zones in London and Tokyo. Ellie Barnholme had told her that Bob hardly ever got home before ten.

It was odd he hadn't called to warn her, but when those switchboards shut down, maybe you can't call out, either. She went to the window and looked down at the museum. Although from the front it looked like the museum, with pillars and flags and stairs, from above all the ugly vents and skylights made it look like a factory or an airport. Mary scowled. The museum got bigger every year, eating up what had been a much nicer view of the park with the expanding steelyard of its junky roof. Would this new roof they wanted be any nicer? Probably not, because people couldn't see it, and nobody wasted money on things that didn't show in this cheapskate age.

The stupidest thing Mary thought she could ever possibly allow herself to do was even to consider the existence of the Montgomery slut. Vincent had drunk way too much at that party, and that show-biz whore was clearly the prom-queen type who probably loved to show how she could have any other woman's man. Mary thanked God she'd stopped that in time, and that a new mood of making marriage work had appeared. She considered how their so-called friends would gossip if anything went obviously wrong with the marriage. People were so pleased by poisonous observations, especially when there was a lot of money involved, as her father was always warning her.

Wallace was awake but wasn't crying. He was wide-eyed in his crib, stiffly waving up his legs and arms as if they were cranes and pulleys that could hoist him out of the hold of his crib into more interesting surroundings. Mary shoveled him out of his crib, pleased by his wonderful little grunts and coos of pleasure. She paraded him into the sitting room, happy everything seemed to be going so well.

"I have to tell you something, Mary," said Vincent, crossing the room rather formally to where she sat. To make matters more painful for him, she had the baby in her arms. When he realized she was concentrating on something else and missing his words, he felt so relieved that he decided to postpone any announcement until some occasion when she wasn't holding Wally.

"Darling, why don't we get a really, really good picture and get rid of this?" she said, standing like an officer on a battlefield in the grand sitting room they used for big parties. She was referring to a portrait of an ancestral Brigham that included two parrots. In mocking symmetry with Queen Elizabeth at Laura's, it hung over the fireplace. Of course the fire had to be lit, as it usually wasn't, to make this comparison obvious. Vincent dropped down to light it.

"What do you mean?" he asked, ready to acquiesce in any manner now that he had truly, physically betrayed his wife. In his own mind he was groveling before her with matches, as if he were begging forgiveness.

"I mean, get something you like." On his knees beneath her,

he considered how he was not a husband in this tableau but a parody of a husband.

"You mean, a picture?"

"Really nice. I sold my Bible stock, and I was thinking, why don't we get something really nice? You know? Instead of just buying more stock. Everybody always says what a great eye you have."

Wallace seemed to be considering Mary's proposition himself. He looked up critically at the picture of his ancestor.

Why didn't the damn fire light up? Vincent moved the faggots around until the wood turned into gasoline. When he stood up, everything looked chidingly serene and mockingly familial. The blood left his head and he reeled. Mary seemed to want a hug.

Even though Vincent had bought a pack of alcohol-based scented napkins on the West Side and rubbed his face, neck, and hands in the taxi back through the park, he was sure he still reeked of making love with Laura. He hugged Mary with the stiffness of a mechanical man. Never before had he felt such palpable insincerity in himself. Absurdly, he gave Mary a peck. Then he jammed his hands in his pockets and looked up at where the new picture would hang, posing as if he were considering her suggestion. In his pockets, the scaly foil wrappings of the scented napkins with which he'd daubed like Lady Macbeth at his lovestains nipped at his guilty fingertips.

"There are some Old Master sales coming," he said. "I just got the catalogs." Once again he heard his own voice as if it were a conversation coming from another room. Vincent made them both strong drinks. It was a family scene by the fire, including a monster only he could see.

Wallace, provoked by what Vincent could only guiltily

imagine, began to cry furiously. Mary rocked to and fro with the emphasis of a dancer, and the baby's cries subsided. She was the mother of his child. He had made those old English promises to her, knightly vows he'd just truly broken—no, shattered.

"You know, I was reading how babies believe everything is them," said Vincent, approaching Mary and taking Wallace —who was kicking and groping and suddenly smiling—off her breast.

"Wally, Wally, Wally. They think the world is made of them, their sheets and crib and room and the people who come and go are all just like more toes, aren't they, Wally? And supposedly it's the realization that they're not everything, that they can't control everything, that makes them get mad as they grow up."

At this moment Mary looked especially pleased and practical. She held a cocked elbow over a hand on her hip. His story about being late because of the museum hadn't put her out at all. She had stew, which could wait. Adultery seemed so accommodating.

"That *would* be fun," Vincent said, looking at the picture she had indicated they could replace, as if he saw dotted lines around it. He shuddered as he was able to picture Queen Elizabeth hanging there instead.

Wally didn't want his mother, either. He wanted the rug, and he spanked this great floral plain with noises of curiosity. He loved to "creep," as Mrs. Keswick called it. Vincent and Mary stared at him like two enormous and complicated sides of an unsolved equation admiring the tiny equal sign creeping between them.

Chapter ❧ 10

"*H*ello, Miss Montgomery?"

"Yes?"

"Pauline McFall's office, Miss Montgomery. Could you hold a minute? She's finishing up another call." The voice was male and campy.

Laura was pleased to note that her call to Pauline McFall was returned an hour later. Highly placed pesons have *A* and *B* and even *C* priority lists of calls and callers. An hour's wait for a return call from Pauline McFall, editor-in-chief of the country's preeminent fashion magazine, was proof that Laura was *A*.

She was furthermore pleased with herself for how quickly and powerfully she'd rearranged her circumstances after Toby Hyman's humiliating termination of her career at the network. She now considered how she was ever so much better off in every way.

For as long as she could remember, people had told Laura how great she'd be at fashion. She had looks and style and connections. She appreciated beautiful things and handsome gestures. With its arch homosexual contingent and escapist focus, fashion occurred to Laura as a place full of relief and relaxation—a safe haven from the achievement-oriented lust and hard news of the network.

But this "hold" Laura had been put on for Pauline McFall was going on too long. She considered hanging up. At last there was an electronic switching noise, after which Laura found herself sucked into the nullity of a dial tone. Angrily she dialed right back, using the private number she had from Daddy.

"Terribly, terribly sorry, Miss Montgomery. This is Peter, Miss McFall's assistant, and she has gotten insanely tied up, but she wonders if you could have lunch on Thursday the ninth at one at the Four Seasons?"

Laura added this date to her schedule. Purring mightily, Florida kept stepping delicately on Laura's calendar. Laura readjusted her cat's placement and puzzled over all the provocative new opportunities in her life. She had appointments with newspapers, television channels, networks, and magazines. Book publishing? Too much reading. The movies? Never, because anything she did in the movies would of course have Daddy written all over it.

The phone rang, and Florida jumped and ran.

"Hi," Vincent said in a tone whipsawed by torment and bliss.

"Hello," Laura answered with mock formality.

"Well."

"Did you get back all right?"

"Sure, great, and this afternoon I've got this errand over at the Brooklyn Museum which I figure is going to take up the whole afternoon."

"That's all right, I have appointments," Laura replied.

Vincent's heart leapt. She was already talking as if they were together. They were scheduling. It was the conversation of a love affair.

He really was seeing her! Why is it called *seeing* when it's more felt than seen? Blind, he'd feel no less with her. In fact, when they made love, sight became a sort of banality. Eyes clenched shut, soaring into the dark space of self where she drew him, he wasn't seeing her. Love is blind because it's more fundamental than sight. It precedes sight in the blindness of the womb—all the love some of us will ever know.

"What I mean is, I don't have to be at this museum this afternoon," he elucidated.

"I thought you said you had to go to Brooklyn." Vincent could hear how her smile deformed her pronunciation. His own smile was so broad, it crackled in his ears. "Isn't it wonderful?"

"It sounds very naughty."

"Have you had lunch? I'll bring a picnic."

"Over here to Brooklyn?"

"Exactly," said the utterly exultant Vincent Booth.

Chapter 11

"Y ou really look spectacular, Laura. What on earth are you doing?" asked Pauline McFall two and a half weeks later at lunch. Doing? Laura thought instantly of Vincent. His passion was the most desperate and total she'd ever experienced. Toby Hyman seemed merely grabby by comparison. Men had wanted Laura, loved her, coveted her, and bragged about her, but never had any of them loved her with such private, personal, violent passion as Vincent. With him, Laura witnessed the astonishment of love.

Their love seemed to dovetail every jointure of their meetings. Taxis were always available, even in the rain. Phones, never busy, answered on a ring. Traffic lights changed to green at once to save them time together, and everyone who saw or attended them when they were out and about smiled and adored them and helped them along. A great force seemed to guide their molecules right through the spaces between those of the barriers set up by reality.

If it was the fact of his being married that intensified this passion, Laura was glad of it. His marriage also kept him from getting possessive. It made their romance not only secret but also intensely private. Intensity and freedom and no connection but that of love made Laura happier seeing Vincent Booth than she ever had felt with anyone.

"I don't know why," Laura said, using a matter-of-fact tone to answer Pauline McFall's question. "I'm job hunting."

"What happened at the network?"

"I lost *It's Morning.* I was going to be the host, and then they changed their minds, and you can't stay on if you've lost when you've refused to do anything else."

"That's awful, darling."

The restaurant where they were having lunch drew an important crowd. The familiarly famous faces lunching there hadn't become so by acting. They were news-famous faces, the ones you see trembling in strobe lights as they disappear into the backs of limousines, or hovering over the sculpted cobra attack of a hundred microphones, blandly institutionalizing the horrendous curiosities of modern civilization. Less famous faces of pleased and powerful insiders, and the transient guests of this amalgam, completed the inevitably complete booking of tables.

Since she was the youngest and most beautiful person in the place, Laura got glances from people who were more accustomed to being glanced at themselves. The particular radiance Pauline McFall had noted caused even the happily married billionaires in the room to stop thinking about their deals for a moment and wish she loved them. When Toby Hyman came up the stairs and saw her, he went straight back down. He telephoned the captain from the street-corner pay phone, telling him to tell his lunch date he was ill, which he, in fact, did feel after seeing the fucking beautiful Laura Montgomery.

"What kind of degrees and all that did you get?"

"Oh, God. I actually quit college to do an expedition in Ladakh. Is that a problem?"

"Where?"

"Ladakh? In the Himalayas? It's incredibly beautiful, Pauline. These monasteries have been there since Buddha."

Pauline McFall was put off by Laura calling her by her Christian name with such instant equality, even though she would have hated hearing this overadvantaged daughter of her onetime lover call her Miss, Mrs., or Ms. McFall. Pauline McFall had a similar reaction to the unexpected rutting glances directed to their table by the usually smug power champions lunching around them. Laura seemed so effortlessly lofted right up next to Pauline's hard-won station—and even beyond it, considering the rampant desire she stirred up. It didn't seem just.

What could you do with a creature like this? She was beautiful, and probably bright and certainly stylish, and she knew everybody. She could be an attraction of some sort for some enterprise. The way she had just said *Pauline* wouldn't have disturbed Pauline at a party, and she chided herself for feeling jealous. For chrissake, she'd slept with Laura's father twenty years ago when Laura was what, five or ten?

Laura loved the taste of the lobster ravioli. She smiled again, thinking of Vincent and how they seemed to cause such magic in the dull old world. She wondered what he was eating and what he was wearing and where he was and when she would see him again.

"What kind of thing do you see yourself doing for us?"

"Interviews," Laura said. "That's really what I was hoping to do at the network. I'd love to just make kind of a collection of people, special people."

"Like?"

"Well, that great landscape architect in Brazil who did, you know, that modern city they built, and the parks and all those modern gardens, and the Dalai Lama, and all sorts of people who don't seem to get any coverage now that everything is just money."

"That's kind of interesting," Pauline said with an ironical smile.

"I can't believe this lobster ravioli," said Laura, oblivious to her companion's expression.

The irony Pauline felt derived from the fact that she had met James Montgomery by interviewing him. When a twenty-six-year-old with a graduate degree in journalism enters a handsome, world-famous forty-five-year-old rake's hotel suite to discuss his achievements, beliefs, adventures, experiences, regrets, memories, loves, childhood, ideals, and sense of artistic purpose for three hours, it's not inconceivable that the subject, as well as the reporter, might begin to feel something like love, as the great and wonderful identity that will rise up in print appears between them. Twenty years ago, after such a magnifico had risen up from her interview with him, Laura's father had nudged the heroic vision of himself just off-center atop the pedestal Pauline's questions had built under it.

"Now, darling," he had said, "let's not make me too good to be true, or I'll never be able to have any more fun. Fact of the matter is, I hit a woman once. Still ashamed of it. My second wife . . ."

Pauline's heart had already turned toward this man, and she'd found herself in his arms like someone awakening in a strange and wonderful room.

After that, of course, the romance had not continued at such a pinnacle of admiration. The bastard had betrayed her quickly enough. He had always been thoughtful and helpful and available, however, which Pauline found useful and attractive attributes—probably necessary ones for a man who had no heart.

Pauline couldn't help remembering all that as she listened to his daughter explain her desire to do interviews, but she masked her telltale smile with a water goblet. On reflection, Laura reminded Pauline of her father: the outrageous attractiveness was there, and maybe the heartlessness too.

"How's James?" Pauline asked just before realizing she'd rather not know.

"He's coming to town in a couple of weeks," said Laura.

"Is he? He didn't tell me."

"He only told me this morning. He's meeting some people about a movie in Brazil."

"Is he now?" Pauline remarked with a sad smile.

"Could you come to dinner?"

"Sure," Pauline answered faster than she would've liked. "Is he married or anything these days?"

"So disgusting." Laura shrugged and grinned forgivingly. "He uses this term he says the jockeys at the racetrack have for when they're not riding. He says he's between mounts."

Chapter 12

*A*ssociate editor? Missy shook her head, causing the corners of the blond helmet of her new bobbed hairdo (an attempt at the intense sophistication she'd decided was in order after Laura's party) to dab her cheeks. Here she was, still in the typing pool after two years, and Laura Montgomery enters the magazine world as an associate editor! Missy might have just hated Laura for it, except Laura had asked her to a dinner party she was giving for her father.

The other oars in the slave galley of the typing pool at Missy's magazine were manned by recent college graduates who, like Missy, had higher ambitions than cleaning up other people's messy manuscripts. There was John, who wore the red-and-black checks of the ecology movement and was a poet on the side. Gigantic Margo, the earth mother, wanted to pull up governmental rocks for a look at the vile bodies squirming beneath them. Alice Maguire, like Missy, was a boarding-school blonde who wanted to write. Alice's goal was fiction, however, as opposed to Missy, who wanted to be a journalist.

A private dinner for James Montgomery! How could Missy tell her fellow workers, whose own high points of the near future were probably on the order of going to a movie—maybe one of James Montgomery's—or guiltily and orgiastically eating a quart of ice cream alone? But she did want them to know of her exaltation. The magazine might return her submissions (Cheese and Alitalia, An Evening Out, An Arty Lunch) and keep her in the typing pool, but it could not ruin her social life.

Despite its relentless rejections of her submissions, Missy considered working for such a distinguished magazine worthwhile. At parties, when others identified their careers—and consequently their characters—by naming institutions devoted to dull money grubbing, she was pleased to name a magazine whose reputation combined artistic quality, liberal-mindedness, and luxury advertising, giving her selection of employment an idealistic but luxurious air, like a Bohemian deigning to appear in a posh restaurant with a smitten millionaire.

Big Margo had just finished toiling considerably on a mountainous piece of nonfiction on plumbing. The potentially disgusting aspects of this report had necessitated so many changes that Margo had to retype practically the entire article. Outsiders said the magazine's elderly editor was losing touch, publishing too many endless, esoteric articles like this one, but the employees were uniformly loyal to his rigorous, old-fashioned standards. Other magazines didn't even have typing pools anymore, nor did they still bother to use scissors and paste.

"Finally, finally, finally," said Margo, having handed the plumbing piece over to production for typesetting.

"Feeling better now?" Alice asked.

"People are just going to laugh us off the newsstands for this one," said Missy.

"No they won't," Margo snapped. "It's actually quite interesting."

"It's a subject you can't get away from." John smirked.

"The Mountain of Gold," Alice joked to Missy, because this happened to be the title of James Montgomery's most famous movie.

Missy could keep her secret no longer. "I'm having dinner with him week after next."

"Who?" asked Alice.

"James Montgomery. His daughter's a friend of mine."

There was a very satisfactory moment of silence.

"Neat," Alice finally said. For the rest of the afternoon Missy sensed the envy and distance her announcement had caused. James Montgomery was just the sort of grand figure to really get to the typing pool. John had bragged about meeting a famous poet, but the others had found that merely sweet. Margo's interview with the mayor for a neighborhood newspaper had been a coup, but nothing to merit personal envy. Alice, as she herself often remarked, had never met anybody in her whole life.

Naturally the typing pool would be especially impressed by James Montgomery. Because of his highly publicized liberal politics, artistic career, and high living, he was a sort of fabulous, exaggerated personification of the very qualities of the magazine that had attracted all of them to work there in the first place. Not surprisingly, Missy's fellow workers felt tiny and plain-fated alongside a person who was about to dine with the great man himself.

Even so, it irked Missy that Laura had been offered associate editor for her first job in magazines. It certainly did seem to be who-you-know in the matter of careers. Laura had probably never written much more than a letter, if that, in her whole life. She'd quit college to go off and take pictures somewhere in the Himalayas—and no one had ever seen Laura Montgomery's pictures published anywhere, Missy reflected. Maybe they stank. Her eyes were glazing over as she looked over twenty hideously scratched-up pages of manuscript by the writer she hated most, writing as usual about his dismal, minutely recollected boyhood again.

So Laura was moving into journalism right at the top, just like that. A camera makes anybody into a photographer, and a tape recorder makes anybody into a journalist. Laura could drift at will from the top of television to the top of a magazine, and on top of all that, she never had looked more ravishingly beautiful.

At four in the afternoon, when John went down to get decent coffee from the espresso place on the corner, he did not, as he always used to, ask Missy if she'd like a cup.

"No wonder they made envy a sin," said Missy when John returned and handed each of the others a cup.

"What do you mean?"

"It's all right," Missy said loftily. "I didn't want any."

"You were in the bathroom when I asked," John replied.

"Please," Margo said, "don't anybody mention that word."

Then, grinning, John produced a cup of coffee for Missy, who blushed. "I'm buying for everybody today," he said, "because I just had my first poem accepted by *Poetry* magazine."

Now all the envy drew back from Missy and turned into congratulations for their rising colleague. It was wonderful news and, Missy figured, a nobler enterprise than talking about having dinner with a celebrity. Furthermore it meant John had suddenly advanced ahead of her in the world of letters.

Laura called and asked Missy to lunch all the time now, because she could talk to her about Vincent.

"Be careful," Missy had advised. "There's always a pattern. They always tell you they're going to leave their wives, but they never do." While Missy had no direct experience of married men, lately she'd been struck by how frequently life seemed to obey clichés.

"But I don't care," Laura had chuckled back. "I sort of like having someone else do the hard part."

"Typical Montgomery," Missy later told Alice, her own confidante. "But I'll bet she won't always be so glad he's married."

Chapter 13

*W*illiam Willoughby habitually carried his courtier's smile thorugh the huge, hatefully common crowd in the museum's lobby. They coagulated mainly there and in the shops and restaurants because, Willoughby reasoned at dinner parties, they felt most at home in malls.

When they ventured into the galleries, it was usually to the latest show in the latest wing. In the museum's original rooms of great masterpieces there wasn't much traffic, although on this particular morning Willoughby had come upon a group of adolescent black girls bubbling up into profoundly sexual shapes which Willoughby found astonishing and ludicrous. He scowled at them. They were swatting each other and giggling as they took notes on the Vermeers.

Halfway down the stone steps in front of the

museum, Willoughby spotted Laura Montgomery sidling out of the park. He felt a painful tweak of jealousy. So now Vincent Booth was leching at work. Willoughby self-righteously pictured himself firing him the moment Mary Brigham announced the inevitable divorce. He certainly deserved to be knocked down a peg, Willoughby concluded as he watched Laura flutter up through the hunkering herds littering the stairs.

Vincent wanted to stand his goddess before Aelbert Cuyp's *Landscape with Cows,* the picture with which he was currently infatuated. He'd doted on it for months, staring at it from different distances, coming upon it with staged unexpectedness, and sitting with it a half hour at a time. It was one of the few instances of absolute beauty in his mind that wasn't Laura or Laura-related. He now wanted to introduce his two absolutes of beauty to each other.

He had decided not to announce it but instead just to walk her into the room and see if she would discover it. And before he had finished rebuking himself for even thinking of testing the love of his life this way, Laura made straight for the cows and turned back to him with the same smile that broke onto his own face. Nodding, he couldn't help embracing her and, through her, Cuyp, beauty, eternity, and the hope and courage that moved men to leave behind such compliments to life.

Rita, a rather cow-proportioned person herself, even when buttoned into her museum guard uniform, stepped into the gallery in time to witness the embrace.

"That ain't half," said Horace, another guard, when Rita told him what she'd seen. "They was in them Lehman Rooms, and he put down the drapes."

"What?"

Horace nodded and laughed, forcing whistles out between his teeth.

"Go on," encouraged Rita.

"Fuckin' they asses off."

"Where at?"

"Them little bitty dark rooms with all the bullshit that got the drapes and the little stairs goin' nowhere," Rita's colleague managed to explain before the two of them began laughing too hard to talk.

The grandeur and mischief of making love in one of the string of rooms reproduced as they'd stood in their donor's mansion —appropriately the one with Diana watching Cupid getting stung by bees at its entrance—left Vincent astonished. He felt he had found an extraordinary new form of living hidden brilliantly inside the plain shell of the old one. He truly had come upon and opened the sort of secret door found in the enchanted forests of such knightly tales as *The Faerie Queene*.

Then he'd shut it, leaving Laura and himself in the opulent treasure trove the late financial magnate desired the public should know had belonged to him. They both blushed and grinned and sank to the floor. Laura stuffed her panties in her purse.

To make love at such risk of being discovered was intensely erotic for both of them. Vincent felt the atmospheric pressure in the room actually increase the moment he closed the curtain. The shape of the structure they inhabited imprinted itself on one part of his brain, the sentinel part, as the rest of his concentration went over the falls. Laura felt a surprising, voluptuous rush of intensely satisfying exhibitionism as he entered her. She could imagine the whole world watching. It made her feel extra naked, inside-out naked.

The colors of the objects and pictures in the little room were deep and rich. The ludicrousness of such a setting for the total intimacy of copulation encouraged complete abandon, and Laura began to buck like a bronco. Before she foresaw it, a great orgasm shook her, the first she'd had with someone else in ages. Her eyes squeezed shut and she screamed silently as Vincent gripped up with all his might and joined her in apocalyptic release.

Afterward Vincent walked Laura to the main entrance. Flushed and smiling and noticeably beautiful, they passed through rooms of mortals looking at pictures of immortals. Vincent and Laura felt somewhere between these two states. Vincent and Laura couldn't help noticing how even guards like Horace and Rita broke into broad grins as they majestically passed by.

Chapter 14

A physicist might chart Sidney Laval as an accreting body in motion. The rush and growth of his millions had quickly buzzed him into considerable notoriety. Vincent fancied he could hear the busy dynamos of money-making at work as the plump young financial manipulator walked purposefully over to the painting of flowers hanging above Mary's desk.

"Fantin-Latour," he said, mispronouncing the name with defiant conviction. He turned back to Vincent, eager for confirmation, which Vincent readily gave him. Sidney nodded impatiently and inquired, "Where did you get it?"

"Wedding present from Mary's father. I think his grandfather bought it from the artist," Vincent replied.

This answer caused the millionaire a rapid series

of nods before he turned back, squinting toward the picture. "Joe Lebenthal's asking half a million for a smaller one than this." Vincent knew the picture the dealer must have shown Laval. "Lilacs?" he asked, getting another rapid-fire burst of nods. "I don't think he'll get it," he suggested.

Now that he'd seen Fantin-La Tour ratified by old money on this wall, Sidney apparently had decided to buy the lilacs. But after Vincent's demurement about the price, Sidney decided not to go over a quarter of a mill.

Sondra Laval looked splendid and expensive. She had been minutely prepared for the occasion by clothiers, jewelers, and beauticians. She was a full head taller than her husband.

"What a beautiful room," she said to Mary, whose toilette suggested little more than a hairbrush and a bar of white soap. Mary had on her horn-rims and a dress she wore as if she'd been ordered into it by a nanny.

William Willoughby entered the sitting room with a dowager who moved with the marionette motions of an advanced but determined member of old age.

"Sidney," Willoughby said with a smile so avid that one would've guessed these two had passed through Groton together. "Sondra has been absolutely fabulous on the committee," he continued, taking Sondra's hands and kissing her. Everybody was beaming.

"Mary, darling," said the elderly lady, approaching the hostess with her arms raised scarecrow-style. "Hi, Rainey," said Mary familiarly, maneuvering into the approaching fork of bony embrace and kissing the fragile, silky rouged cheeks above which Lorraine "Rainey" Phillips's eyes were still greedily bright.

Vincent was glad for the distraction of these guests. It made the transition between his home and the intensifying surrealism of his love affair that much easier. Mary could entertain herself with these other identities, leaving his unexamined. A brief, diverting intrusion of guests, and then sleep was all he wanted in this world after his matinee in the richly appointed little make-believe habitation of the Lehman Rooms.

Vincent never looked more beautiful to Willoughby than he did this evening. Sondra also found him pleasingly attractive, having decided she and Vincent had something in common. They were both more beautiful than their rich spouses. They were bound to come togther in society more and more, and might someday have a fling.

Sondra also observed the objects, service, and procedures of the Booths' dinner party with noticeable intensity. She was surprised that Willoughby seemed more like the principal at the table than Vincent. At their own dinners Sidney usually dominated. But here Vincent seemed as languid as a cat dozing in sunlight, completely and uncompetitively content to let Willoughby do the social sparkling.

Sondra found his behavior calm and appealing. She vowed to teach her husband not to press himself so avidly on everyone —to let the professionals like Willoughby gossip and prance. It seemed so much softer and more elegant and above it all.

"James, this is divine," said Willoughby, ordering more wine from the butler, using his name with authoritative familiarity. Although the way Willoughby rode over other conversations and disdained any opinions but his own was nearly obnoxious, the richness and authenticity of his gossip made everyone indulgent. With bland authority he revealed the inner workings of all sorts of notorious marriages, arrangements, and personalities. Sondra was quite delighted by so much inside information.

Life with Sidney had brought to Sondra's attention first the names of people considered socially important. After she got the names the possessors of these identities were pointed out to her. Tonight, in William Willoughby's gossip, their personalities were nakedly revealed. The museum grandee's revelations made Sondra feel as if she were already on a first-name basis with the people she had decided she would know.

In every regard the evening was helpful, instructive, and fascinating for Sondra. She watched how Mary and old Rainey Phillips went through their parts in the social function like a couple of venerable ecclesiastics at a Mass. Apparently the butler (should she call him James too?) had been borrowed, like an extra chair or some silver, from Mary's parents. How grandly old-family that seemed to Sondra, who cannily decided that it would be going too far too fast to give her own parents a butler she and Sidney could borrow.

Sidney was not unaware of his wife's interest in their sleepy-looking host. Sondra's sleek white flesh had extruded considerably from its bright silk boundaries. But she might as well flirt with a portrait in the British Museum, Sidney concluded. The languorous putz worked in a museum himself, married to money and dead to the world.

Because of a popular movie, the topic of dinner conversation turned to the Vietnam War.

"Rainey was in Vietnam," Mary prompted, and everyone turned in delighted surprise to face the old dowager.

"Indochine," she said with pleased authority as the spotlight struck her. Her delicate skin was wrapped over sheaves of bones and sinews that shifted with her animation.

"My husband Walter was the chargé d'affaires when it was still a French colony. I loved it. I loved the marvelous lettuce, the *laitue* we had from the embassy garden. You know, wherever the French were, the food really was excellent, and the French, of course, brought that lettuce."

Vincent, meanwhile, had happily noted that Sondra's considerable physical attractions could not touch him. His admiration for her beauty was as objective as if she were a sunset or a gorge. Before Laura, such looks would have made him tense from yearning. Before Laura he had considered sleeping with many women, more and more as time went on—friends, people's wives, baby-sitters, even whores. But he had not. He had resisted and tormented himself with frustration and masturbation. A few months before, this Sondra could have made him very unhappy. But not tonight, he thought, very nearly saying it aloud as he yawned deeply and moistly into his napkin.

"I asked the gardener to show me how he managed his wonderful lettuce." The ancient *raconteuse* smiled broadly as she paused and shrugged to suggest that something naughty was on the way. Her teeth looked fine and rare, and her use of pauses and intonations was entertaining.

"When I went out to the garden and saw why the lettuce was so successful, I was shocked," she said with facetious horror, causing Mary to lead the rest in a round of appreciative laughter. This gave Sondra the opportunity to offer Vincent her widest smile.

William Willoughby hated noticing all this. He hated being infatuated with the insensitive ingrate who worked for him, who had half this table in love, who had such extraordinary good looks, the Brigham fortune, and, as his sensuous lassitude throughout the evening all but proclaimed, Laura Montgomery all afternoon.

"Night soil," Rainey Phillips explained, causing an even stronger round of laughter.

William signaled the butler to bring him more wine. It was excellent wine, burgundy—a Corton? A Vosne Romanee? James poured it from a crystal beaker with his white-gloved hand. William Willoughby lived awfully well himself. Why should he resent Vincent's comforts? Especially considering how short-lived Vincent's might soon prove to be.

" 'Tron,' I said to him, 'you must not put that on lettuce. Understand? *Non* on the ambassador's lettuce.' 'No like?' he said to me. 'No!' I said. 'All right.' " Rainey Phillips spoke the gardener's part in an Oriental voice everyone found hilarious. Now even Vincent was laughing to the point of tears. Sondra's laughter was surprisingly authentic. It seemed like a newcomer, a stranger to her elaborate getup. Mary, too, laughed with a deep pleasure. Rainey Phillips really could tell a story. Sidney winked at Sondra, showing how his promise of the fun they would have if she married him was being kept. Only William Willoughby laughed mechanically, but he had heard the story at least twice before.

"The lettuce continued to be abundant and jade-green and completely delicious," Rainey Phillips continued with happy authority from knowing her audience was all for her.

"And I asked to see the garden again. Tron, I thought, must have some very valuable ancient secret here, and I shall learn it and take it home with me to my little garden in Middleburg. Well, there was the lettuce, and there was the night soil. 'Tron!'

I admonished him. 'Tron—I told you no and you still do it—night soil—did I not tell you no?' 'But this all from house, missus. This not Vietnamese, this all you family—all white.' "

The old marionette had performed again. She smiled into the acclaiming laughter with real delight. She'd sung for her supper.

Chapter 15

*A*fter that initial period when their passion seemed to rearrange matter itself to give them to each other at will, everyday obstacles had regained a certain amount of authority over Vincent and Laura. But the difficulties of getting together had added a sweet rush of gratitude to the joy of each successful meeting.

Vincent felt his life had been jerked into a magnificent new posture. There was something grand about loving someone as passionately and boundlessly as he was loving Laura. Every new tryst led quickly into symphonic spasms of mutually fulfilled lovemaking.

Laura decided in the smiling aftermath of one recent occasion to rehang a picture in her bedroom.

"Everything seems so much clearer now," she said, rising up off the bed upon which Vincent lay like an Etruscan figure on his tomb. Her body amazed him more all the time by its shapes, proportions, and motions. Rehanging a picture, she looked to Vincent like a conductor leading the physical universe through a brilliant performance of some wonderful music. He could almost hear that music echoing around earthly corners as it fell softly down from paradise.

But for Wally, he would have asked Laura to run away with him a hundred times. Remembering this as he watched the picture hanging gave Vincent pause. He didn't disapprove of himself for cheating on Mary because the passion he felt spoke to him of absolute truth. It was too grand not to follow. Occasionally, however, this passion did hold up a terrible mirror to his marriage and make him look into it.

"I'd die for him," Vincent said to himself, lunching alone late one afternoon at a sushi bar. But was there a way to die for Wally, a way in which Wally would know his dad had died for him? Because he loved him? That would be nice. It would be noble to die if you came out as a proud memory for your son. Over his sushi Vincent felt a little like a samurai considering a hero's seppuku.

Suddenly, a cockroach crawled into sight, moving like a dot in a video game. Before Vincent could blot it into oblivion with his napkin, this supreme urban tactician had effected an automatic, untouchable retreat. Disgusting, Vincent thought, but at the same time he realized it was far more important to live for his son than it would be to die for him.

Out on the avenue Vincent felt more pleased than depressed by the progress he'd just made in his study of loyalty and devotion. After all, objectively considered, things were going extremely well. Laura actually seemed relieved he was married, and Mary managed her household with pleased aplomb. In

Europe, Vincent's current arrangement was said to be the norm. He concluded that, historically, the idea of combining love and marriage had never even been considered until American sentiment came along and developed the technology to finance and enforce its delusions.

In the windows along Madison Avenue were things for sale that might make happy presents. Vincent saw a belt he was sure Laura would like and, two stores farther on, a china platter he sensed Mary would adore. Since he wasn't up to the cynicism required to buy both presents at the same time, he opted for the platter. It was English, nineteenth-century, and its color and configuration matched Mary's taste exactly. It was much more expensive than Vincent expected, but he sprang for it with a pang of husbandly devotion.

Before returning home with this surprise present, Vincent decided to try Laura's phone one last time. In their morning phone call she'd warned him it was unlikely there would be any conveniently free time that afternoon. Yet on his way home, bearing a gift for his wife, Vincent found himself squeezing a quarter in his pocket.

By now a regular patron of the pay phone, Vincent had decided that the vast majority of this facility's clientele were messengers and adulterers. He lowered into the cold steel box, already anticipating the hopeless whir of Laura's unanswering machine. Instead, to his grand delight, she picked up on the first ring and told him to hurry right over for another of those wondrous hours they were privileged to work loose from reality.

Under now familiar conditions, Vincent loped toward the street that crossed the park, hailing taxis as he ran. He was unlikely to find one in rush hour, so he was overjoyed to catch a crosstown bus waiting like a confederate at the corner. It vaulted him across the park to Laura.

"What's this?" Laura asked, delighted.

Vincent had no choice but to push the present into her hands. She rewarded him with a kiss upon opening it. After they made love she picked the platter up again, studying it. "You know, I never would have picked this out, but I really like it. Seriously."

Chapter 16

*L*ike a politician, William Willoughby sawed his way through a crowded reception at an auction house with handshakes. He enthused and opined and cased the crowd as he did so. Damian Trent, a dealer of Willoughby's age and style, was approaching. William knew his real name was something guttural and depressing, and Damian Trent, of course, knew that Willoughby knew.

Damian wore a pin-striped suit that was fussily oversculpted. His tortoise-shell eyeglasses were actually cut from the shell of a tortoise. His white collar could be detached from his striped shirt. He had experienced a twinge in his scrotum when the handsome young bootmaker felt the fit of the bespoke shoes on his silk-stockinged, pedicured feet.

"William," Damian said, "you look fabulous."

"Thank you, Damian. Aren't you nice. You're lucky to always look so great. It only comes my way upon occasion."

"Is it anyone I know?" offered Damian with a smirk. Damian had a Southern drawl, which, like his name, had replaced an earlier model. He, too, scouted the crowd as he spoke, giving the pair of them the air of explorers keeping their eyes open and chatting amiably as they pass through new country.

"Just clean living, Damian," William retorted affably.

"God, that boy is beautiful," said Damian in a low voice. He was referring, of course, to Vincent, who was transfixed by a painting on the far wall. He was the only one in the entire room actually looking at the pictures.

"He works for me," said Willoughby with greater edge than he'd intended. By now William's infatuation had jelled into a sour mixture of obsession, jealousy, and frustration.

"Good God," said Damian. "Lucky you."

This double-barreled stare made Vincent look up from his study of the picture. Caught, Willoughby and Damian actually bumped into each other as they looked away.

The picture attracting Vincent was the life-size, three-quarter-length portrait of a musician. It was attributed to an obscure eighteenth-century Frenchman, with an estimated value of between three and five thousand dollars. The subject of the portrait was pulling his bow across a violin with fine hands extended from the beautifully painted billows of his linen shirt. On his face was an extraordinary expression, like that of angels in an adoration picture. Whether the portraitist meant to imply that the note stroked out by the beautiful hands caused rapture, or that this musician was not entirely or happily human, was an open question. The effect of his weirdly wonderful facial expression struck Vincent personally: He felt as if he were seeing himself at orgasm with Laura.

Laura had utterly changed Vincent's sense of reality. Loving her gave him a secret identity, which in turn made his ordinary self something slight and amusing. He had stopped writhing in despair as Mary's overprivileged, underloving husband, stepping easily into his happy-husband disguise whenever he wasn't with Laura. Vincent clearly heard the musician's otherworldly and possibly unholy note. Yes, there was something just as possibly diabolical as angelic in this ecstatic, possessed expression. Vincent decided he had to buy this picture.

When he found Willoughby was staring his way with his dandy friend, Vincent wondered for the first time what Willoughby would think if he knew about his affair. It seemed like a belated concern, but Vincent was stung with anxiety when he remembered his performance at Le Bordello. The whole affair had begun right then and there. Willoughby was standing across the room in a gossip's duet; such men are dangerous. Vincent's happy-husband disguise could be pulled down. Mary could divorce him and arrange it so he would never see Wally again. And everything was going so well the way it was!

"He's married to Mary Brigham," said Willoughby in a way that provoked Damian to chortle as if he'd known all about it for ages.

"Is he yours?" asked Damian with a rutting, guttural burr.

"Nor would he be yours, my friend," Willoughby assured him. "He's besotted over a girl called Laura Montgomery."

"As in James Montgomery?" asked the clever and curious self-made Southern gentleman.

Willoughby nodded as Vincent walked their way. "Damian

Trent, this is my associate, Vincent Booth. Vincent, Damian is a fellow Virginian. I'm sure you two are cousins of some sort."

"What's your name again?" Vincent asked.

"Trent, but that's Daddy's family, which is down from Canada, but it's mother with all that crazy inbred Virginia blood," Damian said with an air of self-deprecation.

"Well, what do you think?" asked Vincent, after Damian Trent ambled off. Willoughby looked at the picture Vincent was indicating. "I'm going to buy it." Vincent said, "I've never wanted anything so much in my life."

"He looks like you," rejoined Willoughby.

Chapter 17

Mary and Ellie Barnholme walked their baby carriages in Gracie Park today because Ellie didn't have time to get over to Central Park. Ellie was particularly concerned about Mary because Janie Gilmore had heard something from her hairdresser about Vincent having an affair, allegedly with some movie star. This prospect concerned Ellie for her old friend's sake, but it also sounded immensely thrilling. It tied their own Park Avenue world to Hollywood, which was fun.

"How's Vincent?" Ellie finally asked after they'd discussed several other people. Both Wallace Brigham Booth and Robert Benton Barnholme III were asleep in their carriages. Both mothers were admiring their very young men. Such illustrious names for helpless mites—would they grow into the problematical adults their fathers had become?

"He's fine. He's working awfully hard," said Mary in a confident way that bore no suspicion of philandering. "I think he's finally trying to get somewhere. It's very hard because in a museum the fags all try to keep it to themselves."

Ellie, who habitually hoped for the best, wondered if the whole rumor might not actually be just the sort of homosexual plot to which Mary had just alluded. After all, she reasoned, Janie Gilmore had heard it from a hairdresser.

Ellie was glad her Robert worked at an investment bank. The only thing he liked to do outside deals was shoot ducks. A museum must be a very queer place, she reflected as they maneuvered their parallel baby buggies. Museums, after all, were sort of the final form of the antique shop, an enterprise notoriously attractive to bachelors.

Ellie preferred this explanation of the movie-star rumor both for her friend's sake and for the sake of the institution of marriage. If Mary's husband could be unfaithful, so could Ellie's. She would much rather have him in a duck blind than in some ravishing young receptionist's firmly molded upper arms.

"You were great to march all the way over here," Ellie said to begin her farewell.

"Don't be silly, I love it," Mary said. "I love to walk around and I think your park gets a much better class of exhibitionist." She did enjoy poking around different parts of town, as long as they weren't too scary. She stopped Wally's carriage on York Avenue.

In the window of an old, European-looking sporting-goods store she spotted an extraordinary pair of bright orange and blue baby shoes, presumably inspired by American basketball and executed with Italian chic.

The smallest size in stock was still a little big for Wally, but of course she bought them. Mary loved to spot things outside the predictable emporiums where her friends bought fashionably expensive baby clothes. She'd found Wally a pair of remarkable suspenders in a thrift shop on Second Avenue, and his favorite toy, a lacquered Japanese doll, had come from an antique store in Greenwich Village run by an elderly Russian couple. Having a baby offered a new theme for exploring New York's infinite supply of dry goods, and these tiny Italian high-tops were a real discovery.

The old Neapolitan storekeeper didn't know if her almost violent smile was from delight, or from some sort of scornful American hilarity. Mary shook her head in wonder as he wrapped the little shoes in newspaper and tied the parcel with string.

She put her prize in with Wallace, who was still sound asleep in his carriage.

The clerk responded to his uncertainty about this customer's motivation by treating her with elaborate, almost florid, courtesy. If she were so enthusiastic about the shoes, maybe other rich young American mothers might come along to relieve him of an item that until now had not been moving. If she bought them in a spirit of mockery, as an Italian joke, he would not allow her to leave without first seeing the manners of his ancient world. He performed an elderly, slow-motion rush to reach the door before her. He opened it, bowed, and offered her the outside world with his free hand.

Framed dead center in the door across the street from the Italian sporting-goods store were Vincent and Laura in a writhing embrace, joined at their grinding mouths.

"*Viva l'amore*," the Italian shouted across the street at them.

The aroused couple turned to smile at this compliment. As they waved and walked away, she slid her hand into his back pocket.

"Horrible," Mary said to Wallace. The speeding, jerky movements of his buggy had woken him, and now he was howling. Mary moved as rapidly as she could over the dirty, cracked sidewalks through the midday crowds.

When he'd cried for a full block, Mary pulled her baby up out of his rough ride and rocked him softly. Passersby looked away so as to avoid noticing the embarrassing intimacy of the fat, fierce-looking little mother rocking from foot to foot with her child. She replaced Wally in the buggy and continued toward home at a more reasonable pace.

What galled her was what a beautiful couple they made, her husband and the slut. She was a big, flagrant-looking bitch, thought Mary, like a collie in heat. How nice it would have been not to see it. How preferable just to hear about it. The bastard was doing it out in the streets for anyone to see. Did he have no respect for his wife? There he was, mounting like an animal in the gutter, right in front of his son.

Mary's first act after turning Wallace over to Mrs. Keswick was to call her lawyer.

"He's in conference, Mrs. Booth."

"This is important."

"Hello, Mary. What is it?"

"Hello, Dick. I want a divorce."

"I see."

"I want him out."

"Can you come in tomorrow morning?"

"That's fine."

"All right, Mary, tomorrow at ten, and I'm sorry."

Mary next called the doorman and told him the locks were

to be changed at once. The doorman winced, realizing the elevator man had just won their bet.

Mary looked at her social calendar. These days there was always something. Mary slapped down her silver date-book pencil which, although shaped to represent bamboo, had always reminded her of a skeleton finger she'd seen in the Catacombs of Rome as a child. Hot tears traced her nose. She just realized all the damn social engagements were his idea, so she wouldn't notice his love affair. He'd always hated them before, and now they practically went anywhere a crowd gathered.

The date book was clotted with engagements all the way back to—Mary turned page after page of infidelity—November. That's when the complete bastard must have started. A week after the collie bitch's dreadful arty party, the date book started to load up. Nine months of it! What an ungrateful, loathsome, preening son of a bitch he was.

Mary's tears smudged the pages of engagements. Notations of false evenings spread and ran like blood from wounds. Mary threw back her head and sobbed. When her cry was over, she blew her nose with a couple of noisy blasts and remembered why she'd picked up her date book to begin with—to find out what was scheduled for this evening.

What she found made her cry again, but somehow laugh at the same time. Jonathan Bushwick was in town on business from Cincinnati, staying at the Union Club. They were taking him down to Soho for dinner, then meeting up with another couple to look at all the characters and celebrities that collected down there to while the nights away.

Mary replayed the terrible scene again: the open shop door, the gnomelike old Italian grinning and waving his arm as he croaked out *"Viva l'amore."* That's when she saw Vincent loving up the arty movie whore she knew had seduced him way back last fall at her dingy Bohemian party. Vincent didn't even see his wife and child in the store across the street. He waved like a celebrity to a fan and sauntered away with that bitch's hand in his back pocket.

Could he have *not* recognized his wife and child? He clearly hadn't. Could Mary be wrong—might she have mistaken this disgusting pair of strangers for her husband and the slut?

The front door closed, bringing Mary to her feet with such a start that she dropped the heavy silver pen, which struck her toe and made her shout. How should she act? Should she ask him where he was three hours before, or would she be able to tell just by looking?

Mary wanted a look at Vincent before she decided. If it wasn't Vincent, she was a fool, and he would know how jealous she was. The gray tweed coat she remembered with such horrifying specificity would either be on him or not.

Mary's heart was slamming her neck with rhythmic bursts of blood. If Vincent stood there in his gray coat in the vestibule, everything was over between them. She stepped around the fateful corner.

"Door's open," said an intimidated-looking locksmith, sneaking glances at the highly decorated canyons of space in which rich people dwelled.

"Skip it," Mary said. The locksmith was as skinny as a key himself. Mary gestured him back toward the doorway through which he'd stepped. "Plans have changed."

"Yeah, but—"

"Charge it," said Mary as she closed the door.

Was it Vincent? Or was she so suspicious that she'd conjured up that spectacle across the street. *Viva l'amore?*

As a child one Christmas Eve, Mary had extrapolated a physical Santa Claus so genuine, she could have taken a witness's oath and described him. She must have created this phantasm out of the intimations of Santa's existence presented to children by advertising and their nannies and families.

Lowering his sack to the floor, he was rotund, wearing a red suit trimmed in white fox like a mummy's stole. Mary couldn't actually see his face. He breathed in loud, dry drafts, like Mr. Wilmer, the caretaker in Maine. He pulled out five presents and placed them at the foot of Mary's bed. She held tightly still, so Santa wouldn't suspect he was being observed.

On Christmas morning Mary sprang for the spot at the foot of her bed, but there was nothing there. The five presents in a line were the chimerical gifts of a chimera. He had seemed so real, like relatives and employees, and he hadn't been at all. There *was* no Santa.

But *"Viva l'amore,"* the old man had said. Mary had her witness, unless of course she had only imagined the little Italian shop as well. She went quickstep to Wallace's room, and the apparition of that afternoon did appear to have left behind a present wrapped up in newspaper. Tearing up again, Mary pulled string over corners and pulled down the newspaper to look at the brightly factual orange tennis shoes.

The front door of the apartment opened and closed, and footsteps approached. Vincent opened the nursery door and smiled. He wore a blue blazer.

Chapter ❧ 18

*P*auline McFall delegated Laura's work at the fashion magazine to Regina Wolkstein, who had worked long and hard at making the work of many well-known writers appear professional. Regina's office was small and only slightly, almost dutifully, decorated. It was principally a workplace.

"Is that your cat?" asked Laura, going straight to the framed snapshot next to the phone. Regina instantly reconsidered the young woman she was so well prepared to despise.

"Do you have one?" asked Regina. Laura nodded, studying the picture of Regina's beloved Beanie. Regina was delighted. "Have a seat," she said. "Would you like some coffee?"

They talked about what Laura would do at the magazine. Aside from the grandeur of her connections and some wide-ranging editorial notions,

Regina couldn't find any particular focus or point of view in Laura Montgomery's descriptions of proposed projects.

"Do you know Natasha Glebov?" Regina asked when the name of the famous ballerina put in an appearance among Laura's speculations of subjects for interviews.

"Real well," said Laura, nodding. "She had a thing with my father."

Regina could only smile conspiratorially at such a starry cause for acquaintance. "Do you think you could get her to talk about it?" Laura's broody silence made Regina regret having asked, though she didn't know why Laura had offered the information if she wasn't prepared to use it.

"Well, isn't she here or something?" Regina asked, shuffling through the papers piled on her desk for a flier from a public-relations firm announcing which celebrities were where in the current week. "Here she is. She's at the Sherry-Netherland. I think that might be an interesting interview—I don't mean about your father, but just in general. Isn't she supposed to be having a big fight with Mikhail Scherabin?"

"I guess," Laura said vaguely. Now Regina was truly baffled. Did Laura Montgomery not want to interview Natasha Glebov at all, or just not about her father? The beautiful and problematical Miss Montgomery had picked up Regina's snapshot of Beanie and was studying it as if the cat alone had the answers to Regina's questions.

The interview at the Sherry-Netherland had gone very well. The ballerina was in an expansive mood and well disposed toward the daughter of her old friend.

"Where is he?" she asked after detailing the advantages (material) and disadvantages (spiritual) of her defection from Russia to the United States.

"He's coming next week. If you're in town, would you come around for a sort of a casual dinner?" Laura asked.

"Such a naughty boy," responded the muscular, polished, Slavic-cheekboned dancer. Her trained posture and international celebrity made her seem make-believe. When a telephone call arrived at a moment appropriate to end the interview, Natasha rose and kissed Laura good-bye in a way that suggested they were sisters—an attitude Laura had felt before with other of her father's girlfriends near her own age.

The two women next turned from each other to deal with their respective machines—Natasha her telephone and Laura her tape recorder. Natasha proceeded to erupt in a Russian tantrum as Laura simultaneously discovered that her tape recorder had not stored any of the hour and a half's interview. She'd pushed the wrong button. Its stupid spools hadn't moved a tick.

Vincent simply couldn't understand how Laura could be so cold toward him. It was to be an entire weekend, a glory that had come their way only twice before, both times with the most gorgeous results.

After a fairly mild argument Mary had announced she was going to spend the weekend in Connecticut with Jonathan and Natalie Bushwick, an event Vincent was only too happy to avoid. Jonathan golfed, and Vincent didn't. Jonathan worked with money, which he imagined Vincent despised as an occupation as much as he enjoyed it as a marital convenience. They detested each other as thoroughly as two mismatched five-year-olds in a sandbox.

But Mary could relax with Jonathan and Natalie. They had lived the same lives and knew the same people. The Bushwicks even had a baby who was Wally's age—Jonathan IV, whom they called Jackie. With Mary enjoying herself somewhere else, Vincent could wholeheartedly be with Laura.

Under such fortunate circumstances how could Laura be acting almost as if she wished he wasn't there? She sat frowning, legs akimbo. When he kissed her, she wasn't interested. Instead, she walked to the window. All the inviting shapes and motions of her body might as well be on film, so dimensionally removed from him was she by her foul mood. Vincent began to get angry himself. Anger was the last emotion he could have imagined happening on this weekend.

"What's the matter with you?" Vincent said harshly. In all the time they'd had together, he'd never before spoken in such a tone. The precious, highly compressed time they managed to share had squeezed all their minutes into diamonds. How had broken glass formed instead?

Vincent got up and walked from the room. Because of his mood, her apartment, that onetime Xanadu, took on the frowsy aspect of a theater the morning after a performance. Dishes were piled in the sink. Blanched by daylight, not even the portrait of Elizabeth looked as great as he felt it should have.

To complete this dismal atrophy of illusion, Laura's cat started coughing in a spasmodic way that made her rush to its side. It threw up a big broken roach and collapsed with its sides heaving, its eyes rolling back. "Jesus Christ, the vet's closed," Laura shouted in mortal terror.

"What's the matter?" he asked, bending down with her next to the heaving cat.

"Oh, God," she cried, "what can we do?"

Vincent was so repelled that he stood back up. She was as desperate as if the cat were a child. Vincent found it shocking, indecent, and distorted, as his mind filled with the death of his own first child. This was a cat. How dare she scream so?

"Oh, holy shit," Laura said. Tears were sprinkling out of her eyes. "Will you do something?" she shrieked at him. He made for the Yellow Pages.

In the taxi on the way to the animal hospital the cat made an abrupt and total recovery. Laura went limp with relief. The cat went to sleep in her lap. Vincent told the driver to take them back where they started.

"Look, I think we just want to be alone," Laura said.

"Sure," Vincent replied.

"A lot of shit is coming down at the moment," she added, but she didn't tell him about the mechanical failure during her interview with Natasha Glebov. She looked at Vincent, whose expression was cold, then got out and loped across Central Park West, holding her cat like a baby.

The emptiness of Vincent's apartment seemed positively monumental. The weekend he had expected to be the bower of bliss had turned into the maw of nullity. His presence in these big rooms seemed incidental—irrelevant, even, as if he were just a passing roach himself.

Chapter 19

*T*he phone was ringing when Laura got to her door, screaming at her as she tried to work her keys with one hand and restrain her cat with the other. When she managed at last to get in, Florida launched himself off her shoulder with a painful claw clench. Laura wondered what form of bad news the ringing telephone wanted to stick on her—Vincent on the corner from a pay phone getting even snottier than he'd been through Florida's crisis? Pauline McFall asking after the interview which Laura must somehow inform her had been stillborn? Or maybe it was Daddy, pulling out of the dinner party she'd constructed in his honor.

"It's Tom Harrison," said the voice after she picked up on at least the tenth ring.

Laura waited for some elaboration.

"Remember, from the network?" Tom said.

After a moment Laura realized it was the fellow who had taken her to the theater in what now seemed like a former life.

"Just thought I'd take a chance and see if you could have dinner. Some friends of mine are putting something together at the last minute."

"Oh," Laura said, wondering what any of this could possibly have to do with her.

"Sam Beecham, actually," Tom added with pride. Sam Beecham was the network's principal anchorman, a figure as famous in America as any popular make of car. In Toby Hyman days, Sam Beecham had made more than one pass at Laura.

"Who else is going to be there?" Laura asked, checking her first instinct of refusal.

"Sam and his wife Elaine and this archaeologist who just found a lost city in Mexico." Tom sounded as if he could only half believe that this list of famous personalities included himself. Should he mention he was now a vice president? Why bother?—his guest list spoke for itself.

You never knew what the cat might drag in on a Saturday afternoon in New York City, he thought to himself, beaming with glee after hanging up the phone that had just transmitted to him Laura's acceptance of their second date.

Even among the members of the public rich and rare enough to be found in a restaurant like Lutèce were grandmothers unashamed to approach Sam Beecham and advise him they were viewers. "Well, I don't care, I'm just going right on over there and tell him I love him," said the one waving away objections from her companions, and the waiters obliged to protect the celebrity.

"I love you." she beamed at Sam Beecham.

"Thank you, ma'am," he replied earnestly.

With a palms-up shrug the maître d' indicated that the grandmother had somehow outflanked his defenses. Sam Beecham closed his eyes and smiled through his grimace, nodding his head to signal his forgiveness.

"Laura," he said when he rose to clasp her shoulders and kiss her on the cheek. Tom Harrison blushed with pride over their reception. Everyone in this smashingly important restaurant was watching them. Tom only wished his mother could witness this, the supreme event in his life so far.

"You know my wife, Elaine," offered the anchorman, "and Laura Montgomery, Bernie Stein. . . ."

Laura did not instantly place Bernie as the archaeologist she had expelled from her bedroom over a year ago. She took in his presence casually until she found he was glaring at her as he wordlessly squeezed her hand.

"As you know, Bernie has just made the most sensational discovery in the history of Mexican archaeology," Sam Beecham said, delivering this line exactly as he pitched the news.

"Recent archaeology," corrected Bernie, brightening after the crushing surprise of seeing the very woman who had inflamed and rejected him, the woman he actually had used as a cursed inspiration to keep digging on those days when it was too hot and he was too tired. "Fuck you, fuck you," he'd shouted at rocks in the humid heat, thinking of her locked in her bathroom.

"Itzpapalotl," he said to Laura. She looked as puzzled as the rest of the table. "The obsidian knife butterfly, Goddess of Agriculture."

"Oh, my God," said Laura, striking each word individually, like a chime.

Bernie nodded like a parent encouraging an infant.

Sam Beecham flashed the same slight smile he used whenever the news broadcast closed with a cute item instead of a sobering atrocity. "Don't tell me you two know each other?" he asked. Bernie nodded, beaming, as Laura shook her head in surprise. "You were at that party at my house," she said casually.

Bernie's archaeological dreams had just come true. His name and face were in the news—all the news, everywhere. The idea that an ancient city still could be found had tickled the universal fancy, a wondrous distraction from the threat, rot, and angst of modern times. Bernie's discovery implied that sweet old mother earth still had some treats in her apron pockets for her generally terrified children.

Laura immediately considered how an interview with Bernie could exonerate her from the approaching opprobrium of her unrecorded interview with Natasha Glebov. She gave him her best smile.

Suddenly, Bernie's outrage seemed insubstantial and parenthetical, the anger he'd formed into a pearl of inspiration now incidental. That smile bridged his bitterness and delivered him to this glorious moment of fame and fine food. He shook his head at her like a good sport.

After a bleak hour alone in his apartment following the cat incident, Vincent had decided he couldn't not call Laura. Approaching the phone, he managed to believe everything was as it had been, his family safe in Connecticut, his love ablaze on

Central Park West, and the recent misadventure shrunk down to its appropriate size. He was back in the merely naughty game of adultery, considering even how it might be fortuitous for his alibi if Mary called to find him at the apartment.

"I'm going out to dinner," Laura informed him.

Vincent felt knifed. "What do you mean?"

"Just that. I'm going out to dinner."

"Who with?"

"Sam Beecham and some people at Lutèce."

"What people?"

"Network people."

"Toby Hyman?" Vincent asked coldly.

"No, not Toby Hyman. People I don't really even know. It's a break, actually, and I'm going to do it. Look, I screwed up that interview with Natasha Glebov, and that's why I'm in this mood," said Laura. "I feel like getting out with strangers tonight to a nice place. Don't you understand? And you couldn't take me there if you wanted."

"I love you, you know," said Vincent, surprising both of them.

"Oh, darling. I love you too. Look, why don't you come over at eleven or something, okay?"

"Okay."

"Or midnight. Better make it midnight, darling, because dinner isn't until eight. All right?"

"Sure," Vincent said, hoping it was. It wasn't just the cat, it was everything about loving Laura that felt misdirected today. She was inviting him in after presenting herself to others. He was her thief in the night, which didn't seem nearly as mischievous and amusing to him as it once had.

Uncomfortable at home, Vincent set out on an aimless walk that eventually brought him before the picture of the musician at the auction gallery. The enigmatic, magnificent picture struck Vincent even more powerfully than it had at the reception. He had an uncanny hunch that this picture was of great personal importance to him, a sort of sign indicating a choice he must make.

"Nattier," he whispered. The painting was suddenly, quite clearly, by Jean Marc Nattier. Vincent grinned. His pulse tapped happily. "School of Nicolas Lancret" is what the catalog said. He had found a Nattier they were estimating to sell for between three and five thousand, which was at least five hundred thousand—if not more—short of its worth.

This brilliant discovery removed Vincent from his romantic and domestic confusion. The picture had to do with nobody but him. It spoke to his neglected professional side. Recognizing it made him feel clever and responsive to his instincts. It gave him reasons to like and admire his own capabilities and possibilities, which the sordid events with Laura didn't.

In this revivifying spirit of self-enhancement, Vincent put in an hour of overdue gym exercise and invited himself out to a restaurant for dinner. He would arrive at Laura's at midnight —fit, fed, and full of energy and conviction. He could make his own fortune with this picture, and a new kind of life could begin.

In a rich French restaurant in his gilded frame of solitude, Vincent savored a bottle of Burgundy. Gloved hands wheeled dishes into place before him. He felt gleefully different. He felt independent and overdue for success. He only wished it were tomorrow, and the auction over and the picture his.

When William Willoughby saw Vincent across the restaurant, so clearly alone, he accepted the plea of the old heiress with whom he was dining that he just see her to her car.

"I was born in Oklahoma clear back when it was Indian territory. I'm pioneer stock," she assured him. As William walked the rich old scribble out to her car, he pointed at Vincent and mouthed the words *I'll be right back.* Vincent nodded, glad enough, actually, to interrupt his reveries.

Outside, the dowager now departed, William thought a minute before reentering the restaurant. He warned himself to be careful, that his infatuation would pass, that he'd had quite a lot to drink, and that he could expect nothing from Vincent.

"I'm going to buy that picture," said Vincent after Willoughby finished describing his dinner partner's links to the petroleum industry. Because of the cocktails, wine, and cognac he'd doctored himself with to endure an evening of Oklahoma girlhood memories, William caught himself staring at Vincent with unguarded passion.

"This is awfully good. Let me get another bottle," he burbled, turning away as if looking for a waiter, in case he was blushing.

"I think it's really, really quite a picture," Vincent explained. "They have it cataloged all wrong, and it's a pretty crummy auction, and I think I'm in luck. At least I hope so. I can buy it with my own money."

"Oh, come now," rejoined Willoughby, alluding to Mary's wealth.

"The only way I'd do it is with my money," Vincent said, proudly proclaiming the stipulation.

"Vincent, I just think you ought to be a lot more careful about your life," said Willoughby. "A hell of a lot."

"What are you talking about, William?"

"I mean, about Miss Montgomery. You know it would be quite a disappointment for Mary, and without Mary you might find life surprisingly less agreeable."

"What do you mean?" Vincent's voice had a hint of anger.

"I mean, you ought to be more careful," Willoughby said softly. His hand touched Vincent's sleeve, and his leg ran up against Vincent's, which moved away. Insanely Willoughby pressed his leg on after Vincent's. It was the wine, combined with that damn beauty. He just didn't care, and couldn't help it.

"Stop that," said Vincent.

"You're just a spoiled, spoiled brat," shouted Willoughby, flecking the astonished young man with spittle and causing other diners to turn for a look. "Without Mary Brigham you'd be nobody, and you certainly would not be working for me." He threw down his napkin and bolted from the table. Despite a mean crack on the hip from another table that he dislodged on his listing passage out of the restaurant, Willoughby kept working at buttoning his coat all the way out the door.

Chapter 20

*A*t eight o'clock on Sunday morning, the telephone rang. Vincent listened to Laura fumble the receiver, causing a clatter of plastic on plastic, before offering an admonitory "Hello?" Then she said, "Can I get back to you? What's your number?"

Vincent had heard Laura take many such phone calls in bed. It amused him to be there, the both of them naked in what often was the middle of the day. "Ain't nobody here but us chickens," he'd said one time. Laura had two ways of handling callers when Vincent was in her bed. The basic one was the "Can I get back to you?" she'd just employed. The other option, actually dealing with a call, was generally too demanding.

"Yes. Uh-huh, right. Okay," said Laura at intervals, measuring for Vincent the substantive length of the incoming dialogue. Evidently the caller wasn't willing to wait to be gotten back to, and Vincent found this suspicious. Obviously it was a man. Her voice was as cool and poised as it would have been if she were alone. With a twinge of jealousy Vincent wondered if he'd ever been on the other end of a call like this. She was so convincingly alone-sounding.

"Okay, great. Bye," Laura said, concluding the obscure conversation without revealing the identity of the caller.

"What was that all about?" Vincent muttered, picking up a bedside clock and using gruffness to make it seem he was cross about being woken up so early.

"Nothing," she said, lying back down, her big breasts reshaping as they spread away from each other. Vincent pulled her to him, but she wouldn't comply.

"It's too early in the morning," she complained, stalking to her bathroom.

Vincent realized unhappily that he mainly wanted her out of possessiveness, because he now felt jealous and unworthy.

Chapter 21

*W*illoughby realized Vincent was absolutely right; the picture was superb. It had been consigned by "a Midwestern educational institution," where it must have hung somewhere dusty for fifty years. Once cleaned, it would be quite a spectacle. Of course some pictures suffered from cleaning, since grime can serve a picture like dim lighting on a woman of a certain age. But not in this case, Willoughby realized with a shiver. Vincent seemed to have found something brilliant.

William's smile lengthened, and happy crinkles radiated from the outside corners of his eyes. Vincent Booth didn't have it yet, this picture he had so proudly proclaimed he was going to buy with his own money. He wasn't even smart enough to keep quiet about it. This young pup expected everything he wanted to rush directly into his arms, and maybe it was time he learned a lesson.

"Stop that." What a humiliating remark. Stop what? Willoughby had done nothing. That urge to cleave to Vincent, even at the risk of humiliating himself totally, did not deserve the ingrate's dismissal. Vincent's desultory performance at the museum had more than once been covered up by William Willoughby—and what was his reward? "Stop that," as if the lucky fool were addressing a puppy pumping his leg. He had said it so abruptly and callously that William easily concluded he must buy this portrait of a musician out from under the overprivileged nonentity who had presumptuously issued his superior that bleak order.

William moved briskly out of the auction room an hour before the sale, having made arrangements to bid by phone through an employee of his acquaintance. A bonus in his scheme was the musician's resemblance to Vincent. Soon, Willoughby hoped, his infatuation would end, and then he would have its perfect souvenir, *Portrait of a Musician*.

Entering the auction house, Vincent was nervous, worried that a dealer who knew him as an employee of the Met might start bidding against him for that reason alone. Museums were probably the most vital cog in the machinery of art speculation, since a museum purchase represented a sort of sanctification for a picture and its artist. Museums took goods off the market at prices that became official, then dangled them as trophies in palaces, increasing the public's impression of their value. Without museums, art would have remained a decidedly obscure commodity. But with museums creating demand, even as they shortened supply, the market grew more lucrative all the time.

Vincent was glad not to see any major dealers. He saw instead some of the clowns and weirdos of the small-time antique world. A fat man in checkered trousers taut as full sacks with a meticulously barbered Vandyke beard under a Mets baseball cap and dark glasses blithely ate an egg-salad sandwich and sucked at a container of coffee as the English tailoring of the auctioneer and his assistants swept past him to take the podium.

Three women went to the telephones to the right of the auctioneer's podium to receive bids. Spotters took their stations to catch bids from the variegated mob spreading through the seats like an evangelical congregation. The mechanical scoreboard registering the bids in the world's stronger currencies fluttered some testing numbers before freezing at zero.

The crowd grew to include wealthy young wives out to show their interior decorators they had minds of their own, interior decorators out to keep up their inventories, lesser dealers, big dealers' assistants, and amateurs who had seen something they liked.

Portrait of a Musician was Lot 21, which Vincent hoped was near enough to the beginning of a morning sale to eliminate bidding from casual latecomers. The first lots, he noted with pleasure, were regularly failing to make even the low end of their estimates. If Vincent could get *Portrait of a Musician* for less than three thousand, his capital would still exist. He'd have his cake and eat it too.

But maybe it was an awful picture and he was an awful fool. Maybe it wasn't Nattier, or anything like Nattier. He looked up at it, hanging on the side wall of the auction room as the inventory started selling off from the stage in front. It was a staggering picture, no more appropriate among the dim company sharing the wall with it than a Russian Grand Duke was driving a Paris taxi after the revolution. It was Nattier, Jean Marc Nattier. It had that way of his, that casual way of dropping the sublime like a flirt's handkerchief.

The twenty lots preceding Vincent's prize were diminishing fast. They were ridiculously bad pictures, and Vincent found it surprising that they'd ever sold once, and astonishing that some of them had survived hundreds of years of transactions. Apparently people just wanted a little color from a dead hand on their walls. After all, people also collected and preserved postage stamps, beer cans, books, dolls, and barbed wire for some related, artifact-yearning reason.

"Portrait of a Musician," called the auctioneer, but he added, "change of attribution here," interrupting his rhythm with this statement and causing Vincent's heart to stop. The auctioneer raised his eyebrows and squinted at the card one of his associates slipped him. "Albert Bordonnais, Lot 21 now attributed to Albert Bordonnais," he said. A deft and distinguished middle-aged black man in a domestic sort of uniform placed the picture on a velvet step and stood beside it like an acolyte at Mass.

"I have fifteen hundred dollars," said the auctioneer, and there was Vincent's picture out running naked before the howling pack of wolves around him. The most glorious sound in Vincent's imagination at this moment would be that of a speechless, lengthening pause, some creaking of bored hams on the seats, then a repetition of "Fifteen hundred dollars," at which point Vincent would raise his identifying paddle and get the *Portrait of a Musician* for sixteen hundred.

But that's not how it went. Sixteen hundred was bid at once, as were seventeen, eighteen, nineteen and two thousand. From two thousand the auctioneer jumped increments to two hundred dollars. Bids were coming from all over the room. The three women on the telephones kept their callers informed of the bidding and stood by.

Vincent raised his paddle at five thousand dollars and kept nodding to seven thousand. The bidding continued moving up. Vincent looked again at the picture, with the pleased guard who placed it before them standing respectfully next to it as if he were listening to a choir in heaven—or the note of the violin in the picture, that sound of a masterpiece.

At twelve thousand Vincent returned to the bidding. After fifteen thousand the auctioneer sped up to five-hundred-dollar rises. At twenty-five thousand he began moving the sums fluttering across the scoreboard in half a dozen currencies by the thousands of dollars. At twenty-five thousand, the bidding was being carried between a woman on the phone, who nodded immediately after each increase as if money were no object to her caller, and Vincent, who had lost all sense of anything but his necessity to get that picture. The auctioneer was now driving the bidding along before him in grand, five-thousand-dollar strides like a happy, expert coachman.

"Thirty-five, do I have thirty-five thousand dollars?" Vincent nodded, as if he had that kind of money. "Forty thousand, at forty thousand, forty thousand," intoned the auctioneer. Horribly, the woman on the phone nodded instantly.

"Forty-five thousand," said the auctioneer, as softly as a line in a sonnet. At the second request for this gross sum, Vincent nodded.

On his end of this extravagant telephone call, Willoughby kept asking, "still him? Still him?" Vincent had been the only other bidder since twenty-five thousand. Then, out of nowhere, a different bidder raised his paddle.

"It's somebody else," warned Willoughby's representative. The crowd turned around for a look at the new bidder. It was the fat clown in the dark glasses and baseball cap.

"Who is it?" Willoughby demanded.

"Don't know," answered his agent.

"Fifty-five thousand?" asked the auctioneer, pleased by the handsome number—ten times the original top of the auction house's estimate. The auctioneer looked to the young woman on the phone with Willoughby. "All right," Willoughby said somewhat less automatically than before. The odd bidder had made Willoughby pause to realize that fifty-five thousand dollars was much more than he had in mind when he'd conceived of this lark. Now that the other bidder had interrupted his passionate numerical intercourse with the unknowing Vincent Booth, Willoughby's sense of proportion returned. "Last bid," he said into the phone. It was crazy to risk fifty-five thousand dollars just to rebuke Vincent Booth. After he had released this bid and switched from thinking of having his way with Vincent to an imagined accompaniment of Wagner's "Ride of the Valkyries" to thinking of cash, Willoughby wished he had not approved the appalling sum. He prayed to be outbid.

"Sixty? Sixty thousand dollars?" asked the auctioneer as politely as if he had picked up a handkerchief and inquired, "Is this yours?" He looked at the fat man in the cap, who shook his head, then came back to Vincent, who nodded.

"Sixty-five thousand?" The auctioneer's voice swooped lower, as if preparing for another great climb. He looked to Willoughby's young woman on her phone.

"Is it Vincent Booth?" Willoughby asked.

"Yes."

"No more," he said, and the young woman shook her head.

"I have sixty thousand dollars. At sixty thousand dollars," the auctioneer repeated, but he was pretty sure he'd squeezed this lemon dry. "Going once at sixty thousand—and all through at sixty thousand dollars." He gave one more glance for a last-minute bidder, then slapped down a turned and polished walnut disk against his mahogany pulpit. "Number 322," he said as Vincent held up his paddle.

The fat man felt a spasm of something like sexual release after Vincent's bid. He came to auctions to throw in a bid as close as he dared get to the last one. He stopped way short more often than not, but he'd once managed to bid next to last, and today he finished only one bid down. It gave him a violent sense of gratification. If he ever won a bid, it wouldn't matter, because all the information he put on the paper to get a bidding paddle was false.

William Willoughby was relieved not to have paid fifty-five thousand dollars for a picture estimated by experts to be worth between three and five thousand. The perverse, pleasurable spell of secretly bidding up Vincent Booth had been quickly broken by the surprise outsider's bid. Thank heavens Willoughby had come to his senses; fifty-five thousand dollars was more than Vincent Booth was in essence worth. Best of all, Willoughby considered how he had just placed Vincent in considerable financial jeopardy. Vincent had nowhere near sixty thousand dollars to his name. He would have to go to Mary for it. He would yet again have to grind his nose into the pile of money Willoughby knew Vincent hated. This gratified Willoughby enormously. His little revenge had all worked out much better than he'd first planned, and it hadn't cost him a cent. "Stop that," indeed.

The girl who retrieved Vincent's paddle offered her congratulations. Behind him, the auction continued. He left the auction room and went to the cashier with his ears ringing and his limbs tingling.

Pictures can be removed minutes after they are sold. All you have to do is pay for them. In Vincent's case he only had to tell them to send it to his office at the Met. The Brighams had done many millions of dollars worth of business over many decades at this auction house, and the Metropolitan Museum of Art was not exactly a fly-by-night destination.

Vincent suddenly appeared in his office with no memory of how he'd gotten there. Ever since he raised his paddle-bearing hand for the winning bid, his sense of where he was had been vague, and most of his movements automatic.

The picture had followed him over directly, almost like a dog at his heels, because he was such a distinctly preferred customer. He pulled back the bland, tan-colored paper and plastic padding to expose his purchase. There was a faint odor of neglect about the painting in its dingy frame, a smell of mushrooms or attics. It seemed so surprisingly physical when he held it up in his hands that it wasn't like holding something living, but it wasn't completely dead-feeling, either. It had the spiritual life of a sacred object, buzzing with received devotion.

For a moment Vincent felt the base but pleasant excitement of victory and possession. Then he examined the attached bill. With tax and commission it came to $71,280, roughly fifty thousand more than Vincent had in the world. He stood the picture on a chair. The immobile bow pulled forth its mute chord, drawing the violinist into his slightly sinister ecstasy. Vincent rose up from his desk and paced back and forth in front of the painting.

Just as it struck Vincent that his relationship to the violinist was something like a rat to the Pied Piper's flute, Willoughby opened the door.

"Vincent?" he asked. Vincent stopped his pacing and looked up. "Sondra Laval wants you and Mary for dinner Wednesday week. I told her I was sure it was fine, but I'd check."

"Remember that picture?" croaked Vincent.

"What's that?" asked Willoughby languidly as he stepped into Vincent's office.

"That picture. I just bought it."

Willoughby sidled around to look at it propped on the chair across from Vincent's desk. "Oh, yes, the fiddler who looks like you," Willoughby said, as if he only vaguely remembered the incident. "Very nice. You get a good price?"

"Sixty," Vincent said hoarsely.

"Sixty what?" Willoughby asked diffidently.

"Sixty thousand dollars." Vincent was close to whispering.

"Good, good, so Mary's buying it, after all." Willoughby's sidelong glance was perfectly timed to take in Vincent's distress. Vincent shook his head and Willoughby smiled. To watch the young man try to come up with sixty thousand on his own was bound to be endlessly amusing.

"What about a week from Wednesday?" Willoughby asked innocently.

Vincent was nodding, but God knows at what. "Can you think of anyone who might be interested in it?" he asked. "Maybe I'll sell it."

"You know, Sir David Thompson is over here for a year

at the Frick. He's an old friend of mine, and he'd know better than anyone who might like it."

"Could you get him to take a look?" Vincent asked.

"I'll see what I can do," Willoughby answered, gratified and revenged by such blatant distress. Though he even felt a little sorry for Vincent, it had been a pleasure to offer him Sir David as a thin ray of hope.

Vincent realized $71,280 was due in ten days. He could give them a check which the bank would undoubtedly back for the usual reason, the Brigham bundle, and have another thirty days before it was all over.

He started pacing again. To own this picture he had to come up with $61,280 he didn't have. Of course, he could get it from Mary, but wasn't it his sense of indenture that was squeezing him to death? He was ashamed to think he'd bid on into grander and grander figures because of the subliminal backing offered by Mary's money. That's what kept him bidding—those enslaving Brigham millions. On his own he would've been out at ten. The beautiful violinist played on. *Portrait of a Musician* was a prize and a rebuke, a piper who would eventually have to be paid.

Vincent smiled a sour, cynical smile and sighed within the great stone prison of the museum. He was there because of Mary's money. He was everywhere he was because of this rich passport—except, of course, for Laura's arms.

He had to sell, and fast. It was a little ironical for Vincent to think of selling *Portrait of a Musician,* of becoming a dealer, because he had regularly castigated that profession. He had often run down their connoisseur's pretensions and digital souls.

But the profit would set him free, and he'd have a stake to

start prospecting for himself again. He loved Laura so terribly that this former opinion of dealers was now revealed as just a snotty pose. This was real life. He needed some money, for himself and for Laura, and here was the picture.

How could he pay for it? He was sure it was a Nattier. Ostensibly, at least for now, he owned it. But could he find a buyer within thirty days?

Mary's millions came from profitable transactions. The gimlet eyes of the wealth's founding speculators had since rounded and faded (except when Albert pointed his gun at a panicked woodcock). Vincent now needed that original financial facility and avidity for this transaction. He had a Nattier. He had to sell it so he could buy it and make a profit, just like old T. D. Brigham and his coal and steel trusts at the turn of the century.

Vincent had originally thought of Mary's money as something which would free him. He'd thought about how he could paint, how he would be free to pursue scholarship, how he and Mary could travel and explore. Their issue would be rich and privileged, their surroundings magnificent, and their transits luxurious. Mary was comfortably offhand and ungrand about her "dough," as she sometimes called it. She had never made him uncomfortable about it.

"Let's get out of here," she'd murmured when he began to fret at the wedding reception, which was mightily weighted by her family's side of the guest list.

"Why don't you get a loft and we'll live in an apartment," she'd suggested when their living arrangements were plotted. It all had seemed like nothing but a boundless advantage.

But in truth his painting had begun to fail before the first baby died. That death became the official explanation for his switch from painter to scholar. To be too hurt to continue painting because of an infant's death was an irreproachable motivation, but the canvas had dried up like a desert long before. Everything Vincent threw at it was sucked into mediocrity. His critical eye, he suspected, had outgrown his hand.

All those little decisions nudged Mary's way by the conveniences of wealth had buried him deeper and deeper, until there he lay, entombed and in debt with his overreached purchase in his office at the museum. He frowned and pushed a knuckle into his teeth. Could he sell it? How?

The picture had a strange, cold sort of magnificence that wouldn't go easily with wallpaper and chintz. How do you sell something, anyway? Vincent wondered. He'd watched art dealers lounge about on important furniture in tailored suits telling anecdotes about painters and transactions as buyers moved tongues about their mouths or grimaced, debating whether or not to sign the check. Vincent had no such emporium. He did, however, know the names of serious collectors of eighteenth-century pictures from his work at the museum, and Willoughby was going to speak to Sir David Thompson. Vincent was sorry he'd fended off his advances so abruptly, but Willoughby was certainly being a gent about it, helping him out this way.

Setting out to sell *Portrait of a Musician* didn't feel giddy and grand, as he'd felt when choosing the loft in which to paint great pictures, but it wasn't entirely unfanciful, either. As Vincent walked to his phone to arrange for the picture to be cleaned, he heard martial music and thought of panzer commanders moving toward their machines on a gray dawn.

Chapter ❧ 22

William Willoughby telephoned Sir David Thompson, widely regarded by those in the field as the world's foremost authority on eighteenth-century painting. Willoughby knew Sir David was in New York at the Frick for a year's stint as a visiting scholar because he'd literally bumped into the distinguished old gentleman on the dance floor at the closing party of a club called the Shaft.

In the conservation department of the museum, where Vincent had left his painting to be cleaned as soon as possible, Sir David pitched forward and squinted hideously to raise his heavy glasses up his bony nose. Then he jerked backward, stood up, and walked in a brief semicircle, much as dogs do before they lie down. Then he nodded. "It's a very nice picture, isn't it?"

"Do you have any idea who painted it?" Willoughby asked rather blandly.

"Nattier, I should say. Isn't it a nice one? See how he cleaned his brushes up here in the corner. Always did it right on the canvas, rather insolent in a way. Bravado, I suppose, but he knew he was a great master."

Willoughby was stunned.

"Beautifully painted, of course. Where did you find it?"

"It just came up in an auction," said Willoughby, smiling weakly, furious it wasn't his. Why hadn't he bid another five or ten thousand?

"Arresting expression, don't you think?" Sir David looked closely again at the musician's face. The connoisseur's much-folded neck extruded from his collar like a tortoise's. Willoughby knew about the young man from Burma with whom Sir David lived, and in fact had adopted as his son. He knew that Sir David had chosen most of the two greatest collections of pictures formed in modern times. He knew all about Sir David, as he did about so many other people of use or interest in the world of art, and Sir David Thompson seemed to know just as much about this picture, which he never before had laid eyes on.

"A musician could not have afforded to have himself painted by Nattier, of course—and there is something erotic about it, don't you think? You know, William, I am hearing a faint sound—a little bell going off somewhere in the distance. This is a portrait of a rather important person's lover. A violinist. Now who could it be? It seems almost familiar in some way." The old tweed tortuga smiled as his neck retreated.

Throughout lunch afterward with Sir David, Willoughby

wished that outside man hadn't entered the bidding and broken his concentration. He had been one bid away from a picture very likely worth a million or more; that's all he could think of for now. He forgot all about how and why he'd come to bid on it in the first place—until he saw Laura Montgomery enter the restaurant and sit down at the same table, with the same person, as she had a year before.

"Déjà vu," said Willoughby.

"Who?" Sir David asked.

"Sorry, I just had a little déjà-vu sort of feeling." Brightening up, Willoughby was considering how he might get the picture away from Vincent yet. All he had to do was tell Mary Brigham about Laura Montgomery and, *voilà,* Vincent Booth's access to the Brigham credit line would be over. Then he could call the auction house and warn them about Vincent's check.

If Vincent couldn't pay up, the property would be offered to the next highest bidder, a normal auction procedure that in this case, Willoughby thought, happily, was truly just.

With a bolt of enthusiasm Willoughby called over to the captain and ordered a bottle of champagne for himself and Sir David, and another for the two young women across the room.

"Who might they be?" asked Sir David, startled that his long acquaintance would send champagne to pretty young women.

"Imps, I think," said Willoughby. "Sprites sent down from Mount Olympus to give me a great and glorious bit of inspiration."

Chapter 23

"*L* et me see if I understand this," said Regina Wolkstein, squaring the corners of the manuscript Laura had presented to her. "This isn't an interview with Natasha Glebov. It's an interview with somebody who found a lost city in Mexico?"

"Right," said Laura. She couldn't think of much to add.

"But weren't you going to interview Natasha Glebov?"

"I did."

"So?" asked Regina, raising a palm on each side of the stack of transcript pages. "So what's this?"

"The tape recorder malfunctioned," said Laura, frowning petulantly.

"And recorded this instead?" Regina's smile strengthened with sarcasm.

Laura stood up and sat back down when she

realized there wasn't enough room in Regina's office to pace. "The whole interview with Natasha didn't get recorded because of the machine, so I got another one, and when this opportunity with Bernie Stein came up, I jumped at it."

"Why didn't you go back and just record Natasha Glebov?" asked Regina, who no longer cared whether or not Laura Montgomery liked her picture of Beanie. Laura didn't answer, and Regina concluded she was rather too proud to succeed in journalism. "That's not the way it works, Laura. We have these meetings where we agree on what we want, and that's what we put in the magazine."

"I got some photographs too," Laura said, offering a second manila envelope to the editor.

Regina flipped through the pictures without a smile. "Very cute man. I like a beard, as long as they're good with crumbs. Did you take these?" she asked, and Laura nodded. "And these are the Mexican things he dug up?"

"No," Laura said. "Those are just some things of mine in my apartment."

"Oh, so you shot these at your apartment?" Regina said.

After Regina explained Laura's fiasco to the editor-in-chief, Pauline said, "Let's give her another chance." She wasn't about to fire Laura just yet, not before her party for James Montgomery.

Missy finally sold a piece to her magazine. It was about the Foot Ball, a benefit given by a group trying to prevent adoption of the metric system in America. Their motto was "Don't give an inch." Missy was very proud. She'd cashed the whole check for a spree, starting with lunch with Laura at Le Bordello and then shopping for something to wear to Laura's party.

Missy's soaring spirits made Laura's feel even worse. "Just so completely shitty," she said by way of explaining the reception given her interview with the archaeologist. "People would kill for that interview, and all they can think of is boring old stuff like Natasha Glebov."

Laura looked comparatively awful, which was still enviable. Missy had a hard time understanding exactly what was wrong, and an even harder time announcing her own great success to her depressed friend. Laura was knocking back a lot of wine, so bitterly absorbed in her own problems that she seemed oblivious to Missy's news.

"I'm honestly thinking about just taking off for a while," Laura suddenly announced.

With a touch of unexpected and, she was glad to observe, unnoticed sarcasm, Missy said, "Where to, Laura?"

"Mexico," said Laura.

"Really" was Missy's miffed response. Laura hadn't offered a word of congratulations or praise for her splendid accomplishment. Then the champagne arrived, and Missy, thinking it was a congratulatory surprise from Laura, reached across to kiss her thoughtful friend.

But before she could, she heard Laura ask the waiter, "What's this all about?" The captain indicated a table where one middle-aged man, and another genuinely aged one, sat at lunch. The younger one raised his glass their way and smiled. Laura acknowledged the gesture by returning the toast. She'd seen him somewhere.

"Is he someone you slept with, or someone I slept with?" Laura joked to Missy, coming out of her funk for the first time.

"Which one?" rejoined Missy with the wit of her increasing worldliness.

Laura decided it had been a mistake to fall in love with

Vincent Booth. His behavior toward Florida during the crisis revealed him to be heartless, and it was a pointless affair, anyway. It was time to think about actually living with a man, maybe even getting married and having children. Laura had had five abortions, which she knew was way over the limit. She'd never met a man as understanding and rational, determined and nurturing, as Bernie Stein.

Especially with that patriarchial undergrowth of beard, he seemed as massive and dependable as the pyramids he unearthed. He wanted a home and children. He wanted her to be his wife, whereas Vincent had never mentioned marrying her. All he wanted was love and the life of now, and it was time to think about beyond now.

"Hey," said Missy, "come back."

"Sorry," Laura said. "So much has been coming down on me lately, I'm afraid I'm not much good for company."

"That's okay." As always, Missy chose to be supportive.

"Have you ever thought of getting married?"

"Of course," Missy answered, "as soon as I meet someone who's not still walking around on all fours." Missy was more and more confident about using her wit. She loved sitting there in this expensive restaurant drinking champagne, being funny, and getting published. She regretted her decision not to wear a hat for the occasion.

Missy was also looking forward to Laura's party, where she expected to cut a very different figure than she had the first time. But she returned her concentration to Laura, who throughout lunch had not concentrated on anything or anyone else. "Are you?" Missy asked. Laura nodded.

"Vincent Booth?" she asked, softly and reverently and hopefully, for she had been deeply, romantically impressed with her friend's passionate affair. Laura shook her head, and tears spilled from her big blue eyes. Missy felt the huge velvet sadness she'd experienced reading *Wuthering Heights* long ago. Then her sadness was erased by curiosity. "Who, then?"

Laura wiped her eyes with her napkin, smiled, and told Missy all about Bernie Stein.

Chapter 24

"Good morning, William, it's David," said Sir David Thompson with news in his voice. "You know I told you I thought I heard some little bell when I saw your picture, and I did." Willoughby felt his whole being drawn up at the telephone receiver.

"Last year—in Arizona, of all places—I was visiting Bedivere Fox, Sir Bedivere Fox, who's married to an American—Tammy is her name, I couldn't imagine what it stands for, Tammy . . ." William had never heard Sir David ramble so; it was torment. "In any case, Bevvy and this Tammy person are out in Scottsdale, in something they call a community—you know, everyone's rather old. Had they warned me about where they lived, I never would have accepted their invitation, but it turns out to be rather lucky for you that I did."

William felt sure Sir David was enjoying himself at his expense, dangling this information just out of reach. "Get to the point," Willoughby nearly shouted.

"Bevvy's condo is half a house, all of a level—I imagine because of the unpopularity of stairs among the aged. His model is duplicated in every third structure on a curved driveway. Sprinklers are going constantly, but the gardens are stark, almost industrial-looking products with not a trace of individuality in front of any of the regularly repeated series of three models. Because of the advanced age—"

"Sir David," Willoughby interrupted, afraid the old bugger would lose the point of his call.

"—walkers and wheelchairs standing outside the clubhouse and restaurant like bicycles outside a school—and the security precautions, William, the security precautions are of a military thoroughness and accountability. Do you think of your self as old, William?"

"I certainly don't think of *you* as being old," remarked the instinctively complimentary Willoughby. Sir David's mind had sailed out to sea.

"Nor did I, until I found myself in this place. You know, ironically, the whole community seemed determined to be youthful—dances and socials and lectures in some mad attempt to keep everyone entertained. And the dressing! They dressed like fishing lures—ladies who at a distance looked sixteen from behind were eighty on the other side. It was Swiftian, William, a very strange land in which this Gulliver found himself, and one I wouldn't trouble to describe to you except in it, in Bevvy's condo, in his library—which was no bigger than a sewing room—was a framed autograph of Catherine the Great."

Willoughby felt testy in the silence Sir David here drew out for dramatic effect. He was a crazy old bird, dancing the night away with his Burma boy at that closing party at the Shaft, as well as author of the irreproachable scholarship that produced half a dozen foundation texts of the history of art and now he was also this rambling dotard on the phone.

"I'm not sure I understand, Sir David," said Willoughby, smiling blandly.

"It's a receipt, William, with order attached. Bevvy's autograph of Catherine the Great is, in fact, a receipt addressed to Jean Marc Nattier for *Portrait of a Musician*. I just called Bevvy to get the size. You might check. The Empress's picture is three and a half by four spans, which is, as I make it, something like twenty-eight and three quarters by thirty-four inches. The Empress signed it all with orders for strict confidentiality."

"It must be our picture," William blurted.

"Unquestionably," Sir David said definitively.

"This is wonderful news."

"Such a graceful painter," said Sir David. "So relaxed and sophisticated."

William Willoughby was as excited as a hound at a kill. A documented Nattier commissioned by Catherine the Great was worth far more than a million dollars. "Fabulous news."

"I thought you'd be amused."

"Do you think Sir Bedivere might sell the document? It would be rather amusing to have them both."

"He might trade it, William. I'm sure it's more a question of desiring some sort of variety, living the way he does, rather than a question of money. Tammy takes him on cruises, but I do think the condo gets Bevvy down. Why don't you look about the museum and try to find something to trade him?"

"I can't tell you what this means," said Willoughby, now standing, holding the phone in both hands and smiling wider than ever.

"Well, I thought it might, and that perhaps you might do me a small favor in return."

"Please."

"Nak Oo, my ward. Could you get him a scholarship to Columbia? He's getting frightfully bored, and I do have an entire year here at the Frick. Idle hands, you know."

In the conservation lab, Willoughby checked the dimensions Sir David had given up against those of Vincent Booth's painting. According to Rudi, the restorer whose German accent lent great authority to his opinions, it was a perfect match.

"When do you think you'll have it finished?" Willoughby asked casually, although his heart felt huge and loud.

"It's not so bad, really—just dusty. I'll have it next week unless Phillips demands the two Philadelphia portraits have to come first. Booth says to jump over him and get this out, but I am waiting to ask Phillips."

"You must wait!" said Willoughby. "We have to have those Philadelphia portraits for the American Wing party. You simply have to get them first. Booth's picture is his own. Let's not put private interests ahead of the museum."

Figuratively, the Teutonic technician clicked his heels.

Willoughby now paced his office, wondering how to get Vincent's painting away from him. If the highest bid failed to purchase, the lot would be offered to the next highest bidder, who was, of course, himself. Vincent would soon deliver a check he couldn't cover, if William told Mary about Laura Montgomery.

A fortune was at stake, a sum between a million and two million—an authenticated picture by Jean Marc Nattier commissioned by Catherine the Great. But what if Mary backed Vincent's check, anyway? Or what if Vincent suddenly found out exactly what picture he had?

The alternative was simply to buy the picture from Vincent as soon as possible. This would prevent Vincent from running to Mary, and for this Vincent would have Willoughby to thank. And if William gave him a small profit—not a lot, because that would only make Vincent suspicious—everyone would benefit, at least temporarily.

Willoughby put in a call to the auction house that resulted in the following call to Vincent from a young woman in the billing department.

"We don't seem to have a payment yet on Lot 21 in the Ariadne sale," she said with a note of concern.

"When is that due?" Vincent asked with forced casualness.

"Well, our records show it's in your possession, so I guess it's like past due."

Rudi hadn't even begun to clean *Portrait of a Musician*. "I'm sorry, Vincent, but they say the museum work must come first," he explained. "I will try to start Monday, best I can do."

With gratifying precision Willoughby's plot quickly produced Vincent in his office, questioning him about the collectors most likely to buy the painting.

"When is Sir David Thompson going to look at it?" he asked.

"He already did. Sorry we couldn't get you—he just had a minute. He said it was very nice—he really liked it."

"Did he say anything about who he thought might've painted it?"

"I'm afraid he was a little vague."

Vincent was pacing now, throwing back a lock of hair with his hand each time it returned to his forehead. "Did he have any ideas?"

"Well, he said he'd think about it—but you know, something occurred to me."

"What?" Vincent demanded, stopping in his tracks.

Willoughby watched hope flicker in his subordinate's beautiful blue eyes. "Would you let me show it to someone else?"

"Of course," Vincent answered, resuming his pacing. The cleaning had slowed down, the payment was being hurried, and the mechanics of producing the picture for inspection by a potential customer was being delayed. Mary was staying on up in the country, and Laura had gone to see her mother. His life seemed to be the sort of dream where you're running to escape pursuit in a thickening, hardening suit of concrete.

"I think it's by Nattier," Vincent announced. He'd debated playing this card, but he was desperate to gain Willoughby's interest.

"Really?" Willoughby feigned disinterest. "Mary *is* coming to the Lavals next Wednesday, isn't she? I mean, they are giving the thing for you two," he said languidly.

"Meeting me there," Vincent replied. But why was Mary meeting him there? For that matter, why was Laura acting so distant? And finally, how could he sell this damn picture?

"Is everything all right?" Vincent asked Mary on the phone the next morning. He'd called her every night since Sunday.

"Fine," she said noncommittally.

Now that she was staying away from him, Vincent began to consider how much he'd hurt her. The distractions of Laura and the picture had made him oblivious to the limbo into which he'd pitched his wife, the mother of his son. Once he had hung up, the phone rang immediately, like magic. He was sure it was Laura, and his heart sang as he reached for the phone. She hadn't called in days. He had already rehearsed his apologies for behaving so badly during the cat's seizure.

"Will you take a hundred thousand for your picture?" Willoughby asked.

Vincent was astonished. "What?"

"I showed it to old Princess Lovbetskoy, née Gloria Grunbaum, and she wants to give it to the Julliard School of Music in memory of her son George. I hope you don't mind. I was showing her the conservation department last night after the Donors Gala."

"Are you serious?"

"Her son was killed in a car crash. She gives tons to Julliard."

Toward his forgiving friend Vincent felt both gratitude and admiration. "This is wonderful. I am really grateful."

For a short moment Willoughby felt like a complete shit. But Vincent's thankful tone reminded him that he had, after all, saved the boy's neck. After all, he could've just taken the picture away from Vincent and ruined his marriage in the bargain. In this respect, by removing Jean Marc Nattier's *Portrait of a Musician* from the possession of Vincent Booth, Willoughby was doing him a favor.

Chapter 25

*I*n Connecticut, Mary realized right off the bat on Friday night that she could still have a damn good time. After dinner they played charades, a game Vincent hated, and on Saturday morning she played golf with Jonathan, Natalie, and the pro. Afterward she treated her guests to lunch at the club. Vincent, she realized, would have roundly hated every minute of it.

Saturday night, under the canopy of a bed she'd piloted down many sleepless nights in the country, Mary decided to start thinking seriously about divorce. The worst part was how they looked together now. He made her feel old, fat, and pea-brained. It seemed fairly pointless, so starkly considered, to stay married to him.

Instead of bringing them together, the first baby's death screwed everything up. Maybe it was her fault for getting depressed, despite what the shrink said, but he hadn't been much help anyway. Wally had put everything off, but here it all was again. The bill, as usual, passed to her.

"Ladies and gentlemen," a drunk and crazy friend had announced at lunch. "I am here for no other purpose but pleasure. I hope I give it by getting it, but if I don't, that's too damn bad." Before falling back down into his chair, he had smiled and held up his glass. Though everyone had disapproved of his attempt to be outrageous, he had privately evoked a Dionysian theme that everyone recognized.

Remembering this toast as she thought over her marriage, Mary decided she'd deprived herself of considerable pleasure by catering to her moody husband. Why shouldn't she enjoy the people and things he seemed to despise—or anything she could enjoy? God knows, she was paying for it.

Mary had a lawyer drive up to the country (a service no other client could expect) to begin his work. A certain amount of anger is required to build up the steam necessary to power a divorce through its clattering work of demolition, and Mary's lawyer, a major predator in the field, kept shaking his head at the villain who emerged during their conferences.

"He kept that studio for a year, but no paintings were painted," he observed with indignation.

"He was depressed. So was I. We all were."

"I see," said the lawyer, plainly imagining someone snoozing in a loft costing two or three thousand a month, only to kill time until he got home for dinner.

Mary felt a little guilty when Vincent called just when her lawyer was preparing him like a lamb for slaughter. She told Vincent she would come directly to the Lavals' party, because she didn't want to see him alone. After the party she would give him the bad news. The process-server would be waiting in their lobby, and Mary would return immediately to the country. It all seemed rather theatrical, but the theater of a wedding is how marriage is begun, and dissolution seems to beg for its own equally stagy ceremonies.

When William Willoughby bought *Portrait of a Musician,* Vincent Booth felt his life mark a milestone and turn direction.

Although his first sale of a picture was for a hundred thousand dollars—nearly twice what he'd agreed to pay—it really didn't turn out to be much money. After settling with the auction house and the restorer, he got less than twenty thousand for his efforts. But still, there it was, more money than he'd ever made: twenty thousand, straight into the bank. After adding and subtracting and projecting, Vincent gained a new sense of awe for the feat of monetary accumulation. It seemed much more baffling after his first deal than it had before.

"Is everything all right?" he asked Mary on the phone.

"Fine," she asserted again in her blandest tone.

The hell with her, thought Vincent after hanging up. It was maddening to have news he couldn't tell anyone—how he'd made money by his wits alone. Laura was still at her mother's, and she'd asked him not to call her there. She said she would call him at three. It was all so annoying.

Still, a hundred thousand on his first picture! He did have an eye, even if the hundred thousand had only come out to be twenty thousand in actual money. It still was almost twice what he'd bid, which was ten times the auction house's estimate.

But things had changed. Why didn't Laura call? She swore she'd call at three, and he'd skipped lunch to wait.

Vincent decided to get Laura's mother's phone number up in Massachusetts from information and call, anyway. He had to talk to her, to tell her how fantastically different the world had gotten since their awful weekend, how different he was, how he'd sold a picture for a hundred thousand dollars. He wanted her to know he had decided to move out, that he was a new man, his own man. And her mother might as well know too.

"Who is this?"

"Oh, it's . . . Mr. Willoughby of Booth Investments. Miss Montgomery is one of our clients." As soon as he'd done it, Vincent wondered why he'd lied and chosen this preposterous pseudonymn.

"She isn't here," said Laura's mother, hanging up.

Vincent couldn't imagine why he hadn't said, "I'm her boyfriend, I love her, where is she?" He felt instantly cheap and sneaky.

It all seemed so monstrous, feverish, and tipsy just now. He'd sold a picture for a fortune, only to gain virtually nothing. He was ready to leave his wife to be with a lover who wasn't there. And why was Mary staying in the country?

There could be no more frustrating time to be alone than the Monday and Tuesday before they all came back to their parties. Yes, of course, in the goofy symmetry of current events —like Elizabeth over one fireplace and Mary's ancestor over the other—Laura's party was Wednesday, the same night as the party the Lavals were giving for the Booths. Laura was having a party for her father. Maybe Vincent simply should stay at Laura's and send word to Mary at the Lavals' that he was never leaving Laura again.

*   *   *

"Very fine picture," said James Montgomery. "Very fine."

Laura never accepted this style of her father's compliments without a twinge of anger. He acted as if he were approving an infant's efforts.

"Will I meet your friend?" he said with his useful grin.

"He's coming, but just for a drink because he's having dinner with his wife and family," Laura answered, glad to see at least a twitch in the great man's distancing grin. She was showing her father a limpidly recognizable picture of her naked self that Vincent had painted six months before. She wanted to shock him, but he looked back closely at the picture again, as if she were a child showing him some work she'd just accomplished in a coloring book.

"Isn't this attractive," he said about her apartment. "I'm so pleased, dear."

Missy was the first guest to arrive, bringing forty dollars worth of smoked salmon. She couldn't help losing all the sophistication she'd rehearsed when she saw the famous movie director in the flesh. Missy had just finished reading the story of his life. She knew everything about him.

He bowed, giving her a horsey grin from a handsome face seamed with a calligraphy of expressive wrinkles. "So glad to meet you, Missy. Lolly's told me all about you."

Guests arrived in a drove, and Missy decided to stick close to James Montgomery as long as she could. She couldn't wait to begin to reveal to him how much she knew about his life. He bowed in a poetical, personal way and seemed intensely interested in what others said. Missy got the idea—what the hell —of doing her own interview with him. Here he was, a living opportunity. An interview with James Montgomery would carry its reporter into print.

Tom Harrison felt familiar enough to kiss Laura upon his arrival. Bernie Stein kept nodding and smiling like a man who knew the evening's secret. Pauline McFall managed a proper entrance, a corridor instinctively clearing itself between herself and James Montgomery. She strode down it as if she were on a big white horse.

"Pauline," the director enthused.

"How's the world's completest bastard?" she asked.

"Worried about his prostate," was James's answer, and everyone laughed.

Missy saw that James Montgomery was such a big star that Laura was in nearly total eclipse. No wonder she was so mixed up about him; he outdid her.

"Daddy, this is Vincent Booth," said Laura. James Montgomery gave Vincent a jovial, studious greeting, although in fact he'd missed the young man's name and had no idea this was the painter of the nude, which Laura had put away before the party.

"And Bernie Stein," she continued, bringing Bernie to her father by the hand.

"Not the archaeologist?" marveled Montgomery, to both Bernie and Laura's delight. The two men at once discussed pre-Columbian matters, and Vincent felt superfluous. Laura was too busy to talk to him.

Natasha Glebov arrived in a sable coat she would later be disgusted to find a cat sleeping on. Sam Beecham wore a dark sport jacket, instead of a suit like most of the other men. He called James Montgomery "sir," and told him it was a great honor to meet him. Beecham's wife wondered throughout the evening whether her husband had ever slept with their hostess.

With his typical social serendipity William Willoughby was also invited, on the strength of that bottle of champagne he'd sent to Laura's table at Le Bordello. But he and Vincent could both only stay for a drink, because they were due at the dinner that Willoughby was sure would produce a check from Sidney Laval for the museum's new roof.

In the presence of her father, Laura looked striped with pain. Vincent wished he could express to her his stalwart love and sympathy, but she almost seemed to be dodging him. Finally he managed to whisper "I love you," his lips briefly touching her firm, coiling ear. She reached up to brush away the tickle of it, and her ceremonial smile didn't budge.

Vincent quashed a start of anger at this iron distance she'd set between them. He did not want to recreate the horrible ill will of the last weekend, and wrote it off to her father's presence. She was a tormented daughter, and he must understand and eventually be her solace from this original, unhealed wound.

Despite her pain, or perhaps because of it, Laura looked especially beautiful. It softened her with vulnerability. She wore a lovat-green tunic with purple frogging and a long, darker green skirt—an outfit she'd obviously made up herself with great success. On the tunic was an extraordinary piece of pre-Columbian gold jewelry. Vincent felt personally proud of her good taste. Fathers were hard on the personality, he was sure. He hadn't really had one himself, so he especially respected all the documented problems they raised.

"We slowed to a walk coming over a bridge . . ." Montgomery was projecting like an actor, apparently talking to

Laura's friend Missy, but no less aware, Vincent was sure, of the attentive rings of silence accreting around him. Out of loyalty to Laura, Vincent disliked him.

"It couldn't have been much over four feet down to the water, which scarcely was deep enough to cover your ankles. Suddenly the groom looked gloomy and said, 'Man threw himself off this bridge last Sunday . . . suicide.' Well, I laughed. I thought it was a joke, that little bridge and water about as deep as a movie producer's carpet, but one glance told me Paddy was dead serious, and angry with me. Perhaps he felt I'd shown a lack of respect for the dead. Anyway, he'd have nothing more to do with me, until we started hunting. We went over the first jump. It was a double, a hell of a mess, and I believe he'd run me to it to dispatch me. I've never seen country like that for hunting. It's lovely and utterly mad."

Missy was sitting with a straight spine. Her head was cocked toward the director, and her eyes were shining. Vincent looked around at how many of Laura's guests were listening to her father's tales. Laura herself wasn't there. He had a feeling she'd gone to her bedroom. The door was locked. Through it, she told him, "I can't talk."

"I understand," he assured her through the wood. "It's just that I have to go now." Willoughby was herding Vincent to his vital appearance at the Lavals.

Laura appeared outside her bedroom door, shutting it behind her, and tentatively returned Vincent's good-bye kiss. Then, perhaps feeling the intensity and sympathy he was feeling for her, she embraced him. Her body was so warm, and her color so high, that Vincent decided she must've been crying in her room.

Poor Laura. Perhaps she'd watched how her friend Missy

had gone over to her father's side, and it had galled her. Vincent felt a rush of love, sympathy, and optimism. Now he understood her so much better. Now he would be able to be her friend as well as her lover. It was so stupid of him to have despised her for the frantic attention she showed her cat—perhaps cats were the only vessels of love in her childhood, when her father probably competed with her for affection and attention.

When Mary saw Vincent at the Lavals', her resolution to spring the divorce—already in place, with the process-server assigned to intercept Vincent on the way home—was shaken. They had been apart for nearly a week. The separation objectified her perception of her husband's appearance. He once again had that vulnerable look she loved—the look of someone who needed protection in this dangerous world.

Vincent was glad to see Mary too. There was a relaxing haven of familiarity about her. Being with Laura was like walking a tightrope, dazzling and dangerous and exhausting. The irony of that last episode at Laura's party suddenly occurred to him. It was through the same door through which he'd just called Laura that Mary had called to him when he lay rolling in Laura's arms.

To William Willoughby's bemusement, their greetings were happily cordial. After all, hadn't he just brought Vincent over from his mistress's party? As usual, his inside information enriched his appreciation of the social scene before him. He gauged the hypocrisy of the domestic contentment alleged by the Booths' smiles and pecks. But Willoughby was more than willing to indulge his colleague, because Vincent had unwittingly just made him two million dollars.

Sondra Laval, with a cleverly restrained dose of bright colors on her dark dress showing off her white skin, took Vincent around her party to meet her guests. Mary retreated to the bedroom, where she telephoned the doorman and told him to dismiss the process-server.

"He won't go unless you tell him," he said after an interminable pause. "Hold on a second."

"W. B. Moore," said a mature Southern voice.

"It's off," said Mary.

"Who is this?" he asked.

"Mary Booth," she answered.

"Brigham?"

"That's right. Mary Brigham Booth."

"Off?"

"Thank you, you can go home."

"I don't get paid unless I serve him."

"Please put the doorman back on."

While Mary arranged for the tenacious process-server to be paid off, Vincent and Willoughby were being led by Sondra toward her husband, when suddenly Vincent saw Willoughby turn red. His grin didn't twitch, but his head filled with red like a glass pitcher of tomato juice. Sidney Laval was standing at his fireplace in a velvet smoking jacket and needlepoint evening slippers, talking to Victor Churrasco, the art dealer. Above him, brilliant with restoration, hung the *Portrait of a Musician*. Freshly and delicately lettered along the bottom of the frame was the name Nattier.

Willoughby had forgotten how quickly money can move things along. He hadn't expected the picture to appear in Laval's possession for months. He now turned his smile toward Vincent.

"You son of a bitch," said Vincent.

"Oh grow up, you adolescent bore," William snapped.

Sondra was aghast. Her dinner party was so ingeniously and laboriously planned that she couldn't imagine any part of it going wrong. Now this nasty exchange. What should one do?

"Whatsa matter?" Sidney asked, moving pugilistically forward.

"Where did you get that?" asked Vincent, pointing at the portrait.

"Victor Churrasco," Sidney answered, patting the dealer on the shoulder. He was puzzled but not displeased by the emotion stirred up by his new prize.

Victor offered Vincent a corrugated smile. His eyes were as black as holes.

"Do you like it, Vincent? It was commissioned by Catherine the Great. He was her lover," Willoughby said with sudden, mockingly triumphant composure. Vincent just nodded, glaring.

"Not many Nattiers on the market," Sidney observed.

"It must have been expensive," observed Vincent.

"Two million," Sidney said, "but including the letter she signed ordering it. Sir David Thompson found the letter." He reached his arm around Sondra's waist and beamed with pride.

Mary was astonished to find her husband completely furious. Had he somehow gotten wind of the process-server? She approached him guiltily, but he was staring at a picture over the Lavals' fireplace.

When they got home, Mary had expected to be the one full of brooding and anger. But instead Vincent was.

"What is it?" she asked.

He exhaled a sigh and wouldn't even turn to face her.

"Vincent, I've been thinking about a divorce," Mary said, startling herself. She was fed up with this mood of his, which she felt she deserved far more than he did. She wished she hadn't dismissed the process-server after all. He was awful. "You are just hell all the time."

"You're right."

"So I talked to my lawyer."

"That's fine."

"It is not," she said. How dare he be so willing? Mary burst into tears. "You're seeing someone," she bawled when the bedroom door was closed. "You big bastard."

"I love her," Vincent said.

"Get out of here," cried his wife.

"Party's over," said Laura's doorman.

"I know," Vincent said, moving anxiously into the elevator.

The doorman paused, as if he were going to refuse to take Vincent up, but then he smiled and entered his elevator. All the way up the old attendant was nearly giggling. He couldn't stop himself. On Laura's floor he left his elevator open as Vincent rang the bell. He rang and rang. He could hear the bell sounding inside, but why didn't she answer?

At last footsteps approached from inside, and bolts unlocked. The door only opened a chain's length. Through the gap, Vincent saw a strip of Bernie Stein. His teeth, bared against his beard, were like an animal's.

"Stop that and get the hell out of here," growled the archaeologist. He didn't appear to be wearing any clothes.

Taking Vincent back down, the elevator man mopped at

tears of repressed laughter. When Vincent looked back into the lobby from the sidewalk, he saw this witness to his shame grin and wave as meanly as a member of the mob at an eighteenth-century execution.

Part 3

Chapter ❦ 1

*F*rogs' eggs were what Wally saw in the dark when he closed his eyes. It was like frog's eggs, the way all the little dots cohered in a mass. But unlike frogs' eggs, the tiny specks were as bright as sparks. They floated past when his eyes were closed on certain nights for as long as he could remember, a dazzling filigree that appeared only when it wanted to, and usually went away if he tried to study it.

As soon as he thought of frogs' eggs, the vision disappeared, so Wally started thinking about the extraordinary events in the ditch that afternoon. "Are you awake?" he whispered.

"Yeah," Jackie Bushwick answered from the other bed.

"We sure killed a lot of frogs," Wally observed.

"Yeah," said his accomplice, "the Dance of

Death!" Both boys giggled helplessly at these words. They had sung and shouted this phrase every time a blow of their switches killed one of the hundreds of tiny, newly formed frogs they'd found trapped in a drainage ditch.

Every mortally struck frog obliged its annihilators with a jerky little dance. Eventually the boys' murderous frenzy subsided. Some victims wouldn't dance, and there was something depressing about the growing slaughter. The little bodies floated.

But saying "the Dance of Death" again got them to laughing in the dark. When this laugh gave out, Jackie stealthily approached Wally's bed with his pillow raised. Then he shouted "Dance of Death!" and brought it down with all his might on his unsuspecting guest.

The ensuing pillow fight attracted Mrs. Bushwick herself, a silhouette of angular adult tension in the doorway. "Stop that this instant! If you do not stop, you are separated and grounded. Uncle Harry and Wally's mother are coming tomorrow, and you are not to stay up all night with this horseplay."

"Yes, Mummy."

"Yes, Mrs. Bushwick."

When she shut the door, there was a respectful silence. Both boys sensed Jackie's mother was waiting outside in case they didn't behave.

" 'Night, Jackie," said Wally. He did not like this Uncle Harry seeing his mother. Wally felt his mother had more than enough to do with her affections just by loving him.

"There's this tree tomorrow," Jackie whispered. "Really high—and there's this vine and you jump to it, and if you miss, it would kill you."

Wally opened his eyes, recognizing this as another challenge from his host. He already had tricked Wally into peeing on a strand of electric fence and trying to pet a completely savage killer cow. The frog incident had, for all its ghoulish aspect, been a relief from the unending territorial assertion Jackie Bushwick kept tormenting Wally with on this farm of theirs in Wisconsin.

A year after Vincent Booth ran off, Mary had found herself nodding when her son asked if his father was dead. She decided she could correct this misapprehension when Wally was older. Meanwhile it seemed suitable to explain his absence as death. It was clean, final, and dignified. Moreover, she rationalized, she'd never actually said Vincent was dead. She'd just nodded when the boy asked. So her conscience was clear—or clearish, anyway.

As a female single parent, Mary decided Wally needed all the male companionship she could stir up, so he wouldn't wind up à la Pepe Deschamps. Her father Alfred didn't like children, so she came to depend on the good old Bushwicks to expose Wally to manhood. She was delighted to think of Wally out on their farm, peeing on trees and doing whatever boys do.

When Natalie Buckwick's brother, Harry Buntley (the farm in Wisconsin was the Buntley family farm), began showing an interest, it pleased Mary both as a boy's mother and as a woman. She was delighted to go out to Wisconsin with him to see her son and to see how they got along. She told Harry how important she felt it was for Wally to spend more time around men. "I don't want him to suffer, you know, from overmothering," she told the attentive sportsman.

When Jackie informed Wally about the tree, Wally imagined himself falling out of it. But falling from the tree and breaking his leg, he decided, was not much worse than seeing Uncle Harry, his would-be stepfather. Wally could see himself in white bandages, his mother weeping at his bedside. Even though it's terrifically painful, he smiles, and she begs his forgiveness for the innumerable mistakes she's made over the sad little span of his now broken life. With an heroic effort he lays a hand on her forehead and smiles.

Jackie led Wally up the enormous tree. Vines as thick as a boy's leg ran all around all the trees in what Jackie called his jungle. "See, it is a jungle," he proudly noted, standing at the trunk of the main tree. Wally stared up into the riot of limbs, leaves, and vines, and at the terrifying, bone-breaking height.

Climbing up this tree, from which Jackie proposed to demonstrate what he proclaimed "the Leap of Death," Wally considered how sorry his mother would be when the Bushwicks led her into the dining room and indicated the small black coffin on the dining-room table. Oh, sure, she'd cry plenty then, but it would be too late, too late for her to regret having forgotten her son in the arms of Uncle Harry.

It was very, very high. Wally was huddled in a cleft of the trunk, and Jackie had moved out on a limb by sliding along on his butt. He had a look of fear and pride on his face as he turned back to Wally and gestured at the vine. Then he carefully stood up and jumped, grabbing the vine like a monkey and descending, hand over hand, in swaying spasms. Whooping with victory on the ground, he looked back up at Wally. His head was no bigger than a thumbtack.

"Jump!" he shouted in a voice as far away as China. Wally

looked to where the vine still swayed from Jackie's descent. It was a long way out on a limb just to get near it—and then you had to jump out into nothingness—if you were going to accept the most horrific challenge yet offered by the jealous little maniac down below who obviously just wanted to show off and make sure you knew everything out there was his own personal property.

When Jackie visited Wally in Connecticut and in Maine and in Florida and even in New York, Wally had been wonderful and generous. He had never tried to frighten Jackie just for the sake of it, and he'd always shared all his toys.

Wally scooted out on the limb and reached for the vine, three feet of empty space away. Balancing himself, he rose to his feet and jumped at the vine before he could think it over again.

Hell, it was easy.

Wally hadn't seen his mother in two weeks. She had new clothes and a new hairstyle and, of course, the dogged attendance of Jackie's uncle, this Harry Buntley character. Harry Buntley stood very straight, moved very deliberately, and had a big hawk nose over a mustache. "A Georgian nose," was what Wally's mother would later call it. She thought the big stiff was "incredibly handsome."

"Hello there, young Wallace. "How are you?" said Harry Buntley, pointedly bending down to emphasize the difference in their heights as he crunched the boy's hand in a grip that would have been better employed unscrewing a tight jar lid.

"Fine, sir," Wally answered, dreading his future. Why couldn't his mother just leave things the way they were?

Buntley had a loud, braying laugh to which he constantly resorted over lunch. He offered both Wally and Jackie a taste of wine. "This is good claret, boys," he advised them.

"I think these boys might like some shooting," he said as lunch ended, not to them but to Wally's mother.

"I'm sure I don't have to tell you much," Buntley said to Wally, "not with Alfred Brigham for a grandfather."

Happily for Wally, his grandfather, Alfred Brigham, could not abide children, so he had never inflicted his noisome hobby on Wally. Wally was afraid of real guns.

"This is a 410," Buntley said as he handed Wally a shotgun. "I brought this out especially for you, young Wallace. I was given this shotgun by my father when I was seven years old." Joking, Wally pointed the thing at Jackie and said "Pow."

Harry Buntley snatched the gun from Wally with rage enough to knock the boy down. "Don't you ever point a gun at anyone—ever!" he shouted.

Wally was terrified and humiliated. He followed the rest of Buntley's instructions like a robot.

Harry Buntley didn't seem to want to leave Wally alone. After the scary, deafening drudgery of shooting was over, he announced that they were going for a ride in the jeep. Jackie was not invited. Uncle Harry Buntley put guns in the jeep and got his hunting dog from its kennel. Before allowing the animal into the jeep, he put it through some paces, showing that his mastery was powerful enough to exact obedience even from a dog quivering with prehunt excitement.

Then Uncle Harry explained how to start the engine and how to shift, and asked Wally if he wanted to steer.

"No thank you, sir," said Wally, who would normally have loved such an experience.

"Wallace," Buntley said, "it's not 'sir' with me, okay? It's Uncle Harry, or just plain Harry. I kind of like your mum, young man," he added. "I think she's quite a gal. We might be getting together for good. Now, let's kill some birds."

He pulled a gun out of the back of the jeep. When he whistled, his dog leapt out and started hunting. Buntley was squinting out across the fields with his broken shotgun over his shoulder. The dog stopped zigzagging and froze on point. "Hold it," Buntley whispered sharply. He loaded up and crept forward. He made an animal noise, his dog jumped, and the grouse flew. Uncle Harry very deftly blasted it from a whirring trajectory of escape, then the spaniel returned the blood-laced corpse to their feet.

When they came back from the walk, talk, and shoot, Uncle Harry dropped a brace of birds on the kitchen table and said, "When's dinner? Young Wallace and I have worked up some appetite."

He cupped the back of Wally's skull and nodded the boy's head for him like a puppeteer. Mary beamed at this spectacle, which Wally realized Buntley was staging completely for her benefit.

Throughout dinner Wally dreaded the periodic attentions of the figure who now wore a jacket and tie and chucked him painfully under the chin. The big scary son of a bitch had clearly decided to win Mary Brigham by showing what a great and manly pal he'd make for her son. Wally noticed she seemed to be falling for it hook, line, and sinker.

Once again Buntley offered both boys a taste of wine, which he poured out in a finicky way and watched them drink as if they were lab rats. Of course, it tasted like medicine.

After his divorce Harry Buntley had moved to New York

to manage money, but like all the Buntleys he felt truly at home only on the old family farm in Wisconsin. Obviously he wanted to be "getting together for good" with Wally's mother because she was so rich. You could tell that from all his determination and insincerity. Why couldn't she see it?

Wally liked the farm himself. But it certainly was not worth bringing this tyrant into the family in order to go there. Wally felt his mother entertained the Bushwicks more than enough to be invited to their dumb old farm as much as they wanted.

The changes Harry Buntley's attentions had wrought in his mother were startling. She was going to hairdressers, trying to lose weight, buying new dresses, disappearing for stretches of time, and waiting for Buntley to telephone—actions threatening to utterly shatter what Wallace felt was a fine, successful family unit quite whole enough with her, him, and staff.

"Do you like your uncle?" asked Wally in the dark.

"Sure," said Jackie noncommittally.

"Really?" demanded Wallace. The ensuing silence gratified his suspicions but simultaneously gave him more reason to worry.

Chapter 2

"*H*arry and I are getting married," Mary told her son in the library in New York.

"Fine," said Wally, frostily turning away to study the paneling. So it was true. He'd bagged her like a bird. Pow.

"I think you're going to like him more," Mary said hopefully.

"Really?" Wally said sarcastically.

"I mean it," his mother said.

"I think it's rotten and he stinks," Wally exploded.

Mary grabbed him before he fled, and buried him in the ample upholstery of her defiantly unreduceable body. She spoke softly. "I think it's a very good idea, and I'm sure you'll get used to it."

"What's so good about it?" he asked sullenly.

"I think you should have a man around."

"How did my dad die?" asked Wally. He felt his mother stiffen with a little jolt, as she always did when he brought up that subject.

"He picked up something down in Mexico, and it finished him." His mother's voice was low and dull.

In the ensuing silence Wally let himself be stroked about the brow and nestled about the shoulders. Sometimes the big wound of their broken home was as delicious to probe with his mother as the tender crater left by a departed tooth.

"Was he an artist?"

"Sort of."

"Was he a hippie?"

"No."

"Did he like me?"

"Yes, of course. He loved you."

"Do you think I'm an artist?"

"You draw very well."

"But do you think I'll become an artist, Mum?"

"We'll see."

"What do you want me to be?"

"I want you to be happy and well adjusted, and I think it's a good idea to have a man around again."

Wally withdrew his affections at this fresh allusion to Harry Buntley. A variety of bibelots arranged by Pepe Deschamps stood on the table before them for people to fumble with during pauses. Wally opened and closed a parrot's-head snuffbox.

"Do you love him?" he asked coldly.

"Of course I do," Mary said. But Wally could tell from how she said it that she didn't, which he took as some consolation.

The engagement was announced in the *Times,* and many entertainments were scheduled to fete the new couple. In the

William Hamilton

congratulations Harry Buntley got at his office there were certain allusions to riches. He took it good-naturedly, knowing these people would soon be looking like peanuts to him. They, of course, knew it too.

Alfred Brigham was positively cordial to his new potential son-in-law. The man could shoot. He managed money. It seemed so much more sensible than that crazy artist business which he had told Mary from the start was a bum idea. The only thing that bothered Alfred were the reports he'd ordered which showed Buntley had no particular money. Still, Alfred decided this one was better form. Ultimately he was just plain glad someone who could shoot had turned up in his daughter's life.

Mary was touched when William Willoughby begged her to let him give a dinner for the older connections of the family. Alfred and Lolly came, which was unusual since Alfred detested the city and the sneaks who lived there giving cocktail parties. Rainey Phillips arrived in a walker she called her "playpen." Harry Buntley's father made quite an impression. He called himself "a Harvard farmer," shook his cane at people, and drank copiously. His wife had obviously opted to spend her life as his attendant.

Mary was amazed to see how grandly Willoughby lived. She had always imagined his home as little more than his pit stop, a couple of Spartan rooms into which he pulled for a nap and a change before hurtling back out onto the social racetrack. But his place was large and sumptuously decorated. Mary later voiced her surprise to Pepe Deschamps, the decorator it turned out she and Willoughby had in common.

"Catherine the Great helped him a little," Pepe said archly.

"What do you mean?" Mary asked.

"Don't you remember? He found a painting of one of her

lovers and proved she commissioned it. He got it for nothing and sold it for millions. Willy has an incredible eye."

It was an evening of many toasts, several of them alluding to the hobby shared by Alfred and Harry. So when Willoughby's turn came, he looked at Alfred and his soon-to-be son-in-law and said, "It is a privilege to be able to honor a shotgun marriage."

Throughout the premarital socializing, Harry Buntley kept close track of Wally. He had a way of seizing the boy every so often, an attempt at hearty male affection that struck Wally like a mugger's blows. Wally stopped eating and sleeping right, and began to dream of running away.

One morning Wally fatefully decided to stay home from school, feigning illness. He thought perhaps he could postpone his mother's wedding with some spectacular health tragedy.

"I have a sore throat," he announced.

"Oh, dear," said Mary, about to rush out for a thousand Harry Buntley reasons.

Mrs. Keswick showered him with attention, muttering homilies from the firesides of Scottish girlhood. But no matter how hard he tried, Wallace couldn't get above the fever line on the thermometer, even though he puffed out his cheeks with hot air and held his breath to stretch the mercury.

Even so, Mrs. Keswick attended him with potions, sayings, towels, and trays until her favorite soap opera commenced. Wally then found himself bored and restless. His bed was scaled like a fish with comic books he'd already read. He could hear Mrs. Keswick's soap blaring through the wall, as if she were watching it from a mile away.

Wally stepped into the hallway off his bedroom in his pajamas and socks. He ran as fast and hard as he could down the carpet but could not produce much of a slide on the marble entrance foyer. He ran up and down twice more, then around a corner into the main sitting room, using his momentum to hurtle through the air into the large silk pillows on the biggest sofa. Wally discovered there was plenty of room for him to bury himself under the pillows. From the outside, the sofa looked perfectly normal, but inside it—completely and artfully hidden—was a boy! Wally wished someone would enter the room and sit down on the sofa, someone he could then abruptly scare to death with a scream, or unnerve with a poke on the butt.

But no one arrived, and his trap was getting hot, dark, and sneezy. Wally threw back the pillows and climbed out. He went over to the Louis XV desk that adults like Pepe Deschamps liked to talk about. Atop it, two big elephants marched toward each other with their trunks thrown up like coat hooks. On the back of each was a gold howdah, and in one Wally found a key.

The key opened the desk. Like most pieces of important furniture, the desk wasn't actively used. The drawers were empty and musty, except for old bits of flotsam and jetsam: a piece of chalk, a poker chip, a deck of cards, and something way in the back—letters and postcards bundled together with a rubber band.

Wally pulled out a postcard showing Rio de Janeiro.

My dearest son,

There is something about Guanabara Bay that makes it very easy to picture old sailing ships anchoring here. There is lots of belief in witchcraft, and in white magic. The black ladies dress in white and send paper boats and white roses out to sea for the goddess Iamanjha. These bits of magic and the emptiness of the bay make this a great place to use your imagination, which is what a painter has to do.

I love you,
Dad

It was addressed to Master Wallace Booth. It was from his father! Wally's father was alive! Wally hugged the bundle to his bosom, which was beating like a big bass drum, as he marched back to his room. He arranged and rearranged his treasure, separating postcards from letters and then ordering the collection by dates. The first one was the strangest. It was long, in Spanish, and in a peculiar antique handwriting, but it was signed "Dad." The most recent was six months old. All the letters had been opened.

When Mary returned later that afternoon, she entered Wally's room, saw the letters, and cried out. She began looking through the stack for one letter in particular, and Wally immediately guessed it was the first one, the one in Spanish, that she was after. He snatched it up. Wally knew it was important and that his mother didn't want him to read it.

"Give me that," she cried in a bestial, primitive way that Wally found hideous.

"Liar," he screamed back at her. "You big liar!"

"Give me that!" she shouted. Snatching for it again, Mary almost pulled it away, but Wally hit her with all his might in the solar plexus and ran out of the room as she collapsed across the rest of the letters on his bed.

Wally heard his mother crying in the hall, and doors opening, as he hid the letter in volume one of *The Personal Memoirs of U. S. Grant* in the library. When he sauntered out into the hall, four women—the cook, his mother, the maid, and Mrs. Keswick—were gathered in a circle.

"Give me that letter," Mary pleaded, still doubled over. "Where is it?"

"I won't tell, you liar," said Wally, causing amazement and dismay in all of them.

Weeping, and with a gesture of surrender, Mary turned down the hall toward her room.

"Conchita," Wally said, "can you translate something?"

Conchita, afraid for her job, looked to Mary, who assented. Sobbing, she threw her hands to her head, entered her bedroom, and closed the door.

Chapter 3

"*M*y dear and estimated son," translated Conchita as they sat on opposite sides of the desk in the library, which Wally had locked from the inside.

"Estimated?" he asked.

"Very loved and respected," she explained. Wally nodded. Conchita translated as she went along, and every so often she would scowl and purse her lips before proceeding.

Is three of us here to write to you this letter. Is three because two of us is drinking and one is the writer. Do you like his writing? He is a professional writer of letters for sailors; many sailors don't know how to write, and so Dr. Estéban Peña writes for them. His writing is very pretty, don't you agree? He learned from his father how to write letters for sailors.

Dr. Estéban will write the whole letter for anyone who wants. You don't have to say nothing, or he writes what you say exactly. Also, you can tell him what you want to say or just how you feel and to make it very romantic or very sorry or very mad, and he will. He says the most popular letter is the love letter. Is that not good? But it makes me sad. Sadness!

The other man helping me to write this letter to you is Don Diego Moore. Don Diego is an archaeologist from Minnesota. He is my very good and estimated friend who brought me here to Veracruz. We are all at the port of Veracruz, Mexico, in a bar called La Bamba, because of the misery of love that happened to me.

Don Diego translates my letter to Dr. Estéban Peña, who writes it to you. I have never written a letter this way before, and I think it is a much better way to write a letter than I ever heard of. It gives you a chance to drink and to think, and the handwriting stays completely clear because Dr. Peña does not drink until he is finished.

It is very good to have a diverting way to write this letter, because it is a very difficult letter to write. It is the letter of *adios,* good-bye to my dear son for now. Good-bye, Wally, I am sailing away tomorrow for the Amazon on a ship called *Paradip.*

But this is not a letter of sorrow and sadness because I am too furious to be sad. I am writing not to be sad anymore because now I am rabid and angry, so don't worry, no crying. We are all enjoying being very angry in this cantina. We have excellent seafood and a bottle of tequila with a dead worm inside. The worm is put in the best tequila. He lived in the cactus from which the tequila got made.

I am very glad you are a boy, because we can talk about

things I could not say to a daughter. Only men understand the bad woman, just like probably only women understand the bad men.

You won't be able to read this letter right away because you are a baby now and you can't read yet, and especially in Spanish. But this letter has to be in Spanish, so Dr. Estéban Peña can write it, so Don Diego and I can drink. When you do read it, it will be later for all of us. I will no longer care for Laura.

I think it would be a good idea if you stop reading now and go out and get a record by a good, sad Mexican trio that includes the song "La Que Se Fue" ["She Who Took Off," elucidated Conchita] and if you have enough years, a bottle of tequila. Try to get the tequila that has a worm floating in the bottle.

Wallace, you can't imagine how the world can turn over like a car with you inside. Please understand. I was in love— completely in love. I was in love enough to commit a crime.

Here Conchita's cheeks flushed, and she looked up at Wally, who was listening wide-eyed to this bizarre torrent of information.

I decided that to deserve to be in love, you must not be afraid. You must gamble everything. I believed you can't feel so much love unless love is there, and when you go there, love will appreciate you and guard you and save you, so I went there.

Dear Wally, this is your father's friend Doug Moore. He has to step away from this letter a moment, so I will tell you it is true and that I was there when he came to the excavation, and he is in love. He loves Laura, who is with Bernie, who has the excavation. Bernie does not like the man to walk out of the forest and say, "I love you" to his sweetheart. For one week it is unbelievable, plus there are all sorts of grave robbers now because the excavation is the most famous one in the world.

Now your father returns. I read my addition to him and he doesn't mind. I tell more, but I see he is full of brilliant ideas he got while he was where the king goes alone.

Conchita looked up and giggled, but the next line sobered her.

There is no escape from love, Wally. If you go away from it, you must come back, because if you go, it just goes with you. It becomes all over inside of you, and it hurts everywhere and gets worse and worse. The only way to keep it from killing you is to get it back outside you where you can see it. But if you get it outside and see it—don't hit it with a shovel. Go back where you can see her, outside, standing outside in shorts. Put down anything in your hands. She has on dark glasses. She is so beautiful, you want to embrace her. You think only of her all the time, even when she leaves you. Wally, I loved her so much, I was crazy.

I walked out of the trees and they arrest me. There is lots of security guards for the excavation. Then she sees me. Then at first she is shocked, but I can see she is very happy, and when she kisses me, she lets her body in, like a plane landing on the runway, and I hold her with everything, and I kiss her with all my power.

We make love immediately, like animals. I can't believe she is with me again. We come out of her tent together and look at the trees. It is very hot and humid. I want to say, "Why did you run away" and "Please come with me," but we don't say nothing. We smile with tears in our eyes. The earth is a red color in these patches where the archaeologists are digging. There are little numbers everywhere, and strings. The guards must have gone to get him, this man I can't remember. I can't believe it.

He comes running; he's wet from running. Clouds are rolling like steam. He is screaming at me to get out and go away. He swings back his shovel, completely insane. Laura keeps saying everything is all right, which is probably the most strange time to say that there ever was.

Can you imagine? Nothing is all right, and she keeps saying, "It is all right." That is the trouble with her. She cannot understand reality.

I stay there. She goes with him, she goes with me, and then she goes away. She left him and she left me, and he tries to kill me, and I never even manage to take him seriously.

He says, "She is gone." At first I do not believe him. But when he tries to break my head again with his shovel, I know it's true.

She just left, Wally—"La Que se Fue." She left me in New York, I could not believe it, so I follow and she just leaves again. She goes back to New York on American Express, leaving me with this crazy guy and all the red holes in the jungle he is digging to pull this dead city up out of its grave.

Bernie Stein called me. [Here Conchita decided the words were too dirty. "Bad words," she said.] He is so furious, he cries. Water spits out of his eyes. I can't even believe he is real. Why did she go away with him? Why did she go away from me? Why does she go away from both of us now?

He wants to know, and so do I. There we are left alone

where he is trying to get the plants and mud and earth off the stone skeleton of a dead city with a broken heart. I begin to love him as much as I hate him. Who else can understand?

Finally Doug Moore says people are stealing things because no one is paying attention to the excavation. He can't do everything himself. Bernie must go back to work and stop drinking and crying in my tent.

It is an unusual scene, my son, and I decided to paint it for you with my excellent collaborators, Dr. Doug Moore, Ph.D., and Dr. Estéban Peña of the distinguished family of Veracruz letter writers. I did not leave for no reason. I was the fool who follows love.

But now I feel free. I think I followed love because it was alive. It brought me to a tomb and left me there alone so I could remember that life passes through us, like a breeze brushes up the leaves and goes on to other trees in other fields and stops.

I imagine you now as a young man reading this. Have another tequila, my son. Do you shave now? Wally, I cannot remember the first time I shaved! I am too far from home. Did you know I'm from West Virginia? Have you got a map? Go down from New York and left. Not Virginia— West Virginia. I remember waiting and wanting to shave and to lean against the bars where you hear the sad laughter of adults joking about their bad luck. And now there I am—at La Bamba, a shaver, a joker in a cantina, and you are a young man wondering if the shadow on your lip is deep enough to lather up and scrape off.

Conchita stopped and stared seriously at Wally. He impatiently pointed at the letter. He was like a little man, the little master. Conchita sighed and continued.

I liked feeling like an animal again. Laura made me feel like an animal. I was beginning to feel like a little thing, like that head of the parrot on the table in the library, a little painted thing that sits on tables in rooms where people gossip about each other.

Because of how Laura made me feel, there was a birth, a life in me. I felt not like a little painted thing. I felt like a lover and a traitor, and big and dangerous and living—filling out all the parts of my body and my opportunities. I was a big, bad man. And then I found myself in Bernie's graveyard, making conversation with the other skeletons after life went away. Maybe she is the witch of life, Wally, who looks so beautiful, so you will believe you are not alone and follow her to your doom.

All this will happen to you, I guess. Something like this happens to everybody. From here I look back and I see only luxury and betrayal. That is all those men at the cantina joke about, because the other part, which is love, does not serve for the jokes you need to survive in cantinas.

I love you, Wally—you crawling baby now—and I always will.

Dad

La Bamba
Veracruz

The rest of the letters were nothing like this one. They were mundane and sweet and less inspired. Most of them came from Rio de Janeiro, where he lived. He was a painter, an artist. He became more and more like a stranger as the letters got more recent.

There weren't as many letters lately as Wally felt he deserved, and he began to feel a little sorrier about reducing his mother to such a state. By now it was dark, and she still hadn't come back out of her room. He tiptoed to her door and rapped delicately. "Mom?" he asked.

Mary opened the door and embraced him. "That letter is why I said he was dead," she said. "I didn't want you ever to have to see that letter until you were grown-up." Mary had a better translation of Vincent's letter from Veracruz in a file at her lawyer's for the annulment of her marriage. The bad taste of it is what horrified her most: a drunk writing in Spanish to his two-year-old son about chasing and screwing his whore—it tested the entire digestive system just to consider it.

Vincent had hurt Mary so terribly, and then simply disappeared into the tropics—wasn't it kinder of her to tell Wally his father was dead? Could Wally prefer a truth as disgusting as that letter?

Actually, he informed her, he could. She never should have lied. Even as he said it and forgave her, Wally realized he had just been given a permanent advantage over his mother. "You lied to me" was all he would ever need to say in order to triumph in any argument or disagreement he might have with her.

In his own bed for the night, Wally reviewed his tumultuous discovery with much more delight than he would have expected during the painful and dramatic events themselves. It was wonderful to think of a living father. Before, Wally could only resort to a stock character he'd patched together out of infantile memories: a tall, dark man holding him high off the ground.

Now, from that Mexican letter, Wally knew what his dad

was like—a wild adventurer, the passionate, wandering artist, a man infinitely superior to that disciplinarian bore who was moving in on Wally's mother like a sniffing, quivering hunting dog.

Wally imagined finding his father in the tropics. He amused himself in bed by imagining he had run away from the concentration camp Harry Buntley would undoubtedly make of his house.

Wally was something of an artist himself. Perhaps he and his father could share a studio together, painting on two easels as parrots squawked and monkeys chattered outside.

"Dad? A little alizirin crimson?"

"Good idea, Wally."

In the jungle studio he now imagined, Wally considered another, less amusing possibility: the native wife with naked boobs and hair to the floor and dozens of tan half brothers and sisters. But maybe they'd be fun. Maybe they'd show him how to use a blowgun and dive over waterfalls.

Chapter 4

*I*n art class Wally drew a comic monstrosity of a bird hunter. The art teacher, Mrs. Wilson, singled it out for praise, and many of his classmates complimented him.

It was an ambitious picture with lots of detail. The central figure was hugely equipped for destruction. His arsenal included pistols, grenades, and rockets, as well as an enormous, vividly recreated shotgun at his waist. "I killed a bird," said the balloon rising from his drooling mouth. The disproportion between this stupid-looking, over-equipped giant and his harmless little prey was comically exaggerated.

Mrs. Wilson hung the picture in the school's main hallway, where it won Wally additional praise and attention. One day James Hobart—a big, dangerous boy who had enrolled only the year before and had already formed a gang—approached Wally in the locker room.

"Hey, artist! Are you a fartist?" Hobart said. When Wally laughed politely and tried to move past, Hobart grabbed his arm. Two of Hobart's cronies were with him.

"Are you?" he demanded.

"I don't know," Wally said.

"He's a fartist," crowed one of Hobart's sidekicks. Laughing uproariously, they blocked the doorway.

"A famous fartist," Hobart elaborated.

"The richest kid in the school," said the boy on Wally's right, a fat fellow named Lacey.

When they called him a fartist, Wally was hurt. But when Lacey made his remark, Wally felt a chill.

"The richest fartist in the world," quipped Hobart, giving the three of them another laugh.

When Wally tried to walk by again, Lacey shouldered him into a locker. The clang and sharp pain in his chest scared him. When Hobart picked him up, the feeling of helplessness was terrifying. To his horror Wally felt tears on his cheeks.

"Oh, he's crying, Jim," said Lacey. They sat him down, and Hobart pretended to smooth Wally's brow maternally.

"Oh, little baby's crying," said the third member of Hobart's gang.

"Gimme twenty-five dollars, fartist," said Hobart, "or I'll kick the shit out of you!"

"I haven't got twenty-five dollars," said Wally, hating his tears.

"Tomorrow, punk, or we kick the shit out of you. And if you tell anybody, we'll double-kick the shit out of you."

"Maybe he'll stay home sick, Jim," suggested a member of the dangerous hood's staff.

"That's okay," Hobart said. "We got all year."

Evil has a way of collecting. The shakedown at school happened the very day Harry Buntley was due back from Scotland, where Mary's father had taken him on a shoot.

"Uncle Harry is here," said the maid as Wally walked in the door. Had the staff been bought off? he wondered. Wally was damned if he'd call him Uncle. In fact, he'd decided not to call him anything. Harry Buntley held out his massive paw for another painful handshake.

"Hello, son," he said. Wally silently shook his hand and went to his room, closing the door.

"Oh, he'll be all right," he heard Buntley say to his mother, who had started to rush after her hurt and upset son.

Wally threw himself on the bed, burying his head under the pillows. He had trouble at school and trouble at home. If only he could run away and find his father and live there with pet monkeys and his own grass hut and perhaps a dog or two. By now his father seemed wonderful and magical in Wally's imagination, somewhat along the lines of Dr. Doolittle.

When Wally stepped out of his room, he had, for an exquisite instant, completely forgotten about Harry Buntley. But the big bastard was in the library, in a high old wing chair he occupied like those crabs that steal other creatures' shells.

Mary, spotting Wally, smiled brightly and held out her hand. "Uncle Harry's been in Scotland with Grandpa."

Wally eased into the room and leaned against his mother's

chair while the intruder chuckled and held a glass of Scotch up to his mandibles.

"How was it?" Wally asked, smoothing a lock of his mother's hair back on her forehead.

"Hey, son, unless you want to grow up to be a hairdresser, why don't you come away from your mamma and grab yourself a seat," Buntley suggested.

Wally realized he had to bear this insult, that retreat would only gratify Buntley and ratify his opinions. Wally gracefully assumed a position across from Buntley, with his mother between them.

"How was the shooting?" he asked in a phony, adult way his mother could see right through.

Buntley, however, couldn't. "Great shooting," he reported. "Twelve brace of grouse and six of pheasant."

"Dinner is served," Conchita announced from the doorway. Wally kept up his last pose, the diffident adult, throughout the meal as Buntley rattled on about his shoot, a slightly British inflection now joining his already clattering train of affectations. When Buntley said his friend Alexander was "you know, Lord Hillsborough," Wally looked purposefully at his mother. But she just kept beaming at Buntley as though she couldn't see what a big fake he was.

"You got the money?" asked Hobart, as though some legitimate deal were being discussed. The bully had caught him a block away from school. Wally shook his head. Hobart made a strange little fist and drove it three times into the same spot on Wally's shoulder, with surprisingly painful results. "You gonna get it?"

When Wally shook his head, Hobart struck the same spot

five more times. Things being as they were at home and at school, Wally felt he might as well die or go to the hospital. He swung a punch that missed, and Hobart immediately hit him in the face, clanging a huge bell of pain. Wally swung again, but Hobart was nothing but muscle. It was like hitting a car tire. Hobart laughed as he kneed his puny adversary. Wally flailed out again, and his haymaker chanced to take in Hobart's nose, releasing an enormously gratifying nosebleed.

"You son of a bitch," he snarled.

"Hey, hey—are you all right?" asked a busybody pedestrian, rushing to Hobart's aid.

"I'll get you," Hobart vowed, trying to keep the joyously spreading blood off his clothes as he skulked away.

Except for the considerable pain in his shoulder, and the tender swelling under his eye, Wally felt exuberant. Somehow he'd defended himself.

Mary was gratifyingly horrified by Wally's black eye, and he himself found the wound sufficiently magnificent to spend twenty minutes in the bathroom examining it. Harry Buntley wanted to know who had won the fight and what had caused it. Wally just shrugged.

"How did it start?"

"Called me rich," Wally said.

"And you hit him back," said Buntley admiringly, balling up his own fist.

"Sure," said Wally.

"Good show!" Buntley roared, giving the boy's sore shoulder one of his rough, manly squeezes. Wally doubled over in pain and then, before he considered what he was doing, kicked the man in the shin.

Buntley howled, and Mary rushed up to them.

"What are you doing?" she cried furiously at her son.
"Say you're sorry."

"It's all right," Buntley offered. But he glowered Wally's
way.

When Mary retired for the night, she found Wally's picture of
the monstrous bird hunter on her pillow.

"Don't you like him at all?" she asked Wally after school
the next day. Wally shook his head.

"I think it would be much better for both of us to have a
man in the house," his mother repeated.

"What do you think I am?" Wally answered, indignant.
Mary smiled at her beloved, magnificent son. He turned away
to seem aloof but was secretly pleased by her worshipful gaze.

"I just don't know, Harry," she said to Buntley, who was
trying, he explained, "to get things a little more focused as to
an exact date for the wedding."

Buntley found the boy far more of a problem than he'd
anticipated. He studied the picture and frowned as Mary gushed
about the art teacher's high opinion of her talented son. This
picture was clearly the naked attack of a propagandist and
saboteur.

Little Wally was the only problem. Everybody else was all
for Harry. Alfred Bent Brigham found him excellent company.
Mary herself had clearly agreed to marry him, and now she kept
stalling over the date. Buntley had found it worrisome, and here
she was saying "I just don't know" as she showed him a hateful
picture drawn by her son. What more could he do?

And the little bastard had kicked as well as mocked him.
Hundreds and hundreds of millions of dollars were Buntley's

except for that spoiled little brat who would probably wind up queer as queer could get. Between his mother and these art teachers, Buntley figured, effeminacy and homosexuality were damn near inevitable. "Homo," he grumbled to himself, pulling out his cuff links. If she didn't marry him soon, she wouldn't. The little bastard was clearly working against him every waking hour, and there was no way of getting rid of him—no father to pick him up, no school to pack him off to. Harry fixed himself a highball and swished it through his teeth, an angry grimace etched into his deeply disturbed countenance.

Chapter 5

*L*ike antibiotics, publicity can have unforeseen side effects. An American network news team coming to Brazil to interview the grand old man of landscape architecture, Ulysses Aranha Moro, was itself the subject of extensive interviewing because it represented North American publicity for a nation wooing tourism and, more spectacularly for the Latin imagination, because it starred a famous blonde woman.

Missy Ferguson was filmed arriving both at the airport, where she was presented with flowers, and her hotel, where she was asked to give a press conference.

"I'm not used to being on this end of an interview," she told the Minister of Tourism as they shared a *cafezinho* in the hotel lobby. They sat in fat leather chairs surrounded by cameras and quartz lights.

"How is it for a woman in the media in America?" asked a young woman reporter.

"The opportunities are there, and so are the obstacles," Missy observed. Electronic shutters hissed, and passing tourists paused and went up on tiptoes to see who was causing such attention.

"How did you start?" the same reporter asked.

"Just like you, doing interviews," was Missy's response, though Laura Montgomery had recently put it somewhat differently after Missy had gone to a lot of trouble to get Laura a job, which Laura botched with her usual flair. "She started by sleeping with my father and stealing all my ideas," was how Laura explained Missy's success.

Missy didn't televise exactly as she looked. On the screen she was cool, tailored, intelligent, and handsome. The network gave her what it considered to be the more intellectual assignments. In person Missy looked so different, she was rarely even recognized in public. "It's like the camera brushes her hair and presses her skirt and buttons her buttons," marveled Toby Hyman, whose pass she had instantly and authoritatively rejected when she started at the network.

Vincent did not immediately realize it was Missy on the television in the bar where he sat drinking beer and scoffing with a Brazilian friend at the success of New York City's downtown wunderkind painters. But suddenly he knew exactly who she was.

So Missy was in Brazil. She was famous and had everything that Laura wanted. Vincent felt intensely vulnerable. He had cauterized his wound of romance in the fire of exile, but Missy's turning up on Brazilian television immediately recalled all his painful memories.

Vincent stared with terrible seriousness at the interview, and his friend could not recognize his mood.

*　*　*

Interviewing Ulysses Aranha Moro was Missy's own esoteric idea (sure, she had heard of him from Laura, but Laura never followed through on anything). The network had agreed only because Missy's interview with the Dalai Lama had been so unexpectedly successful.

Ulysses was much better known in the fifties, in the days of modern art and a fabulous future, than he was now. The most important patrons of modern art and architecture had gardens by Ulysses, and he had also designed parks and even cities in those eager days of progress and discovery.

He was a botanist and explorer as well as a landscape architect. His estate outside Rio was famous for its garden and extensive collection of tropical plants, and it was there, the morning after her arrival, that Missy planned to conduct her interview.

Missy's successful programming formula was to interview interesting people in interesting places. "No sets, no swivel chairs" was her motto. As Missy slept off her plane ride, Vincent spent a night of insomnia wondering whether he should try to see her. His life had felt so satisfactory, even worthy, that he feared finding out how fragile it really was only after breaking it.

But if he didn't try to see Missy, Vincent reasoned, it meant he was afraid of himself, still vulnerable to the life he'd left behind. Not seeing her would poison his confidence as surely as reentering the world he had escaped, or falling back in love with Laura, would.

He now saw how impossible loving Laura was. She had left him in the jungle with Bernie Stein, the only other man who understood his feelings—and hated him for them. That was savage. She left both of them like a pair of unfinished executions.

He saw his old self as a monstrosity, like the former lives of the old Nazis still to be found hiding in the interior. Was Missy there to take him back for exposure and trial? Could he return to those scenes of luxury and betrayal without losing the new life he had struggled so hard to create?

Vincent really was a painter now. He painted people. He was working on a full figure of Pedrinho, a cook's son, and it was his best work so far. The picture had immediately started painting itself, and then it had begun to paint Vincent. That character of life, that breeze passing through leaves, flowed through Vincent's brush and hand. He never wanted the picture to finish. This was a joy which, now that Vincent knew it, he never wanted to lose or leave behind.

Would Missy's reality skew the new one Vincent was so proud of making for himself in Rio? Would he still be able to love his pictures? Was his new life just a fiction that could be laughed away by presences from the past? Vincent couldn't sleep, wondering what to do about Missy's arrival in Rio.

Ulysses's flower arrangements were unlike any Missy had ever seen, and his house and garden mixed the curvaceous abstractions of modern art with the finely proportioned, unrefined simplicity of seventeenth-century Portuguese Colonial architecture.

Ulysses himself appeared in a fine white shirt over white trousers. He had white hair, a white mustache, and heavy black glasses.

"How did a child like you ever hear of me?" he asked.

"The Museum of Modern Art," answered Missy.

His collection of plants were in an apparently endless series of walled gardens over which bamboo blinds regulated sunlight, and through which gardeners constantly passed, adjusting, examining, and watering. This tamed jungle was the perfect backdrop for a grand old man who knew how to present himself as grandly as he presented any plant or flower.

"This is a palm that blooms only one time—in fifty years—and then it dies. I planted this one to bloom the day I die."

"And when is that?" Missy asked, instantly regretting her question.

It was the perfect last shot for Missy's interview: the grand old man gesturing up the palm that apparently was going to serve as his alarm clock for paradise. A servant arrived with drinks, as if on cue, and Missy and Ulysses took their drinks off the tray. Ulysses chortled and raised his glass to toast his response to Missy's brutal question.

"When I can no longer fuck young sailors," said the grand old man in his cultivated, mellow English.

Missy's messages were mainly invitations from every quarter of the more solvent realms of Carioca life. She was asked out socially, politically, professionally, and romantically. It was like going through a deck of cards. She sighed. All she really wanted to do was go to bed early.

It had been a good interview, despite Ulysses's naughty finale. Things of beauty were shown, and things of interest said. It was exactly as Missy's pretty, informative interviews ought to be.

Vincent Booth? It couldn't be, but it could—he'd disappeared into some heart of darkness or another. How many Vincent Booths could there be?

"My God, Vincent," Missy cried when she arrived at his studio.

"My God, Missy," he joked back.

He looked older and more gaunt, even more attractive than before. He seemed poor and casual, the opposite of the well-tailored, cynical husband she remembered. And his paintings were wonderful.

"You could make a fortune in New York," she advised him. Missy, too, had aged attractively. Her skin was closer to her bones, her hairstyle less collegiate.

They were pictures of people, mainly children. Missy just managed to stop herself from asking if he painted so many children because he missed his own so much.

"This is where I ate with the first money I got from my art," Vincent explained. They were next door to his studio at a grill in Copacabana where pullets bronzed over charcoal. The jug wine was bluish and served in cups called *canetas,* in the old Portuguese style. It was a welcome change for Missy from the publicity glitz that had surrounded her ever since she'd landed in Rio. It was all so real, and the little birds were delicious. She asked Vincent if they were "free-range."

He didn't know the term. "I guess I've been away for a long time," he said when she explained New York's latest food fad.

" 'Free-range' means they're not raised in those horrible chicken factories, so you get this real taste." Missy gestured with her fork. When Vincent asked the cook, his old friend and Pedrinho's father, where the chickens came from, the proud proprietor said, "From machine farm. They never touch the ground or see the sun in their whole life. Completely scientific."

Vincent told Missy how he had started his career as an artist in Rio by offering people likenesses of themselves on the streets and beaches.

"I was just like a beggar—and they turned me down until this Dutchman gave me ten bucks, some of which I used right here that night. I was so hungry and happy that it was the finest meal of my life."

"Why didn't you go to a college and teach or something?" Missy asked him.

"I would have if this didn't work out, but I wanted to try something with no advantages."

"Except for your talent."

Vincent nodded. Missy now found him the most romantic man she'd ever met. A street artist in the Third World—this man who once had had everything New York could offer.

"Mary's engaged to a man named Harry Buntley, but she keeps putting off marrying him," Missy told him, having kept up on the woman she'd met so long ago in Europe. This conversation seemed to make Vincent defensive, and he wasn't asking what Missy was sure he most wanted to know, so she answered, anyway.

"Laura came back to New York. Then she tried going back to college, because that's what her shrink told her to do, but back at college she bought a horse and started talking about trying for the U.S. Equestrian Team, and then she changed her mind and came back to New York again. She's always getting diverted."

Vincent's dark blue eyes sparkled as Missy rendered the simpler facts of Laura's recent career. He held his breath for stretches of time, letting it out in sighs. Finally Missy told Vincent that she and Laura were no longer speaking, because Missy had succeeded so specifically where Laura had failed. But before the final break, Laura had seen lots of Missy, even asking for her help.

Missy owed her a job, Laura had said, since Missy's career really began with the interview she'd gotten with James Montgomery. Missy finally persuaded Albert Dorn, the book publisher, to take Laura on, which he soon did, in every sense of the word. Laura continued to be attracted to the men who were running things.

"Obviously it's another father fixation," Laura said more than once over long lunches during which little besides herself was discussed. This particular fixation ended when Albert Dorn's wife felt it was threatening her long, wealthy, unhappy marriage. Once again Laura was fired.

After that Laura suggested she should write and produce Missy's shows, but Missy just didn't see this proposal as a good idea. She tried to lay off her rejection on Laura's affair with Toby Hyman, still senior vice president of the network. That was when Laura took up with Tom Harrison, now a vice president himself, and told everyone Missy had slept with her father and stolen all her ideas.

Missy tried not to tell Vincent this woeful side of his old flame's career, but the wine and the easy, humid evening just wafted the grisly details out of her. Back at his studio, they sat drinking that fresh, smooth, bluish wine, with the only illumination coming from the spotlit paintings. The pictures were of a proud boy child, a beautiful little girl in an orange dress that flared out behind her like tail feathers, three young men, and three landscapes of Guanabara Bay, which Missy liked the least.

"The portraits are just great," she said in her bossy way. "You really could make a fortune, you know."

"I don't like fortunes much anymore," Vincent answered.

Everything he said made him even more romantic, this starving artist who had thrown off the chains of wealth. He was obviously so much happier, and he wasn't really starving—the chicken was awfully good, and the wine was smooth and endless.

"Are you ever coming back to New York?" she asked.

"You know," said Vincent, pausing to stare at his unfinished portrait of Pedrinho, "I got this crazy idea I wanted to paint Wally without him knowing it was me. To see what would happen. To be painting him and see if—I don't know, it's kind of a terrible idea."

"Why don't you?" Missy found the idea irresistibly romantic. "You should. I bet I could help set it up in New York. I know all kinds of people with kids who know Mary. And you could paint one of them, and we could show Mary and tell her about this great new painter."

"I don't know. I just feel great when I'm painting someone, this feeling of both of you sharing whatever happens. And I thought, what a great way to get to know Wally again, but I'd really have to think about how to do it and what kind of idea it really is." He looked back and forth from his best picture to Missy as he spoke.

"I think it's a wonderful idea," she said, melted by wine and this melodramatic proposal. Her eyes were moist, and the more usually hard line of her mouth was pillowing up like a bud, and the bee in Vincent buzzed, so he kissed her. Missy rose up out of her chair, clutching him frankly and pushing into him. They stood embracing in increasingly irresistible sexual excitement.

Vincent felt the thrill of his dangerous old past come alive in his arms. Missy felt great romance in hers. His pain and travail and talent called to her; her symbolism and her body called to him. They didn't say anything, they just did it, and the passion of it—along with the enervation of wine, warm weather, and Missy's long day—dropped both of them into swoons of sleep.

Both of them awakened with the realization that sleeping together had been a terrible mistake. Missy felt loose and sodden and ashamed. Vincent felt that he'd done it because of that damn Laura, on whose account he never wanted to do anything ever again.

The manners they displayed on this anxious morning after were as courtly as if they were attendants at a papal audience.

"Good morning."

"Would you like some café?"

"No thank you, I really have to be getting back."

She left as soon as she could. Wearing the previous night's clothes through the lobby of a hotel so eagerly attentive to her was agony. The manager's grin bespoke his Latin-lover congratulations. How absurd—Vincent Booth, another of Laura Montgomery's unfinished ideas.

Vincent sought refuge in his painting of Pedrinho but found none. He was painting with a dead arm. He couldn't concentrate and could think only of how Laura-infested last night had been, how ashamed he was to have told Missy his childish, stagy plan to reopen his career of fatherhood.

In his black mood, Vincent wondered if maybe he had just killed off his whole new life as a painter. He could imagine looking on his life in Rio from New York and finding it too ridiculous to continue. Maybe he would go back to someplace like the Met and someone like Mary, and something like Laura would happen all over again, only worse this time, because he should know better.

Vincent decided he should apologize to Missy. He had invited her up to see his pictures, softened her up with wine, and seduced her like a cad—the complete clichéd routine.

Why was Missy always around when the bottom fell out? Maybe she was a form of witch, too, like Laura—and what else could Laura be but a witch? Vincent found he was sketching a head and getting an idea for a painting, a painting of a witch or witches. The drawing spread quickly with inspiration.

Vincent felt much better. Perhaps it was time to go back to New York and paint all of them: William Willoughby in his yellow leather coat; Mary in her horn-rimmed glasses; and Laura—how? Laura holding up her dress with no underwear. No, just Laura. It was all in her face, anyway—you needed only an artist's objectivity and that face would just come out.

"I wanted to say I'm sorry about last night. I feel completely ridiculous," Vincent said after Missy dropped her solid little "Hello?" like a stone into a pond. He heard nothing but the busy current of the phone line a moment, and then, "Me too" from a sweeter voice, one relaxing on softening lips—Vincent felt a jolt between his legs and a quick constriction of his throat. In the ensuing pause they could hear each other smile.

"What time is your plane?" he asked.

Missy stayed over an extra day. The Ministry of Tourism felt proud about the apparent effect of Rio on this northern media celebrity.

"I don't know what I'm going to do if you come to New York," said Missy with schoolmarmish precision. She was thinking of the big, lackadaisical writer from Texas with whom she lived.

"You've got somebody?" Vincent guessed, and Missy nodded.

"Well, I'm coming up there really because I figure it's to see Wally and, I don't know, have a look back down on it all from now."

"You mean Laura?"

"I guess so. But I sure would like to see Wally."

Missy was relieved. She liked planning and moving things along, and Rio would remain a fling. Missy was determined to produce that meeting of father and son—the father painting a son who doesn't know the painter is his father. It was too wildly romantic not to try. How many chances like that turn up? Not many. Everything is usually so regular. Missy outlined all sorts of ways the enterprise could be successfully brought off.

Chapter 6

*N*one of Missy's projections worked as she had planned, but her instigations accomplished her purpose in an unforeseen way. Harry Buntley had decided to surprise his fiancée with a portrait of her beloved son to show them both what great stepfather and husband material he really was. He got the idea from a lord in Scotland on Alfred Brigham's shoot.

"Painted my way into her corner," His Lordship had joked when the others kidded him about marrying an heiress. Harry, feigning indifference for his would-be father-in-law's sake, was riveted by the man's candor.

"Painted her son, not me. Had him painted by the best man in London as a surprise! The darling boy all painted up, and that's what did it," said the financially rejuvenated aristocrat. "A new roof's going on the castle even as we speak—slate, cut the old way. And the damn picture of the little beggar only cost fifteen hundred pounds." There was a good deal of laughter before the fire in the old lodge.

Missy had shown Vincent's portraits of children to every affluent mother she knew. She included Wally's art teacher at her little reception for the painter, who Missy introduced as Ted Sanchez.

"What's this all about?" complained Missy's boyfriend, Barry, who secretly feared Missy was inviting mothers over and hanging up these pictures in their apartment to reopen her suspended negotiations over starting a family with him. Barry did not especially want to go through the demands of fatherhood again, having done so twenty-five years ago when he was more resilient and ignorant.

Missy told Barry the whole story of who Vincent Booth really was, why she was hanging a show for him, and why his name had to be Ted Sanchez in New York. She told him everything, in fact, minus the two nights of lovemaking in Rio. Barry knew how energetic and intriguing Missy's nature was; he saw how this project would be irresistible to her. All he had to do was stand back and mix some drinks or, if he wanted, he could skip the whole thing.

Barry went instead to the Brook Club, where he explained, at the communal dining table, that he was there for dinner with members of his own sex because "the woman I live with is having a lot of Park Avenue mothers over to look at portraits of children by some Brazilian."

"Portraits of children?" said Harry Buntley, coming up on point like a spaniel.

"This guy's supposed to be the best," answered Barry laconically.

*　*　*

Harry Buntley invited Ted Sanchez to lunch at the club where he'd first heard of the painter. Buntley was relieved to find the foreigner was apparently an Anglo-Saxon who spoke excellent, almost perfect English.

"Harry Buntley," said the bird shooter and money manager, holding out his hand and elevating a pillar of tailoring over a foundation of bespoke cobbling. Buntley's considerable vanity rose with him. Just then Vincent couldn't bring himself to don the mask of his pseudonym, so he only smiled and shook hands with this man who evidently would become Wally's stepfather.

Missy's assistance had moved Vincent's fantasy plan of anonymously meeting his son along much quicker than he'd expected or was prepared for. At the airport he had almost dropped the ruse entirely and called Mary to say he was in town and wanted to see his son. But Missy had met him with a network limousine, and explained that she had already invited six wealthy mothers to meet Ted Sanchez.

Eventually Vincent found it amusing and somewhat of a relief to have this role to play on his return to the scene of his old crimes. Ted felt like a new man, a tourist who could wonder at the increase in dirt, poverty, incompetence, and homelessness he saw in New York City, an innocent who could ask questions to which he actually knew the answers and listen for lies, and play at being an immigrant looking for a second chance, which only he knew was actually his third.

He was more aware of the vividly sexual appraisal of him by the young mothers at Missy's reception than he would have been as Vincent Booth. The detachment of a new and foreign man excited them. He had those looks. And painting their children, of course, would require contact.

"Did you study art?" asked a potential patroness with a smile that had to do with other matters altogether. She had big eyes, dimpled cheeks, and a sheen of fine blonde hair on her folded arms.

"I did."

"Whereabouts?"

"Europe."

"That's really awfully good," she said seriously, reassembling her physique for a look at Vincent's portrait of Pedrinho.

Vincent wondered where Ted would take him. There was something antic about his adventures with a pseudonym. Would he hear a woman cry out "Oh, Ted" in the throes of love—and if he did, who would it leave him?

But meeting Harry Buntley was no fun, even for Ted Sanchez. Buntley looked like privilege and private schooling and hidebound snobbery. Vincent would not have chosen this man to cast his shadow on Wally.

Ted Sanchez was only two thousand dollars, quite a bargain from what Harry's early research on the price of children's portraits had turned up. Barry Matthews—quite a famous writer from Texas who lived with Missy Ferguson, the TV personality—had said Sanchez was outstanding. The poor bastard probably didn't know North American prices. He was probably considering his figures after multiplying them into millions of cruzados.

Buntley decided to go to contract immediately, before the price adjusted itself upward, and said so.

"Don't you want to see something?" asked the incredulous Ted Sanchez.

"Oh, of course," said Buntley, fearing he had appeared unprofessional. Vincent had slides, and they did look excellent. Buntley only wished he'd asked for them before offering Sanchez the job. He hoped the painter had not lost any respect for him.

"It's to be a complete surprise," Buntley said gravely. "A surprise for his mother."

Vincent found Buntley's requirements of secrecy and surprise fit his own with eerie precision. He recalled the unlikely appearance of Romeo's taxi, so eager to bear him into adultery, and all the wedding gowns appearing around Mary and him in Italy. Fate could be awfully accommodating as it drew you around the more dangerous corners.

"Would you like some cognac or something?" offered Harry Buntley after lunch.

"Sure," said Vincent, glad to postpone a call to the number Missy had written for him on network stationery. Laura's number.

Buntley was glad the artist seemed to be a gentleman. A portrait was such a family thought, the perfect surprise for Mary. As long as he could get the little bastard to cooperate, he would have an ingenious weight to pull down Mary's wobbling scales of indecision his way.

Vincent looked up because someone passing across the other side of the paneled room suddenly had stopped and groaned. It was William Willoughby, who quickly turned away and left the room. His face was dead white, as if he had seen a ghost.

Vincent discovered with considerable chagrin that the studio in which he was to paint portraits would cost him more for a month than his first commission. The whole trip was much more expensive than he expected. It would require all his capital and a couple of paintings as well. He dwelt angrily on these considerations to avoid others, right up to the moment he finally telephoned the number Missy had given him. A recording started, and Vincent's heart stopped pounding. But before he drew the phone away from his ear, she answered over her own taped voice.

"I don't believe it," Laura said in a friendly, guiltless way. "It's all right," is what he last remembered her saying—"It's all right," when it certainly wasn't. So "I don't believe it" probably meant she did. He asked her to dinner at Le Bordello.

"How long are you here?" asked Laura in the restaurant.

"Just a month or two."

"Where are you?"

"Rio de Janeiro."

"No kidding. You look great. I'm so glad. I didn't know what happened to you."

"Missy Ferguson told me what happened to you."

"That bitch. You're not seeing her, I hope."

"No, I ran into her in Rio."

"What a parasite."

"I like her."

"You don't know her."

Vincent was pleased to find himself quickly feeling he wanted the evening over with—that he'd already had enough of Laura. She obviously didn't have any idea of her effect on him. She just didn't get it, and never had.

She was older and tougher-looking but still undeniably beautiful. She looked like she still had many lovers to go. But that irresistible sexual beauty of her youth had changed as its purpose moved further and further from a biological to a psychological property of her existence.

"God, we change, but this place sure doesn't," she said, looking around the restaurant.

Vincent would have enjoyed asking himself what he ever saw in her, but he could still see it. She looked like a bottle of vodka to a reformed alcoholic.

"You really look terrific Vincent. God, I loved you," she said, like a bottle of vodka moving toward a reformed alcoholic with its top magically unscrewing. She smiled an old smile and touched his cheek.

Her leg was next to Vincent's. Its configuration was just the way he remembered it. He knew each inch of that leg from every angle. Coming out of the restaurant, she moved into him as familiarly, as if she were putting on an old coat.

Vincent knew better than to sleep with her, but his body didn't. On the way to her place in the taxi, they doubled up together and fell about in the dark cage, groaning as their bodies fell into a sentimental reunion.

Vincent felt sexually attracted but psychologically removed. He wondered if she felt the same, or whether that was how she had felt the whole time when they were together. This thought entertained him. It was she who wanted him tonight, for some reason, and he who felt he could oblige her without enslaving himself as he had. He found an unexpected banality in this needlessly feared encounter.

She told him she enjoyed sex much more now. Her new therapist had gotten her thinking of it in positive ways. Did he remember that time in the museum? Wasn't that a riot? She just wished she had known how to let loose and enjoy it that way every time, back then when they were together.

She had a smaller apartment and a new cat. Vincent could imagine how great a place like this might look to a newcomer. She did have great style and great looks. But Vincent found her attitude preposterous. She acted as if that epoch of time, that geological period beginning with the life-exterminating volcanic eruption of Mexico and the ensuing ice age of exile had never occurred. So the apartment was a little smaller, she'd gotten a little older, and there was a new cat. Is that what she understood to be the extent of changes between Mexico and now?

The telephone rang. Her machine answered. She was a little flustered as an angry voice boomed "Tom Harrison" and hung up with a blow.

"He's a little ticked because I broke a date to see you," she said, putting her head close to Vincent's chest.

She did look so well. "I've got to go," he said abruptly.

Laura was hurt. Vincent did not want to hurt her, now that he probably had, but it was only a little hurt. He didn't mean to excite and reject her. His sexual excitement, however, felt separate from himself. His heart was not in it. He would not treat his old love like a whore, for his sake as much as for hers.

"What's the matter?" she asked.

Vincent just kissed her good-bye.

Cannily Harry Buntley took his secret portrait project to Mrs. Wilson, Wally's art teacher at school. He realized Wally wouldn't willingly do anything he suggested—that Wally believed everything Buntley did was calculated to win Mary over to his way of thinking. But Mrs. Wilson was Wally's favorite teacher, and staring down at the boy's crude artistic affront to himself, Buntley began to smile. There would be an element of revenge in using Mrs. Wilson, patroness of Wally's slanderous portrait of the bird hunter, to bag Wally for his own portrait—a gesture that would surely set the date, once and for all, for the wedding.

Mrs. Wilson was most enthusiastic about his proposition. Because of her presence at Missy's reception, she already knew Ted Sanchez and loved his work. She eagerly lent her imprimatur to the alibi necessary for Wally's secret sittings.

"I think the best way to go would be for you to handle it with Wally, if you could, Mrs. Wilson," Buntley said.

"How do you mean?"

"If he just knows that his portrait is to be painted as a surprise for his mother."

"You don't want him to know you're arranging it?" she asked.

Buntley demurred with piously closed eyes, pursed lips, and a shaking head. "I don't want young Wally to feel beholden, or that I'm intruding in this. It's really just meant to be a surprise for his mother."

"He's a wonderful painter," said Mrs. Wilson, partly addressing herself because of the suspicions Buntley seemed to arouse in her for reasons she couldn't name.

"Wally, this is Mr. Sanchez. Ted, this is Wally Booth." Having made the introductions, Mrs. Wilson was startled to see the painter burst into tears. Wally jumped back toward her, and she instinctively decided to get the boy away from the apparently unstable Brazilian. She grabbed his hand and made to run for for the door.

But Wally jerked away. "Dad?" he asked, and the painter nodded. Wally crossed briskly to his father, and they embraced. Vincent was laughing and crying. Wally was only laughing.

"Excuse me," said Mrs. Wilson, "but what the hell is this?"

"Have a seat," Vincent said, using a handkerchief to wipe off his face and blow his nose. "Have a seat, Mrs. Wilson, and I'll tell you."